Love
by
DESIGN

A ROMANCE NOVEL

Tiffany Landis

Chapter 1

SOME DAYS, YOU WAKE UP KNOWING YOUR LIFE IS ABOUT TO BE different.

In the two years since Jess Tyler had started her own interior design firm, Anicca, she'd had many kinds of days. Days when she had been inspired. Days when she had been challenged, physically, mentally, and emotionally. Days when she had wondered why she ever left the safety of her old firm, Unoa, which was established and past the point of building a reputation, developing a client base, and trying to make ends meet. Days when she had to push herself out of her comfort zone, in ways both large and small, all so that her fledgling firm would survive in the competitive world of interior design.

And then days like today, when she knew it had all been worth it.

"They're here!" Jess heard Charlie, her assistant, call from outside the bathroom door where Jess had been hiding out for the last twenty minutes.

His voice snapped Jess back to the present. She took a breath and focused on transforming her nerves into excitement.

About a month ago, Jess had been notified that 7×7 Magazine, the go-to magazine for all things San Francisco, was profiling Anicca. She still remembered the expression on Charlie's face when he told her the news. She had literally jumped for joy with him, screaming so loud that her other assistant Moira had rushed in wondering if one of them had gotten hurt. But Moira joined the celebration as soon as she'd been filled in. A profile in 7×7 meant big things for all of them, not only more clients but more prestigious opportunities. It was the culmination of everything Jess had dreamed of when she left Unoa.

"Just a sec!" Jess replied. She glanced at herself in the mirror, grateful that she had taken her sister, Bridget's, advice on what to wear. She looked the part, the twenty-nine-year-old founder and CEO of a cutting-edge design firm—a far cry from shy, quiet artist she'd been in her youth, the one who had never quite fit in and had doubted she ever would. In many ways, Anicca existed because of that girl. If Jess had not spent most of her life wondering if she would ever belong, she might not have taken the huge risk of starting her own firm, to create a place where she, finally, felt at home.

"Come on, Jess!" Moira shouted. "They're asking where you are, and Charlie's getting dangerously close to having a panic attack."

Jess smiled. "Coming," she said, bracing herself as she opened the bathroom door. She took in the chaotic scene outside. Anicca's small lobby had been taken over with cameras and studio lighting. There were at least three people setting up various pieces of equipment, with Charlie in the corner directing people where to go while at the same time offering croissants that he had stood in line early to pick up from Tartine, the famous Mission District bakery around the corner from his house.

Jess turned to Moira. "I see what you mean. Let's go save him. It won't look good if a member of the team passes out in the middle of the photoshoot."

"Not exactly what we want to be remembered for," Moira chuckled. "Hey, Jess," she placed her hand gently on Jess's shoulder, "you are going to crush it today."

Jess touched Moira's hand. "Thank you. I think I needed to hear that. Alright, let's do this."

As if through some coordinated dance, each of them assumed their roles. Moira became the de facto project manager. It suited her well. Moira was that strange combination, perhaps unique to San Francisco, of a dedicated yogi and meditator who believed in a higher connection and human potential but who also wasn't afraid to tell you straight up when you were being an idiot. In addition to being a talented artist, she helped Jess manage the design process, working with sometimes challenging clients and coordinating the many steps necessary for a design to actualize. Jess had laughed to herself a few times during the shoot as she caught Moira correcting a photographer on how they could best capture an image. Moira's directness was tempered by a well-meaning nature that let her get away with much more than she might otherwise have. Jess had been lucky to add Moira to her team when Anicca was starting out. Someone with her talents could have gone to any firm she wanted, but she had taken a chance on Jess, believing not only in Jess's designs but in Jess herself. Her faith in Anicca had been crucial during those many times when Jess's doubt had felt overwhelming.

In the meantime, Jess teamed up with Charlie to go through some of the designs they had selected for the shoot. Charlie had also been with Jess since the beginning, recently graduated and eager to take on the many and varied tasks inherent to a new business. He told the crew about the Wabisabi aesthetic that informed much of Anicca's work, which took what might be perceived as flaws in a space and elevated them, honoring them as reflecting its history, something that adding to its richness. Perfect was boring, but a well-designed imperfection made a design beautiful.

It was in homage to that idea that Jess had named her firm Anicca, reflecting the belief that all things are impermanent and changing. Jess loved the concept of impermanence, how everything was just as it was for a moment in time and then it was gone. The philosophy deeply resonated with something that she had felt and appreciated in her bones since she was young, watching the sky and seeing the clouds move and the colors change, feeling like, for at least a moment in time, she belonged. Like it was okay that she too was imperfect, because there was no such thing as perfect, and she was exactly how she was supposed to be.

By some minor miracle, everything that morning went smoothly, and after a few hours, the photoshoot portion was wrapping up. The only thing left now was the interview. Jess separated herself from the chaos so that she could reflect on what she wanted to say. Her mind became still as she let herself imagine the design process, how she started with a blank slate and then felt the energy of the room. It was a visual experience, but also physical, auditory … all her senses alive to capture the essence of her surroundings. Jess felt some of that now. She leaned against a wall in a side hallway and closed her eyes, remembering some of the spaces she had designed, those that had spoken to her. Her skin tingled with that energy, her mind wholly immersed in the memories.

"You look lost in thought."

Jess started abruptly from her reverie to find a man standing next to her.

"Sorry, didn't mean to startle you," he added. He looked at Jess with interest. His eyes, a deep brown, sparkled, matching the amusement in his slightly upturned lips.

"It's okay," Jess replied, collecting herself. "I was just … preparing."

"By all means, don't let me disturb you."

Jess stood up straight from against the wall, too flustered to continue her meditation. She took a closer look at him, seeing his rich chocolate-colored hair that made his brown eyes seem even darker. As Jess studied him more, she found that he exuded a certain warmth, an energy that Jess, sensitive to people as well as environments, immediately found comforting. Her shoulders naturally relaxed around him, which was unexpected given that he had startled her. Yet, somehow, he brought that feeling of relaxation out in her. His demeanor conveyed sincere interest, like she could tell him anything she wanted and feel completely accepted, not judged.

"Ah, you must be the interviewer," Jess said, realization dawning. "Figured I would hear from you soon. I have to say, even though I'm excited for this, I'm also nervous. We'd better get started before I back out! We can move to my office for a little more privacy."

He paused. The corner of his mouth twitched up mischievously. "Well, as much as I would enjoy more privacy with you, I …"

"Oh," Jess blushed. "I mean, I just thought that for the interview, it made sense not to have distractions, but I don't want to presume how you work. We can do this however you'd like."

Jess blushed again. She tried to get a handle on what was happening to her. She was supposed to be making a great first impression with the person whose words could make—or break— her career, and she was stumbling over herself. By sheer force of will, she stopped talking and looked up.

He had a curious smile on his face, like the two of them shared some personal joke; only she wasn't in on it. He extended his hand.

"Jack," he said, as she took his hand. "It's great to meet you, but I think you have me confused for someone else." He let go of her hand. "You must be the person this whole show's about."

"Oh, you're not the interviewer? That's embarrassing. I assumed that you must be one of the crew here, and the only person I hadn't met yet was the interviewer." Jess noticed she was rambling again and, for the second time in as many seconds, recollected herself. "Yes, hi, I'm Jess. Jess Tyler. And yes, this 'whole show," as you described it, is about me. Well, about my firm, which is more than only me, but it's about the work we do."

Jess paused for a beat. Now that she had had a moment to exhale, she saw how strikingly attractive he was. Tall, clearly athletic. His clothes, though subdued, were well made. That confidence, which before she had found inviting, now seemed deeper, like he was a man who knew his way in the world, had always known his way in the world, and simply was on the path to get there.

"Have I seen you before?" Jess asked, tilting her head slightly. She didn't know how she could forget an interaction with *him*, and yet, he looked so oddly familiar.

"I don't think so," Jack replied. "But I—"

"Jack!" A woman approached his side. "Hi there," she said, extending her hand to Jess. "I'm Alex, the interviewer." Jess took her hand, mortified at what had just happened. Alex looked back at Jack. "Sorry, Jack, this is going a bit longer than I'd expected. Do you mind if we start lunch a little later? I'm thinking, what, half an hour?" Alex asked, looking inquiringly at Jess.

"If you're asking me, I say definitely. I can't imagine wanting to spend more than half an hour on this daunting, although life affirming and validating, experience." Jess chuckled.

"Sure thing," Jack replied. "I have some errands I could do in the area. I'll put our name in at the restaurant and meet you there when you're finished."

"Thank you," Alex said. She and Jack exchanged a quick, somewhat awkward, hug as he left.

"So sorry about that," Alex said to Jess. "I thought we were going to meet at the restaurant across the street, but I think our communication got crossed. Not the most professional first impression."

"No problem," Jess replied. "Boyfriend?"

"Oh God, no," Alex laughed. "Or at least, certainly not yet. Still early stages, and, to be honest, it's probably not going anywhere."

"Ah," Jess responded quickly. "He must be pretty interested, though, to brave coming to your work?" Jess found herself curious about how serious their relationship was, which made no sense. She had just met Jack and was only now meeting Alex.

Alex shook her head. "I doubt it. He's nice and obviously a total catch. But I'm not getting too invested in that bachelor-of-the-year type. No, he's for fun but … it's been a lot of fun." Alex's eyes twinkled mischievously.

"Bachelor-of-the-year type?" Jess asked, a vague recollection dawning. She knew she had seen him somewhere …

"Oh yeah," Alex answered. "That's Jack Stinson. You know, SF royalty, one of those born-and-bred-in-SF types. Surely you've heard of him."

Jess shook her head. "No, the name sounds familiar, and it's possible that I have seen a picture of him before, but to be honest, I haven't paid too much attention to that scene. When I think Stinson, I only think Stinson Beach." She shrugged her shoulders, referencing the locally famous beach at the foot of Mount Tamalpais, the tallest mountain in Marin County, an upscale area for SF hiking, mountain biking, wine tasting, and the other recreational yet sophisticated activities that made San Franciscans' hearts flutter.

"Well, yes, exactly," Alex said, looking intently at Jess. "*Old SF money*. His grandfather's grandfather, or his grandfather's grandfather's grandfather, or some grandfather-type figure, is *that* Stinson, the guy who founded Stinson Beach. SF royalty, I'm telling you."

"Wow," Jess said. "I guess I'd never thought about how Stinson must have been a person. I mean, I've heard of Sutro, but ..."

"Yep!" Alex laughed. "That's what everyone says. Sutro, yes, of course, Sutro Tower, Land's End. But Stinson? No way."

Jess appreciated Alex's ease. "Right? It's funny how we choose what realities we easily accept. But, for the sake of your date, I guess we'd better get started. You don't want to keep the one-and-only Jack Stinson waiting!"

Alex tilted her head. "I guess, when you put it that way." She smiled. "You know, I think you and I are going to get along just fine. Enough about Jack. I'm interested in hearing about you and this incredible firm that you've put together. Honestly, Jess, your designs are so inspiring. I can't wait to hear your story."

Jess glowed as she took in Alex's earnestness. "I can't wait to tell you about it. Let's get started."

Jess got home that day feeling that good kind of tired when, despite it all, you feel sated. It was days like this when she appreciated that her apartment had a bay window and that the owner had been wise enough to put a bench underneath it. She had loved that nook immediately when she'd come to view the apartment and applied on the spot, despite the cramped kitchen and the anti-quated appliances.

She went there now to watch the sunset. It was calming, watching the shades of orange and purple and pink that decorated her window. Whenever she felt particularly uninspired in life, she connected to the vastness of the sky. It made her feel like more was possible, like as hard as things were, or as complicated as things seemed, with every day, the world created something magical. She found great comfort in that.

She ran through the day, beaming again at what her team had put together. It was hectic, to be sure, but it all came together in the end. Perfectly imperfect, Jess smiled to herself. She recalled the interview.

"You got your start at Unoa, the top firm in SF. Tell me about that," Alex had asked.

"Yes, I went to Unoa right out of school—"

"No small feat, from what I hear, by the way. I heard Unoa usually only accepts people who've been working in the field for a couple years," Alex said. "Rebecca Morrison is not known for taking chances on new talent. It's one of the reasons people say she's made Unoa so successful."

"That's usually true, I guess, but Rebecca and I had a natural rapport as soon as she saw my graduation show. She took me under her wing, so to speak, helping me hone my aesthetic. I will forever be beholden to her," Jess continued. "But, after a time, I realized I needed to have my own platform to fully express my vision. It was a hard decision to leave Unoa because I was happy there and because, well, starting my own firm was scary, leaving my friends, the reputation that Unoa had, benefits!" Jess had laughed, trying to sound poised and professional while at the same time authentic. "When I look at what Anicca has become, though, it all feels worth it."

Alex had seemed impressed. "It is. What you create is beautiful. And running a business is its own accomplishment."

"*That* is certainly true. But my team makes it easier. They're fantastic. I made mistakes along the way, but luckily nothing so huge that it wasn't fixable," Jess had continued. "Stepping out on my own, though, forced me to learn that I could rely on myself and that the limits I had set for myself were worth questioning. It taught me to believe in myself. I've always been a dreamer. Through Anicca, I've realized that I can make those dreams a reality."

Jess exhaled deeply, steadying herself and remembering that, at the end of the day, she'd lived a life true to her own values. That was what was important. She turned her attention back to the sky, the colors by this time vibrant. The changing patterns in the sky spoke straight to her heart. She felt herself slow down, absorb everything. Reminders of the impermanent nature of things made her want to be present in the moment she was in now, which was beautiful, one of those rare moments she'd felt since leaving Unoa where she felt completely sure that she'd made the right choice.

She let her mind drift off as she watched the sky continue to change colors, a deeper orange now surrounded by shades of pink, turning darker as the day transitioned to night. No matter what was going on in her life, she could always count on this daily ritual of day becoming night, indifferent to the travails of her human existence, speaking to a more ancient rhythm. Jess's thoughts calmed as she let herself be held by that truth, as she let herself take comfort in the bigger picture and in the joy of some- how, finally, finding her place within it.

Chapter 2

THE MONTH UNTIL THE PHOTOSHOOT AND WHEN THE FEATURE came out was one of the longest of Jess's life. Charlie had reassured her that the profile had gone well so many times that Moira had had to put a moratorium on the topic, which had ultimately been for the best. It turned out that ruminating about the profile didn't speed up the inevitable waiting; in fact, to the contrary, it made time pass even more slowly. In the end, Jess had to let go of the need to know and trust that she and her team had done their best.

Finally, the day arrived. Jess hadn't been able to stop smiling on her morning run. The sky over the bay seemed more vibrant, the air coming off the eucalyptus in the Presidio more crisp, her soul lighter. She relaxed into her morning rhythm at the office, making the coffee and mentally running through the day ahead. Moira and Charlie would arrive at any minute, and even though she was dying to read the article, she wanted to wait until they were there to open it. This, after all, was a moment for all of them, and it was important for them to celebrate together.

As she turned on the coffee machine, the two of them walked in. "Well, what if they said something negative, or we didn't anticipate something, or, I don't know … I felt like my outfit was off that day or …" Charlie's words poured out at a rapid pace as he and Moira exited the elevator.

"Or this, or that, or, or, or! Will you chill out, please?" Moira said, sharply turning to face him. "Look, I know it's a big day, and I very much want to be there to support you, but Charlie, you seriously need to calm down."

"I know. You're right. I'm getting worried over nothing … But what if you're not right, and instead I'm right and … Oh hey!" Charlie stopped short, catching sight of Jess. Without skipping a beat, he transformed his furrowed brow into a serene smile. "Jess! You must be so excited! You did such a fantastic job."

Moira rolled her eyes. "You have *got* to be kidding me. Charlie's been a hot mess since I saw him in the lobby, and now he's Mr. Cheer Team." After an exasperated glance at Charlie, she gave Jess a hug. "*Anyway*, Jess, I'm sure you're excited. We all are. Have you looked?"

"No, I haven't," Jess said. "I was waiting for the both of you. Speaking of, can we please psychoanalyze Charlie later? I'm about to burst with anticipation. Let's see what the magazine says! Moira, can you pull it up?" Jess went to stand by Charlie as Moira took a seat by the computer.

A few interminable seconds ticked by as they waited for the 7×7 website to load. And then, there it was—the article, *her* article.

The Nurture of Change

When Jess Tyler, CEO of Anicca Design, sits down to design, she doesn't see a room. She sees a moment in time, a moment of existence that will change the next minute and tomorrow, will be something completely different.

"What drew me to design is relishing in the futility of it all." Jess is seated before me in a fashionable yellow top that perfectly, yet improbably, complements her black scarf and trousers. "Many people think that the room is theirs to design, and it is them who will shape it to their will. They have this illusion that, if they get it right, they will achieve something, like they're in control of the moment and there's an objective and finite design somewhere 'out there' that can activate the potential of a space.

"The truth is, though, that everything changes all the time. You could design the perfect space, and then, a moment later, you could feel differently, or the energy of the room could change. Everything could be different. You could set out with a vision and find that, once in the room, it doesn't feel right. Or you could create a beautiful design and then, a moment later, your pet knocks something over and that piece that you were convinced completed the room is suddenly destroyed.

"The design philosophy of Anicca is to not only accept change as part of life but embrace it as one of the things that makes life worth living." Jess shifts her scarf, reflective. "The idea that we can surrender to the nature of change, that we're all part of it, and that change is not good and not bad but simply is, it's liberating."

Jess sips her tea, a combination vanilla citrus that floats aromatically from her cup. Listening to her, I can't help but feel a little liberated, as well. After all, who needs control? Who needs to feel like they know everything all the time?

I carry this mood with me as I am taken through the whirlwind of her designs. Her assistants, Moira Lucas and Charlie Covington, let me in on the process. Charlie and Moira explain how each of Annica's profiled designs channels something of the impermanent nature of existence. The "Living in Motion" living room design, inset at photograph A (right), feels settled while at the same time conveying a sense of flow. Charlie explains how the slightly angled construction of the pieces, and a subtle increase of more "movement-oriented" colors, compels the viewer to move forward. "Not what it seems" (photograph B, page 3) looks perfect at first glance. Moira points out, though, one blemish, right in the center, obvious once you see it but not there until you look closely. This asks us to question our concept of "perfect," to see it as only a label we have applied, rather than something inherent to the room. Anicca's designs remind us that "perfect" is not part of life. Instead, they value the imperfect and see life as more real through the incorporation of it.

Jess is careful to honor her team as integral to her work. And seeing them all together, it's clear that Anicca is a shared effort. But in the end, it's Jess Tyler who names the game. It's Jess Tyler whose vision makes these works accessible, Jess Tyler who believes in change, who nurtures change as the other side of permanence. In her words, "Permanence is boring. Change or rather giving up the illusion that we can avoid change or even that we would be better off if we could avoid it, well, that's where the magic lies."

Looking at her designs, I fall under that magic spell.

Jess looked up from the screen. She made eye contact with Moira and Charlie for one silent moment before, simultaneously, they all screamed.

"*Aaaah.* Oh, my goodness, that was so good!" Charlie exclaimed.

"Seriously, Jess, do you have any idea what this means?" Moira placed her hands on Jess's shoulders. "This place is going to take off."

Jess couldn't stop smiling. She was lost in the reverie of it all. It felt surreal, that Anicca and her work were going to be ... something, something big. She had no idea what would happen next, and as much as it was overwhelming, it was thrilling. This was what she had always wanted. Her heart erupted, and tears of joy came to her eyes. She looked at the two of them.

"You guys," she said, taking both of their hands, "thank you so, so much." Jess hugged them, not bothering to wipe away the tears. In this moment, with her perfectly imperfect team, she wanted to feel all the joy she could.

A second later, the phone ringed.

"Anicca Designs," Charlie answered. "Yes, of course. Here she is." Charlie handed the phone to Jess, mouthing "Alex" as he did so.

"Hello," Jess said, trying her best to hide the nerves in her voice. Moira and Charlie gracefully ducked out of her office.

"Hey, you! It's Alex, you know, the one who wrote such glowing things about you, calling to be one of many to wish you congratulations today! I assume you've already had a chance to read it? Although, seriously, if you haven't been clicking the refresh button since 5:00 a.m., I'm amazed and want to learn from you."

"Ha! No, I haven't been," Jess laughed. "But even I can't tell you how I restrained myself. Oh wow, Alex, that piece … that piece was … I don't even know what to say. Thank you so much. You might have just made my career."

"My pleasure. I meant everything I said."

"How are you? How is Jack?" Jess asked, hesitantly. She wondered if it was awkward to ask. Alex, after all, was a professional colleague, not a gal pal. Regardless, Jess was curious, for some reason she couldn't quite figure out, about how the relationship between them had panned out. Probably because it was the only thing that she really knew about Alex, she reasoned. And as for feeling awkward, maybe the traditional protocol did not apply here. After all, Jess had only met Jack through him coming to the photoshoot in the first place. Besides, Alex was someone who had maybe changed her life, and if that didn't make them at least acquaintances, she wasn't sure what would.

"Oh, I'm fine; thanks for asking. Jack? I don't know. We didn't last too long after you met him, but … what can I say? I had a good time, no regrets. But this is *sooo* not about me. It's about you! And I've been tying up your line for too long. You probably already have five voicemails by now from people wanting to tell you how amazing you are. Just one favor—please, please, when you're the host of some *avant-garde* HGTV show or something, remember who wrote that amazing piece that helped launch you there, okay? Seriously. I really want to meet Jonathan Scott."

Jess felt her shoulders relax. She was comforted to hear that Alex was no longer with Jack while at the same time sad on behalf of Alex. She wondered if Alex's "too cool" manner was sincere. She thought about asking how Alex really was, but if she had thought asking if she and Jack were together was possibly too personal, asking for a deep dive into Alex's emotional state was definitely going too far. Instead, she settled for a quick goodbye and a vague promise to introduce Alex to at least one of the Scott brothers.

After hanging up the phone, Jess was even more ecstatic than she had been a second ago but in a different way, a more solid way. It was sinking in that this was her life now—hers, what she had worked for. She looked around her office room and felt a renewed sense of possibility emerge within her. So much of Anicca, up to that point, had been about starting a business. It had been hard, at times, to hold on to the dream she'd had when she started the firm. She wasn't sure exactly what this article meant, but she knew it meant something good. It had been a goal of hers to establish not only Anicca as a firm, but herself as a designer, and she was becoming more aware, herself as a human being, more and more comfortable in her own skin.

Her time to revel was short-lived. Jess heard her phone ring again.

"Hey, Bridge," Jess answered.

"*Aaaaahhhh!*" Bridget screamed so loudly that Jess had to pull the phone away from her ear briefly. "You. *You!* Oh my God, Jess, you are going to be so fucking big. *Aaah!* Are you losing it or what? I know I would be. I can't believe I'm being outshined by my younger sister, but then again, you're talented as fuck, so I guess I knew it had to be coming."

Jess sat down, grinning at the familiar voice of her sister. She didn't know what she would do without Bridget in her life. Bridget … the high-powered attorney, always top in school and always full of direction. She and Jess had been close as kids but on decidedly different trajectories. Bridget had been the one to win all the awards. Jess's path had been less direct. She saw the world more in terms of possibility and imagery, a way of being that didn't exactly fit into the linear structure of a traditional school system.

As a result, it had taken Jess a while to find her way. The differences between the two sisters could have driven them apart, but instead, they brought them closer together. Bridget, though only two years older than Jess in age, had fallen into a protector role for Jess, supporting her and encouraging her to dream. Even now, as adults, their dynamic still carried a big sister/little sister tone to it. The how of it changed, but the energy of it stayed the same, permanent and impermanent, all at the same time.

"Aw, Bridge," Jess said, tearing up. "You have no idea how much this means to me, how much you mean to me, how much having you believe in me has always meant to me."

"Of course, Jess," Bridget said. "I hope you know—I hope you really, deeply, and fully know—that all of this, everything that's happening, is nothing more than what's meant to happen. You deserve it all. You have a gift, baby sis, and now it's time to share it."

"Thank you." Jess was so overcome with emotion that she was surprised the words managed to find their way out. "Hey Bridge, do you ever remember what you told me in middle school?"

"Um, that even though I was destined to marry Jonathan Taylor Thomas, I'd forgive you if you got to him first?"

Jess laughed. "Okay, good, I'm glad you haven't forgotten. But seriously, Bridge," Jess felt her eyes get misty, "I meant what you said on one of those unfortunately many days where I came home from school crying. I had been daydreaming in class, *again,* and a teacher called on me, but I didn't hear. So the teacher kept calling on me, but I still didn't hear, and eventually the class started laughing at me."

Bridget took a sharp inhale. "Yes, Jess, I remember that day. Fuck that teacher, by the way. But, yes, I remember you telling me about what had happened. You were so down on yourself."

"Yeah, I was." Jess was surprised at the intensity of the sadness she still felt at the memory, all these years later. "But I'll never forget coming to your room after that happened. I was so worried that you'd be mad at me, but you weren't. You told me that I was awesome and that that teacher was a mess—"

"Still true," Bridget interjected.

"But that there were different ways of being in the world and that I was in the process of finding mine."

"Also still true," Bridget said. "You've always had this unique and inspiring way of seeing the world, Jess. I think you're finding your potential, and I don't know where it will take you, but I know that the moments where I've felt like I've seen the world through Jess's eyes? It's like the world I thought I knew has been cracked open, and I've been let in on this secret rhythm to life that I thought existed only in dreams. You taught us all to be the dreamer that we've forgotten how to be."

"Thanks, Bridge." Jess heard her voice soften from emotion. "I love you."

"I love you, too." Jess was surprised to hear Bridget sound choked up. She was always so strong, never a moment away from a witty retort. "Now go on, get off the phone with me, crack some champagne, get a little day drunk, and soak it up. I'll check in with you later."

Jess smiled at the abrupt change. "Okay. Bye, Bridge."

"Bye."

They hung up. Jess looked out her window. The sky was blue, hopeful, as though it too were celebrating with her. Jess felt her chest lighten even though she hadn't known it was tight before. She let the warmth spread through her body, finding a pocket of being present in the midst of the chaos.

"Another call, Jess!" Charlie peeked his head into her office, snapping Jess back to reality. "From Donathan Lewis. It's starting!"

With a small degree of reluctance, Jess turned her gaze from the sky to answer the phone. It was time, she knew, to put on that demeanor she'd cultivated for the past few years: the polished demeanor appropriate for the founder and CEO of a cutting-edge design firm. She thanked the sky for being her constant companion through these years. It made it easier for her to imagine getting through these next few hours, knowing she'd be able to reconnect with it after.

Chapter 3

Donathan Lewis, founder and CEO of Jumbl, a social media platform marketed towards the late high school and college-aged crowd, was on the phone. After building a considerable market share, Jumbl was being touted as one of the top three social media companies in the world. Donathan Lewis, in other words, was SF tech royalty.

"Hello," Jess said, taking the phone from Charlie.

"Hey, Jess, Donathan Lewis here. Just read the article in 7×7 and knew I had to reach out and meet the person who's about to revolutionize design."

"Thanks for the kind words," Jess replied. "Yes, we're very happy with the piece. Nice to meet you, Donathan. What's on your mind?"

"Straight to the point. I appreciate that," he continued. "Okay, okay. So, here's the deal. My company, Jumbl, is about to relocate. We've been growing and growing, and we're getting to the point where our current office space isn't big enough. We need a new office. And I want you to design it."

Jess's breath caught. Design the new office for Jumbl? It was a terrific opportunity to design in the innovative tech world. Ever since Google and Facebook had revolutionized how offices looked through the design of their expansive campuses, tech companies had been climbing over themselves to create offices that were the perfect combination of professional, relaxed, and the ever-elusive "cool." The challenge excited her.

"Wow, thanks for the opportunity," Jess said. "What are you thinking?"

"Well," Donathan paused, "don't thank me quite yet. I need you to design more than the office. I need you to design the entire campus. We're moving our headquarters, and I need the place to be really amazing, a signal that Jumbl is competitive with Facebook, Tik-Tok, Instagram, etc. Also, everyone is going to be pissed as hell when they find out we're moving, and I need whatever you design to soften the blow." Donathan's personality was friendly, a combination of formal yet relaxed, approachable. Jess liked him right away.

"I understand," Jess said. She looked out her window and let herself relax. Designing an entire campus for the tech elite was a big ask, she knew. But more than that, she knew that she could do this. She had done harder things before, starting Anicca, for one. That awkward Jess of her youth, the one who never fit in, was no more. She had to remember that. "You know, Donathan, I think we can do better than avoiding angering your employees. I think we can design something that people will be really excited about."

"Oh man," Donathan said. "If you can pull that off, you're definitely hired. And I probably owe you something, like some small island off the coast of Brazil."

"We'll write it into the contract." Jess caught herself smiling. "Let's schedule an initial consultation. When are you free?"

"Any chance this afternoon could work?" Donathan said tentatively. "Because the other thing is ... Well, the timeline for this is pretty short. We have four months until we have to move."

Suddenly, Jess liked him less. "Four months?" Her incredulous tone couldn't help but slip through. "That's hardly any time, Donathan. You're asking for a miracle."

"I know, but I'll give you whatever resources you need and ... I don't know—I like to live in a world where I believe miracles happen." His charm seeped through the phone. Jess was not surprised that his company was so successful. He was managing to make her like him when she should be strangling him. "Listen," he went on. "I know it's short notice, but honestly I hate this stuff. I should have started a while ago, but I've been putting this off. I'll do whatever I can to set you up for success, and if you come through, you'd really be saving my ass."

"Fine. I'll take a look and let you know if it's possible," Jess grumbled. "Does 2 p.m. work for you?"

"Perfect! I'll meet you there," Donathan exclaimed. He quickly gave her the address of the new campus before hanging up.

"Charlie? Moira? Do you have a second?" Jess felt her heart race as they joined her.

Moira asked first. "What was that all about?"

Jess could barely contain herself, the words pouring out in a rush. "What that was about is that Jumbl is going to be opening a new campus, and we've been commissioned to design it. I'm supposed to meet Donathan Lewis there at 2 p.m."

"Oh my goodness, oh my goodness, oh my goodness," Charlie said. He braced himself against a cabinet and took deep measured breaths.

"Are you serious?" Moira clapped her hands together. "Wow, Jess. That's ... wow. The entire campus?"

"I know!" Jess stood up. The excitement was too much for her to stay seated. "There's just one catch."

"Uh oh," Charlie looked at Moira. "I told you on the elevator, didn't I? That we shouldn't get ahead of ourselves?"

"Charlie, please, this is so not an I-told-you-so moment," Moira told him. "Also, we have no idea what the catch is, so I'd save any comments until after we hear more. What is it, Jess?"

"Well," Jess pushed past the lump in her throat, "the project timeline is only four months."

Moira stopped short. "You can't be serious."

Jess nodded. "Unfortunately, I am. I told Donathan I'd have to take a look before agreeing to anything. I'm supposed to meet him there at 2 p.m."

"Wow," was all Moira could say.

Charlie shrugged his shoulders. "Four months? So what! We can do it. Nothing's impossible when you have millions of dollars to throw at something, and I'm guessing Jumbl is willing to spend on something like this."

"True," Jess replied. "Donathan did mention he could provide whatever resources we needed." She was thoughtful. "Is this crazy, to even be considering this? This is going to be Anicca's first project following that article. Even though it would be fantastic if it turns out great, it could ruin our reputation if it doesn't. I don't know … Maybe we'd be better off starting with something a little more manageable?"

"No!" Charlie exclaimed. "Jessica Tyler, you, honey, are a dreamer. You left a huge established firm a couple years ago to start your own company with this little skeleton crew. If you'd done that back in Georgia, you'd have a whole parade of people coming by your house under the guise of saying hi but really checking to make sure you hadn't lost your mind. But you did it, because nothing about you wants to stay small, and look where you're at now."

Moira, having recovered from her shock, joined the conversation. "I hate to say it, Jess, truly, I do," she paused for emphasis to give Charlie another look, "but Charlie's right. Yes, check it out today to make sure it's not a total disaster, but if it feels even borderline possible, I say we go for it. As much as we all might regret saying yes when we're three months in and haven't slept for the last two, I think we'd regret it more if we said no and Unoa or some other firm got the commission."

Jess's jaw stiffened slightly as she considered what they both were saying. "You know, I think you're right. As crazy as it would be to say yes, it would be crazier to say no. Alright," she threw her hands up. "I'll take a look and probably say yes. Just remember that you both convinced me to do this when you hate me later, k?"

"You got it," Charlie said, at the same time as Moira interjected, "No promises."

"Oh no," Jess shook her head. "We're in for it now. But honestly," she continued, more seriously, "I can't thank both of you enough, really. It's like everything is happening just as it should."

"It is." Charlie placed his hand on her shoulder. "About time too."

"Jess, I hope you know that this is exactly what you deserve. Charlie and I have put a lot of trust in you, and we wouldn't be here if we didn't have faith that you'd succeed." Moira gave Jess a hug. "I hope you have that faith in yourself."

Jess squeezed Moira tightly for a moment before letting go. "Thank you." She felt her eyes tear up as she turned to hug Charlie.

The phone rang again.

"Another admirer for you, Jess," Moira said. "Charlie and I will get everything ready. You bask."

Jess picked up the phone as the two of them went into the hallway. She considered Moira's words. It was nice to believe that everything that was happening was simply no more than they all deserved. Her lips turned up as she took in that possibility, so tender, laying hopeful on her heart.

• • •

A few hours later, after more phone calls than Jess cared to count, things finally calmed down. Jess looked out the window of her office, catching a glimpse of the sky, her old friend, waiting patiently for her.

She had always loved this view. Anicca's office was in the heart of the design district in SF, right next to Potrero Hill. Design felt alive here, possible. The area itself was charged with a certain energy. So many dreams had come to fruition here. Once a warehouse district, Potrero Hill had attracted artists looking for big spaces and cheap rent. Over time, it had transitioned to become a design epicenter, a bourgeois evolution solidified by the opening of that unofficial signature of neighborhood gentrification: Whole Foods.

But Jess liked the neighborhood for its roots. She liked that you could still see the rough around the edges. The warehouses carried some of their original grit, and the hodgepodge of architectural designs reminded her that this place had a history, not polished in the same way as neighboring Mission Bay, with its commercial landlords and intentional urban planning. It had come to be without that, and the resulting mix of commercial spaces, houses, and a park that seemed to always have a baseball game taking place was comforting to Jess. She found it beautiful, its imperfections making it more real, more perfect.

Before every project, Jess had a ritual of walking up to the top of the hill to take in the feel of the city as she let her creativity flow. She loved San Francisco itself as a symbol of change. It had grown so different from how it was when she was a child, but through it all, its heart continued to beat true, that part of change that remains, permanent amongst the impermanent.

As Jess sat in her office chair, she realized she needed to walk there now. She checked the time and saw she had only a little more than half an hour before she needed to make her way to meet Donathan. She would have to be quick, but it would be worth it. She needed to be with herself, to resource herself in the best way she knew how, before taking on what was unquestionably the biggest project of her life.

She put on her shoes and went outside. The fresh morning air touched her face. She took a deep breath and let her shoulders naturally relax. She started walking along De Haro street, absorbing her surroundings. The buildings around her were all unique, a combination of stick-style Victorians and industrial spaces reimagined through a mission-style exterior and more mid-century modern and post-modern designs. Colors popped in a color scheme that perfectly captured the spirit of this area. The colors weren't necessarily complementary—mint green sitting causally next to electric yellow and neon blue—technically violating one of the basic principles of design. Regardless, though, the combination had ... character. The energy of the city here was palpable. It hummed, speaking of how it was possible to transform yourself, but how it took work and how, at the end of the day, you'd keep a little part of the old you. That was yours, always.

Jess walked slowly, making time to look around her. She knew, ultimately, that, although she had officially chosen to have her office in the design district for practical reasons (it was simply the place one *had* to be in if one were to be taken seriously as a designer), the real reason was deeper. She connected with this energy, with this attitude.

The energy of finally finding yourself after so many years of being lost—that was Jess's story, too. The world wanted her to be perfect. Jess wanted only to dream.

She'd learned that lesson early. She'd daydreamed during science class, imagining how the different pieces of lab equipment could be repurposed: a beaker becoming a flower vase, a series of vials artistically hung on a wall to create a space for measuring cups. Imagining what things *could* be was much more fun than paying attention to things as they happened to be at that time. Nothing stayed the same. And to not listen to that other part of the object, the part that wanted to evolve, felt so limiting.

Jess had always connected with the things she touched. She'd also learned, from a young age, that everything had a story, if you let it. Jess had, from a young age, known how to listen.

The world was alive when you let it be.

She'd mostly been okay about being as she was, at least when she was by herself. The problem had come when she tried to operate in the mundane world. She'd gone to college, as one does, and had struggled to find herself, as one does. But luckily, in her sophomore year, she had signed up for a design course, on a whim, as it happens with so many important life decisions, but she had fallen in love. Something clicked. It was like she had been speaking a different language her whole life and had just been given a translator. Design was her path, how she could bring this secret world she had kept in her heart out for others to see.

Jess had devoured design, taking all the classes she had time for and could afford and reading all the books she could read. She created, and created, and created. Her creations had come pouring out of her, the song of her spirit.

Rebecca had told her once that she knew that Jess was bound to change the design world; it just had to catch up to her first. She wondered if that was what was happening now, if maybe that was all that had ever needed to happen, that she didn't need to change to be part of the world, but rather that it needed to change to find a place for her.

Jess reached the top of the hill. She looked around at the city that she loved. She saw Bernal Hill a short distance away, followed by Sutro Tower, Twin Peaks, and a view of the Bay Bridge. She breathed and let the cool air fill her lungs. A smile came upon her face, her spirit responding to the air, the sun, and then the energy. Glancing down the hill, she saw her office, shining out. Her place.

She had created her place within this world.

Chapter 4

JESS ARRIVED AT THE SITE OF THE FUTURE JUMBL CAMPUS. IT WAS on the other side of town, near Lake Merced, a part of the city that Jess loved and looked forward to getting to know more.

After thanking her Uber driver, she stepped out of the car and felt the cool breeze surround her. Amazingly, she'd made it to the site with five minutes to spare. Her eyes caught sight of a coast live oak tree nearby, one of the few native species in the area, and responding to a pull it had to her, she found herself moving in its direction. The energy of the tree felt soothing, solid. This lesser discovered pocket of the city maintained a wild feel, less manicured than Golden Gate Park, more in touch with nature and how San Francisco once was. She closed her eyes and allowed her senses to take over: the cool air, the fresh smell, the warmth of the sun, the hum of nature, of life, around her.

"Hello, Ms. Tyler," a voice called out. Jess felt her heart jump. The voice was familiar, but Jess couldn't place it. Regardless, she immediately felt her heartbeat quicken and her skin tingle. Whoever was calling her name was someone who came with a palpable energy, soft and strong, but with a hardness underneath that offered a challenge, an invitation in, if she were up to the task. Jess's body felt electric.

Jess squinted one eye open. Jack Stinson was standing a few feet away from her, hands in his jean pockets, looking casually confident and sexy. His brown eyes had a greenish tint to them, reflecting the colors of the scenery and making him even more attractive, something Jess had not thought was possible. It was unfair, Jess thought, that someone could walk around the world looking that way. She guessed that he was the type of person that could have anything and anyone he wanted. She thought about what Alex had said, that he was fun but not someone who stuck around. She and Jack were so different, Jess thought. He was someone who had always not only belonged but had set the tone of what "fitting in" even meant. He would never understand what it was like to have to find yourself because he had never been lost. That he was here, in this relatively obscure part of the city, getting in the way of her finding her inspiration, was certainly inconvenient. The electricity that had been in Jess's body before was transforming into something more like irritation.

"What are you doing here?" Jess asked. She paused, realizing she had come across more abruptly than she thought. Despite the energetic roller coaster she seemed to find herself in around him, the only crime he had committed thus far was saying hello. She could, she thought begrudgingly, at least be professional around him.

"Sorry." She turned to face him. "You caught me off guard. Let me start over. Hi, Jack, nice to see you again. What brings you to this part of town?"

Jack laughed. "You know, I think your initial reaction was more believable." He took a step closer. Jess could smell him, rustic and masculine. It was unfair that she responded to him like this, particularly given that she'd decided they were so different. "I'm here for the same reason you are, I imagine," he continued. "Giving my two cents on Donathan's campus. I'd say it's nice to see you again, except on my end, I'd actually mean it."

Jess softened. He was direct; she had to give him that. But in him, it came off as charismatic.

"Busted," she laughed. "I'll have to work on my interrupted-mid-reverie greeting style. So, wait, you're here to design Jumbl, too? I … I guess I didn't even know you designed."

"I don't," he replied. "Donathan asked me to be here, though. I have no idea why. But we go way back. He's like a brother, so when he asks me for a favor, I try to comply." A mischievous look came over his face. "He usually doesn't get me into *too* much trouble."

"Just the right amount, I guess." Jess looked at Jack intently as he looked back. Something about his expression affected Jess. It was like he saw her, all the way through. Even though their interactions had been brief, she could tell that he noticed her, noticed more than she would have liked to reveal. She wasn't quite sure what to make of that.

She suspected that her inclination to dislike him was not entirely fair. He was, after all, a seemingly nice person showing some kindness and loyalty to his friend. That he would show up for Donathan simply because he'd asked spoke well of Jack's character. She wondered what kind of history they had together that would create such a tight bond. Begrudgingly, she admitted to herself that she *might* have written him off a little too quickly. It was possible that he was a little more multidimensional than her snap judgment had allowed. As much of an entitled playboy as she was internally painting him out to be, she had to acknowledge that he was the type of guy who valued the people in his life and wanted to show up for them, people, at least, that he let close enough to earn that trust.

"Hey, you two!" Jess and Jack separated their gaze as they looked to see Donathan running up. "Sorry I'm late. Hope you haven't been waiting too long?"

"No problem. We just got here," Jess said. Jack nodded in agreement. To her unwelcome dismay, Jess was vaguely disappointed that Donathan had interrupted her time with Jack.

"Oh good." Donathan slowed as he approached them. "Great place, huh? Huge potential. Huge." His hands moved emphatically as he spoke. His whole presence was larger than life, but somehow, he owned it and transformed that energy into an undeniable charisma.

Jack looked conspiratorially at Jess. "This, you have to understand, is classic Donathan. We're standing in front of a building that it wouldn't be unfair to call dilapidated, and Donathan's delusional enough to look at it like it's a diamond. Donathan," Jack turned to face his friend, "tell me you're at least being reasonable with her."

"Come on, now," Donathan waved Jack away. Jess took it as a testament to the depth of their friendship that Jack let him. She doubted he was a man who took kindly to being shooed. "All it needs is a little vision. I'm hoping you can help with that, Jess."

Jess shrugged her shoulders. "Well, I'll certainly look. And to answer your question, Jack," she made eye contact with him and felt a wave of renewed energy coarse through her, "he's definitely being unreasonable. The timeline he's given me is four months."

"Four months!" Jack's eyes widened. "Run, Jess. Run far away."

"Ha, ha," Donathan interjected. "I would be careful about what you say right now, Jack, because every word that comes out of your mouth only gives me more to gloat over when I turn out to be right, as I always do. Come," he continued, cutting off Jack's retort. "Let me show you around."

"Whatever it takes to stop this from coming to blows," Jess offered. "Besides, I suppose I should get a sense of what I'm maybe signing up for."

Jack's eyes twinkled at her. "Just try not to burst his bubble too harshly, Jess."

Jess consciously averted her gaze as she gave a stiff nod of acknowledgement. Her attention went back to Donathan who was heading towards the building. Donathan, she noticed, was also athletic, like Jack, but slightly shorter. Jess had seen him in pictures before, but seeing him in person, she became aware of the brightness of his smile and the sparkle in his eyes. His energy was naturally fun and welcoming. Jess could tell that his charisma coupled with what she was identifying as an unrelenting optimism had almost certainly been critical to the success of his company.

Donathan paused in front of the door. "This is what I imagine the main office building would be. There are a few other buildings in this area that could be, I don't know, a cafeteria or gym or something else. Honestly, those ideas feel a little boring; every campus has those. I'm hoping that you can create something truly remarkable."

"Four months," Jess heard Jack mumble incredulously under his breath.

The three of them walked into the foyer of the building. It was, to put it kindly, a dump. In need of significant repair, it had clearly been left untouched for some time. A few light fixtures were barely hanging to the ceiling, subfloor was showing through in a few patches, and what furniture there was looked like it hadn't been used in at least a couple decades. Those issues aside, though, there was something else. The building's size and emptiness came off as harsh, sterile. Jess was surprised that such a plain building existed in such opposition to the beautiful scenery surrounding it, much like what she imagined the buildings in the Presidio must once have looked like when they were still army barracks, before they were converted into residential and commercial spaces.

"So, yeah, this is it," Donathan said. To his credit, his voice, instead of seeming anxious, rang only hopeful. "Listen, I have no idea what this place could be, except that I know it could be something special. I couldn't tell you why I feel that way. Aesthetics, I can't do. But I know what it's like to feel inspired by a blank canvas, like a computer screen waiting to be full of code. I hope that you get that kind of feeling about a place like this." He looked over at Jess. "Let me know if you think it will work. I'm set on the place, though. As soon as I came to this area, I knew it was something special. This is the next site of Jumbl, no doubt."

Jess considered her surroundings. She liked Donathan's energy. There was truth in his words. Even though the site, as it was, needed some love, there was a vibrant hum to the space, that same hum of primordial energy that she had connected with since she was young. "Can I have a minute to think?" she asked.

"Sure. Take your time," he replied, graciously taking a step back.

Jess walked over to one of the walls on the far side of the building. She placed her hand on it and closed her eyes. She focused on her heartbeat and then felt, first the connection between the palm of her hand and the wall and then, more subtly, the connection between her palm and the beat in her chest as it fell into sync with the energy of the building. She felt the aliveness hidden in its walls. The slow hum turned into a pulse. There was a spirit here. There was something this building wanted to say, some way it wanted to shine. As Jess moved deeper into the connection, she realized that, in some ways, her work would be easy. The building was longing to speak, and all Jess had to do was translate.

She opened her eyes. "I can do it," she said. "You're right, Donathan. This building, this place, is special. I believe that the right design can bring that out. I think we can create something magical here."

"Yes!" Donathan clapped his hands together. "Exactly. I'm so relieved that you *get* that. I knew you'd be the right person to design it. I hope you don't mind, but I had my team do some reconnaissance before I invited you over. After reading your profile in 7×7, I checked out a few of your other projects and felt like, if anyone could understand this place, it would be you. So, you'll do it?"

"Well, we'd have to talk about logistics, but excepting something big happening, I'd say yes."

"Great! Whatever you need, we'll make it happen." His enthusiasm was contagious. Jess felt herself liking him even more.

"So, did you need me for something, Donathan?" Jack asked, stepping back into the conversation. Jess and Donathan had been so excited with the possibilities of the space that they had almost forgotten he was there.

"Oh, right, of course!" Donathan said. He turned back to Jess. "So, yeah, there's one more thing. I'm … I'm not great at this design stuff. I really meant it when I said my canvas is a computer screen. But Jack … Jack is actually a great artist. Sure, he had to sell his soul to start his solar company, but underneath that crusty corporate exterior is the next Van Gogh. Or someone equally talented but less crazy."

He intentionally ignored Jack's side-eye as he continued. "Anyway, I want you to work with Jack on this. Not all the time, of course—it's your design. But I'm sure there will be questions that come up about what material to use or which design to choose over another, and I'm telling you right now, I'll be complete crap at helping you out with that. Worse than that, I'd be complete crap but then choose something anyway and then feel regret about what I'd chosen and change my mind about a hundred times before you finally quit because I'm such a pain to deal with. It saves us all a lot of headache and prevents you from throwing in the towel if I outsource to my best friend here. And with all the other things involved with moving the campus, plus the massive hiring spree the company is undertaking—that is the reason we have to change locations in the first place—I'm swamped. Plus," Donathan raised his eyebrows mischievously at Jack, "Jack owes me for helping him work on funding for his company."

Jess felt herself stiffen. She regretted having just committed to do the project. Working with Jack was not something she had bargained for when she'd spontaneously agreed. What's more, she wasn't sure she wanted to work with Jack. There was some charge between them that was best left unexplored, and she needed to keep her distance to accomplish that. This arrangement would put her in close—and inevitable—contact with him.

On the other hand, Donathan had a point. She would need input at certain junctures, and there was nothing worse than an indecisive and remorseful client. Regardless, the idea of working with Jack made her uneasy. She knew it was unfair to have judged him like she did. He couldn't help the family he was born into any more than she could, and some part of her suspected that she was being unfair to him. In all their interactions to date, he'd been nothing but polite, friendly, and charming. But something about him still nagged at her. She kept getting the sense that he saw through her. It made her uneasy. Some part of her, though irrational, she tried to tell herself, remained worried that, if they got even closer, he'd see too much.

Then again, designing the Jumbl campus was a huge opportunity. That she was being offered it on the spot simply because Donathan had Googled a few of her designs after her article came out was stunning. The intuition that had compelled him to launch his own company must, she figured, have been the reason for him coming to such a quick decision now. He seemed to have no qualms about the cost, which meant that Jess could realize whatever vision she wanted, even if fantastical. That was exciting. Beyond that, this was her chance to start working with an entirely different type of client base. The 7×7 profile had been her launch point, Jess realized, to this kind of opportunity.

Perhaps more than that, though, she was called to the space. The stunning landscape needed to be understood and integrated into the design. Jess felt like it was an opportunity she shouldn't pass up.

Which meant, unfortunately, that she had to square working with Jack. "Would you even want to do that?" she asked him. "That's a big project your friend is asking you to take on there."

"Woo, let me think about it." He squinted his eyes. "Um, yeah, I think I don't have a choice. See, first of all, I've known Donathan long enough to know that, when his mind is set on something, he's irritatingly unmovable in his opinion. Second of all, I know that, if I don't do this, he'll be pestering me with questions all the time anyway, and it will be more irritating than if I'd said yes in the first place."

Donathan nodded in agreement. "My friend knows me well, Jess. Irritation into submission is my number one sales strategy."

"And," Jack added, his expression now serious, "it would give me an opportunity to work with you, see inside that mind of yours a little more. I have a deep respect for people who are creative, and I can already tell you are, through and through. No, this is one of Donathan's completely-too-much-to-ask-for requests that I think I would enjoy, if you would be open to having me tag along."

Jess was disarmed again. Jack's candor, while flattering, brought up those same feelings that she had had before, that he was seeing more than she thought he was showing. He said what he was feeling and didn't hold back. If she didn't watch herself closely, she could end up letting him in more than she liked. She'd have to stay watchful. This was a man, she could tell, who could be dangerous.

"Well, okay then. If you're down, I'm down. I'll warn you, though, I'm going to blow your minds with what we can do with this place. You have something special here, Donathan. I think you'll be amazed by what it can be."

"Challenge accepted," he said. "Let's set up a time to work out the details. I can't wait."

Jess tried to match his enthusiasm with her expression. The design opportunity was fantastic, she had to remember that. As she left the site, though, something unsettled remained. Working with Jack ... she hoped she hadn't signed up for more than she had bargained for.

Chapter 5

IT WAS LATER THAN USUAL BY THE TIME JESS GOT HOME THAT evening. It had been an eventful day: the write-up in 7×7, the opportunity to work on the new Jumbl campus and make her mark among the tech elite, and the news that, as part of that venture, she'd be working closely with Jack Stinson.

She went over to her nook by the bay window and let her mind drift. Even with the many events of the day, it was Jack that her mind was focused on. She felt ... unsettled. She didn't have any specific reason to feel that way. After all, she was a professional, and he was a professional, and they were both working together professionally. But she couldn't shake the feeling that the time they would spend together would feel anything but.

Now that she had a minute to herself, she tried to figure out what was going on. Okay, he was attractive. She hated to admit it, but there it was. He was conventionally, objectively attractive. She didn't have to deny it. No, instead, admitting it to herself would give her some distance from it all. He was an attractive man, and she thought he was interesting. That was it. Nothing more than that.

At least, Jess decided, she would refuse to let it become anything more. She refused to have her big day overshadowed by this one insignificant, inconvenient detail. She had worked so hard and risked so much so that she could make her impact in design, so that she could make something permanent through her creative expression, not so she could sit by her window daydreaming about what it would be like to feel his soft lips touch her own ...

Stop! Jess forced herself. She rose from her seat, shaking her head, and went to the kitchen. She needed to eat; that was why she was so distracted. All this confusion could be solved by a sandwich.

The truth was ... Well, there were a couple truths. The Jumbl commission represented a tremendous achievement, and Jess was not about to let some strange vibes off some old-money SF-trust-fund kid overshadow that.

But it was also true that she was afraid, not of Jack himself, necessarily. He seemed fine enough. But she was afraid of what he represented: a distraction, a step away from her thriving career. She'd heard the tale too often of a woman who'd given up her dreams for a relationship. Even her own mother had had to make that choice.

Jess let her eyes drift over her apartment, her body relaxing with each familiar object she saw. The apartment was small, technically a one bedroom, but only in the euphemistic lens of the expensive SF real estate market could it be considered anything other than a glorified studio. The kitchen, though, had the essentials, and Jess had made the interior beautiful. What it lacked in size, however, it made up for in location. The apartment was right in the heart of Alamo Square, the famous SF park that was situated across from the Painted Ladies. The park was the perfect place for Jess to spend a few minutes if she happened to get home early from work. She never had to go further than a block or two from her front door to feel the aliveness of the city. Jess had been lucky to get the place, paying under market because the landlord had an interest in her work and offered to reduce the rate if Jess would agree to contribute to the apartment's design. Jess had been happy to agree and had not regretted it. This apartment, with its bay window that Jess adored, was all hers. It had been her solace when she'd been finding herself and building her firm. She loved it.

As she was assembling the ingredients for her sandwich, her phone buzzed. It was a text from Rebecca: *I know you're home alone right now when you should be out celebrating. I'm at the bar at State Bird Provisions. Come have a drink with me!*

Jess glanced at her half-made sandwich. It was, now that she thought about it, not exactly the most celebratory meal after such a memorable day.

You know me too well! But at least I'm easily persuaded. Be there in 15.

Jess quickly ordered an Uber before putting her sandwich back in the fridge.

In less time than she had anticipated, she arrived at the famous restaurant on Fillmore Street.

Rebecca enthusiastically waved her over. "Hello!" she patted the stool next to her at the bar.

"Hi!" Jess replied, giving Rebecca a hug before finding the hook to hang her purse.

"I only half assumed you'd be home alone, by the way." Rebecca shifted to accommodate Jess's purse. "But even the possibility was sad enough. Glad I got you out of the house! Honestly, though, who better to celebrate this achievement with than me, your old boss, you know, the one who found you and shaped you when you were fresh out of grad school. Just remember me when they ask who knew you when."

Jess's eyes sparked playfully. "Um, yeah, I *think* I remember you. I recall it a little differently, though. Aren't you the Rebecca whose business I infinitely improved through bestowing it with my creative genius?"

"Ha! The very one." Rebecca summoned the bartender over to order two glasses of champagne. "So, congratu-fucking-lations!" They clinked glasses. "That was one hell of a write-up. You certainly caught the attention of the SF design world today. How does it feel?"

"Great! Really great! Honestly so, so great and also," Jess hesitated. She wasn't sure if it was okay to feel anything other than exuberant at the profile. But Rebecca had been her mentor for so long that it felt disingenuous to be other than honest with her. "The truth is, it's great, mostly, but also terrifying. It's like all of a sudden people *expect* something now. When I was only building Anicca, the only place I could go was up. I didn't have to worry about what people thought because, well, they didn't think anything. But now, I don't know … Now I feel this pressure that the next thing I design has to be amazing so that people don't think

I was a flash in the pan. In many ways, the future of Anicca feels more tenuous than ever. Does that make sense?"

Rebecca's expression was soft. "Yes, of course it does. Now the microscope is on you in a way it never was before. Ooh," she took a sip of her champagne, "I do not envy you there. The next few years are going to challenge the hell out of you, and you'll either rise to the challenge or ... Well, there is no 'or.' Not really. Not for you. Jess, you know, you *have* to know, that you were meant for this work. You'll live up to their expectations. Just, you know, don't expect to have a social life for a while."

Jess took her own sip. It was smooth, delicate, with what Jess imagined some might describe as strawberry tones. "Thanks, I think. You've always believed in me, Rebecca. Thank you for giving me the opportunities you gave me at Unoa. I have no idea how I would have gotten started if it hadn't been for your mentorship."

"First of all, you're welcome," Rebecca said. "Second of all, if we're going to be having this kind of conversation, I'm going to need at least some appetizers, so hold that thought." Rebecca waved the bartender down again and ordered some oysters and lamb dumplings.

"Okay, now, where were we? Ah, yes, the post-having-made-it existential crisis. Okay," Rebecca took Jess's hand. "Jess, don't you dare sell yourself short. Real talk—there are a lot of people who are going to make you doubt yourself, my dear, especially now that you're playing on a whole new level. People are jealous and insecure. Some people feel like they need to make you small in order for them to feel big. But you have a real talent. Don't you ever, ever forget it. I saw it in your graduation exhibition, and I've seen it since in every design you ever turned in at Unoa. You're going to make an impact in this world. So, go do it."

Jess listened intently to Rebecca's words, some ache inside her that she hadn't known was there releasing. "Thank you, Rebecca. I don't know what to say."

"Well, I mean every word." Rebecca's demeanor shifted from serious to playful. "Even if I didn't, though, it's some pretty good buttering up, right? Which is great for me. I have to keep my contact with you warm in case I ever need to work for you some day!"

Jess shook her head. "If it ever comes to that, consider yourself hired."

"Let's be real, Jess. If it ever comes to that, I'm finding a new career." Rebecca's humor allowed Jess to relax. "Now, tell me about all the people who've come to congratulate you and ride on your coattails in the past few hours."

"You mean other than you?" Jess kidded.

"Naturally. And it doesn't count if I'm picking up the tab, which I of course am. That's more like a mutual coattail riding experience," Rebecca said assuredly.

Jess remembered why she'd always had a special bond with Rebecca. There had been many designers at Unoa, but Rebecca had particularly mentored Jess. It would have been easy for Rebecca to be threatened by Jess's talent, but instead of their relationship heading in that direction, Rebecca had embraced and nurtured Jess, allowing her to hone her skills and grow.

"Well, by far the most interesting is Donathan Lewis," Jess volunteered, her tone shy.

Rebecca's eyes widened. "Donathan Lewis, Jumbl Donathan Lewis?"

"Mm-hmm." Jess wasn't sure how much she was allowed to share. She was pretty sure that the new campus was not yet public information.

Rebecca noticed Jess's evasion. "Okay, I won't push too hard, although I have to admit I'm intrigued. Probably some grand scale design project, right?" At Jess's assent, she continued, "Alright. Well, you don't have to share details, but I hope it's worthwhile. And Jess, I know you didn't ask for my advice, but let's be honest, when has that ever stopped me? Don't be afraid to put your foot down when it comes to client expectations. We can only do what's possible. That said, what's possible is pretty fantastic."

"It's uncanny how you just clocked that." Jess thanked the bartender for bringing over their dishes. "His expectations could use a little adjusting."

"Maybe," Rebecca considered. "Or maybe it's just that this ain't my first time at the rodeo."

"Could be that too." Jess took a bite of the dumpling, her mouth watering at the complex and delicate blend of spices. "But yes, it's a grand scale project with a nearly impossible timeline. And as for putting my foot down, well I, um, sort of already committed to it."

Rebecca shook her head. "Why am I not surprised? Although I guess, at the risk of sounding patronizing, learning to set boundaries is something that comes with time."

"You know, Rebecca, I liked it better when you were telling me how awesome I was and not making me terrified about the first project that I'm taking on at what you've just made clear is an extremely crucial time in my career!" Jess's tone was playful but serious all the same.

"Okay, you're right, you're right. I'm sorry!" Rebecca somehow slurped an oyster while conveying an air of defense. "You're going to be fine, honestly. You just might, you know, have some hairy moments for a bit, that's all."

Jess raised her eyebrow. "I guess that's real."

"And," Rebecca continued, "you know that you can call if you need support or, I don't know, if you need to collaborate and give Unoa credit on whatever you're working on, too."

Jess laughed as she shook her head. "No! This is Anicca's baby. Unoa has enough awesome projects to work on."

"Can't blame a girl for asking," Rebecca grabbed a dumpling. "Listen, I know you'll be fine, more than fine, but in all honesty, you know you can count on me should you ever need."

Jess felt her insides turn warm. "You know, I really do." She paused, then. She considered telling Rebecca about Jack's involvement but stopped. She wasn't sure if they had that kind of relationship, for one thing. For another, she wasn't at all sure what she would have said. She was still processing that whole dynamic herself.

"I feel like there's something more you're not saying, but I won't push you on it. Anyway," Rebecca sipped her champagne, "something tells me that whatever it is, is not entirely about work."

Jess hated how transparent she could be. "You're right on both counts. But enough about me. Honestly, all day long, all I've done is talk to people about me, and I'm sick of it. Tell me what's going on with you!"

Rebecca's face lit up. "Well, as long as you're asking ..."

Jess relaxed as Rebecca caught her up on everything that had been happening at Unoa. She sensed, on some level, that their relationship was subtly shifting. Rebecca was still her mentor, but Jess, having now set forth on her own, was closer to a peer.

The evening carried on pleasantly, with Rebecca insisting she pick up the check. "It's a write-off! One of my favorite things about running my own business, by the way, is the deductions. Jess, thanks for letting me celebrate you tonight. Now, go home and get some rest. Remember when you wake up tomorrow that everything is different, in the best of ways, and that this is your time."

Jess thanked Rebecca and hugged her goodbye. She decided to walk home along Fillmore, appreciating the consistent hub of activity that flooded the trendy street. As she took in all hustle-bustle on the outside, inside, she noticed a shift. She hadn't known she needed Rebecca's blessing, but having received it, things were complete.

She'd always looked up to Rebecca. Rebecca was a firm believer that there was enough for all and that you never got ahead by cutting someone else down. She had made it clear at the outset that Unoa was never to succeed at someone else's expense. Jess remembered Rebecca telling her once to hold on to her friends, no matter how much work demanded your time. In the end, success doesn't mean much if there's no one there to celebrate with you.

Rebecca had taught Jess design, but more than that, she had taught Jess how to carry herself, what values to operate by, and how to be a professional in this competitive world. Jess considered her almost like a second mother.

Speaking of which, she realized she had yet to return a phone call from her mother earlier that day. She had taken her time doing so, in part out of being busy but, truth be told, in part out of anxiety. Jess knew that Diane wanted Jess to be happy, above all else, but ... She also knew that her decision to choose career over everything else was in stark contrast to the choice her mother had made, and sometimes she wondered how Diane truly felt about that.

The profile's effect on Jess's career could potentially be significant, and although that was fantastic news in one sense, it made the chance that Jess would pursue the family life that her mother had chosen even less likely. As Jess continued to walk down the busy street, though, she started to feel that the celebration was incomplete. More than anything, Diane would be excited for her, and Jess was tired of overthinking it. She punched in her mother's number.

"Jess!" Diane exclaimed, answering the phone. "*Aaaaah!* I saw the profile this morning. And again this afternoon. And I read it again just now. Oh Jess, I am so proud of you."

Jess noticed moisture around her eyes. "Aw, thanks, Mom. Really, thank you. This whole experience has been such a whirlwind,

I've barely had time to think about it. It's like I'm one big ball of tired, but towards the edges, it feels vaguely like happiness."

"I'm sure," Diane's tone softened. "You always were one who had trouble basking in her accomplishments. You deserve all of it, though, Jess. I really am so very, very proud to call you my daughter. Next time you come home, we'll have to have an official celebration."

Jess fidgeted slightly. There it was again, a comment about her not having been home. Sacramento, her hometown, was only a little more than two hours away, yet Jess hadn't been home in six months. More than six months, now that she thought about it. She knew that she was due for a visit. With everything being so chaotic lately, and things showing no signs of letting up, she had no idea when that would happen. She'd have to figure it out somehow. Jess hated knowing that the people you loved the most in life were often the ones you took the most for granted. Fresh from her conversation with Rebecca, she was reminded again of how important it was to not lose the ones who cared about you along the path.

"I'd really like that, Mom." She imagined her mother's eyes crinkling at the corners. "Hopefully we can find a date soon."

"I know, I know. You must be incredibly busy and, with this article coming out, soon even more so. But just know, there's a family here waiting to celebrate you whenever we can."

"Thanks, Mom." Jess felt heavy in her chest. "I'll try."

"Alright, you've had a long day. Go get some rest. I love you."

"Love you."

They hung up. As Jess put her phone away, her tight chest started to loosen. She hadn't realized that she'd been breathing more shallowly, or even that she'd been anxious at all, but now that she had time to herself, all the emotion that she'd been carrying inside for the past day, for the past two years, was starting to come out.

She reached her apartment and leaned on the door after she closed it behind her. She took one hand to her chest, closed her eyes, and breathed. Through the many emotions she had felt that day, one was starting to surface to the top.

Belonging.

The realization that this was finally it, young schoolgirl Jess, who had felt so odd, so ... not normal, finally had a place. *Jess* finally had a place. Scratch that—she had made her own place, through Anicca, and she was going to keep making it, no matter what. She had no idea what was about to happen, but she knew that, whatever it was, she could handle it.

Chapter 6

"JESS!" MOIRA GREETED HER AS SHE ARRIVED AT THE OFFICE THE following day. "There are about a million voicemails for you, mostly from well-wishers of varying degrees of acquaintanceship. One from your sister. Two from Donathan. That guy is … persistent. And one from someone named Jack Stinson wondering what the 'next steps' are, whatever that means."

Jess felt her stomach sink. Jack Stinson—shoot. She'd had such a good morning, still glowing from the day before during her run and even stopping for flowers on her way to the office, that she had almost forgotten about that small detail.

"Thanks, Moira." Jess took a vase out of one of the cabinets. "Looks like we have a busy day ahead of ourselves. I'll get set up and start responding. Can you put together a brief history on the Lake Merced area of San Francisco? If there's any way we're going to make the deadline on that Jumbl design, we're going to need to get started."

"Sure thing, Jess. I was planning on taking a yoga class at lunch today. Want to join?"

"I doubt I'll be able to. But you should go. And Charlie too. Everyone needs to make sure they stay relaxed so that they don't burn out."

Moira took the flowers from Jess and arranged them artfully on the counter. "Yes, I'll force him to go with me. Everyone likes that, right? Being forced to destress? It's usually pretty relaxing when someone's yelling at you that you have to relax."

"Exactly!" Jess pointed to Moira's floral arrangement. "You know, you're really talented at that. Maybe you can incorporate that into a design?"

Moira shrugged. "Perhaps. It's mostly for fun, but if the right project came along … You, Jess, have a lot of work to do, though, and so do I if I want to have time for that class. Let's work on that and talk flowers later."

"Agreed," Jess said. "Check in in a few hours."

Jess shut the door to her office and opened her laptop. While she waited for it to turn on, she checked her phone to see a text from Bridget: *Call me when you can. Want to hear about your fame so I can feel bad about myself while I slave away preparing for this deposition.*

Jess replied: *You're the one who decided to be a lawyer. <3 Slammed today. Yoga/brunch Saturday?*

Bridget's response was fast: *Ugh, fine. I'll do it if that means I can see you. Text details later.*

Jess texted back that she would and then turned to her inbox: 652 messages. Good lord. She didn't know 7×7 even had 652 sub-scribers. There were emails from people congratulating her, a few people wanting her to design their spaces—she forwarded those on to Moira with directions to keep them at bay until more progress had been made with the Jumbl project—five from Donathan, and one from Jack Stinson with the subject line "Jumbl — Next Steps."

Jess's heartbeat raced as she clicked the email open, saturat-ing her with what she could only describe as some combination of dread and excitement, two emotions that she was quickly learning could easily coexist at the same time.

> Hi Jess,
> Wanted to follow up on our meeting yesterday and talk about next steps for the Jumbl project. Let me know your availability.
> ~Jack

Jess's face flushed. It was beginning to sink in that she had really agreed to do this. Jumbl was a significant opportunity, but … She intentionally sat up straighter in her chair and took a deep breath. But nothing, she reasoned. There was no way she was going to let herself continue to question this. She had not worked this hard to turn down this project simply because she might have to run a few things by Jack.

She shook her head.

> Hi Jack,
> Thanks for initiating the conversation. I'm putting together some ideas today and tomorrow, mostly broad and based

on the history of the site and the geographical features surrounding it. After that, I'll get a sense of what you like and talk through what you're hoping to achieve with the design in the space. Usually I'd do that with Donathan, but he appears to have left things entirely up to you. Should be ready for that stage by Friday, but we can push until Monday if you would prefer not to start at the end of the week.

Best,

Jess

Best, she thought. It was such an oddly formal way for her to sign off. She hated how off-kilter he made her feel, even through email. She hated even more how she couldn't pinpoint what it was about him that had that effect on her.

She'd experienced people who made her feel uneasy before. Growing up feeling like she was always the odd one out had left a certain restlessness in her psyche. But usually, Jess was able to analyze, to understand what the person was doing or thinking or energetically transmuting that made her feel that way, and to focus on putting it back on them. It was hard, sometimes unrelenting work, but it had been crucial to her ability to grow professionally and personally too.

But with Jack, she was learning to understand, she had no such luck. His energy was all over the place: soft yet hard, inviting her in yet warning her to keep her distance. She'd have to do more introspection as she got to know him more, to understand why she found him so disorienting. The thought made her grumble. Spending more time thinking about Jack was the opposite of what she wanted to do.

Jess scanned through her other emails: congratulations from some old colleagues, a few possibly exciting offers to pitch projects. A pit formed in her stomach as she thought about how they were going to do it all. She'd have to hire more staff, probably, but that was risky in and of itself, having to agree to pay people who wanted a guaranteed income when she still couldn't be 100 percent sure that Anicca would have a consistent stream of projects, not to mention having to find people she could trust and who were the right fit and, oh yeah, trying to take on the daunting task of hiring when she was already going to be so busy that she didn't know what to do with herself.

Jess took a deep breath and steadied herself and tried to remind herself that this was a good thing as she continued perusing through her inbox. She came across an email from a contractor saying that they were going to be delayed on receiving a shipment of materials for a hugely important part of one of her existing projects, swiftly forwarding the email to Moira with the message, "Fuuuuuck. Please deal with this." It was emails like this that made her miss the sweet safety of Unoa where ultimately, problems like this, while a hassle, were Rebecca's to deal with. Rebecca's reputation was the one on the line. The thought made her have some empathy for Rebecca. She thought of their conversation the night before and Rebecca's warning that these next few years would be all-consuming. She was struck anew by the reality of those words.

By the time she had finished checking her remaining emails, much sooner than she expected, an email popped up from Jack.

Hi Jess,

Friday sounds great. Let's do lunch. And if you want me to be part of the brainstorming process, happy to do that too.

Superlative,

Jack

She stopped short as she considered what it would be like to have lunch with him. It was inevitable, she supposed, that they'd have some meals together, given that he was her *de facto* client. But some voice within her whined. She'd thought it maybe wouldn't happen so soon.

Pushing that part aside, Jess braced herself to respond. She was going to have to get their initial meeting over with, and over lunch was as good a time as any. She wasn't sure how she felt about him teasing her, closing with "Superlative." Then again, she herself had thought it odd that she ended the previous email using "Best" as the salutation. Maybe it was to his credit that he was lightening things up. She was going to have to give him more of the benefit of the doubt if this—what, partnership?—this whatever was going to work out.

She wrote him back saying that Friday was fine and named one of her favorite casual restaurants, Plow, as the location. She didn't acknowledge his desire to be part of the brainstorming process. That was a solid no for her. She needed to have her space to come to her own vision of the project before she let others in. Jack Stinson energy, she could already tell, would certainly not be helpful.

She punched in a Google image search for the Lake Merced area of San Francisco and started compiling a board of images. She was starting to get in the flow.

An hour later, Jess had the beginnings of an idea for the site. The southwest corner where Lake Merced was located was a hidden gem within the city, unexpectedly green and calm and soothing. One of her favorite parts of the city was how much natural beauty it still maintained: the wilderness of Mount Davidson; Glen Canyon, which was a bona fide canyon in the middle of a city; and Lake Merced, a serene lake surrounded by majestic trees. These bits of nature that seemed to fly in the face of the definition of "urban" and, yet, there they were, unabashedly taking up space. She appreciated what they stood for: the unapologetic expression of self. It was a message that connected to that part of Jess that still felt young and out of place, that part that, even after all this time, needed to hear that it was okay to take up space.

The images Jess had pulled online were a great start to her design, but they were missing something: that energy of the place, that feel that she'd had when she put her hand to the wall. There was a vitality that she needed to capture, and she needed to be there to tap into it.

She collected her things and ordered an Uber, letting Moira and Charlie know where she was going. To their credit, they simply nodded and didn't ask too many questions. The two years that they had worked closely together had made them understand her process enough to know when she needed to be left alone.

Within twenty minutes, she was at the lake. She started walking around, quietly, slowly, starting to take in the natural feel of the place. She had purposely chosen to come to the opposite side of the lake from where the Jumbl campus would be because she wanted to be able to experience the scenery for its own self, without thoughts of what the design would ultimately look like. She paused as she was crossing over a wooden bridge and looked down at the water. For several minutes, she stared, noticing the changes within the patterns of the water, imagining the water washing away her thoughts, feeling her heart start to ease as she let herself breathe along with the movement of the ripples. She was starting to merge with this place, to hear its story.

There was something about the lake that wanted more, even though it seemed to suggest that it was comfortable exactly where it was, content to be one of the city's many secrets, experienced mostly by the locals who lived in the area. The lake had patience, a serenity that came with having seen many generations come and go. Jess leaned in more deeply. There was also something else: a comfort in being hidden but a longing to be … *noticed.*

Noticed—what a strange word to have come to her. It was an odd idea for such a graceful place. So many people came to it, saw it, every day. But to be seen is not to be noticed, not truly. What Jess sensed was that the lake's story was about reconnection with something deeper. It was easy to see the lake. It was much harder to experience it.

Jess left the bridge and made her way to a nearby tree. She sat down, took her shoes off, and ran her hands and feet on the grass as she looked at the water, still and far away. She felt the responsibility of telling the lake's story. The presence of Jumbl would change the feel significantly. Done thoughtlessly, it had the potential to herald in a tech revolution that would soon overshadow the simple calm that the lake could provide. Jess tensed at the thought and squared her jaw. She couldn't let that happen. No matter what, the energy, that lifeforce of the lake would have to remain.

She took out her sketchbook and started drawing. Later, down the line, her designs would become digital and client-ready through the mixed blessing of AutoCAD and other software, but for right now, it was just her and her sketchbook. She drew gardens, lily pad-like benches where people would be directed with their morning coffees, outdoor workspaces where the desk areas were intentionally hidden so that someone would have to look up and see not a screen but life.

It was a new thing for her, to begin her design by focusing on the landscape. And yet, with this project, she wasn't ready for the interior or, rather, the thought hit her, the interior wasn't ready to let her in. She had to be invited inside.

Her imagination took off as she settled into the grass. Plazas and interconnected trails started to be born. All of them carried the theme of letting the natural beauty shine. The landscape was the star, and us, humans? Well, we are here for a bit and then we are gone. It was like the reverse of what Anicca meant. This time, the object was permanent and the viewer was transient. Jess couldn't stop drawing.

More green, and more green, and even more. So much more. You had to feel this place. It wasn't enough to have a coffee and then go back to the corporate world, closed off in its cold cement walls and compartmentalized away from life. The exterior of the building itself became a hanging garden, the top a roof decked with plants and tastefully secreted community spaces. This would be a place people could dream, where people could take a break from their coding lives and come outside, tend to the dirt, plant a flower. There would have to be a garden station full of local plants that invited those present to participate. The whole world had become so heady. Telling the lake's story would emphasize their return to the earth.

After some time, Jess felt the invitation to work on the interior. The hiddenness of her surroundings found its way into her design. Each room invited the people within it to pause and simply be with what was around. The energy honored connection, slowing down. Clean, simple lines directed the eye time and again to large windows surrounded by hanging plants and created with reclaimed wood.

The design materials would have to be local, organic, the building created with as little impact to the environment as possible: a tree fallen from a windstorm repurposed for the windowsills and doors, natural woods forming the floors, the softness of the grass preserved through tasteful additions to walls, each room inviting in the outside, as porous as possible.

And the water—Jess imagined the feeling of flow coming into the space, guiding people from one room to the next, taking them from one moment to the next until they came to a room with a wall entirely of glass where the star was the lake, the magnificence of it humbling the ego, so that anyone looking was suddenly aware that they were but a participant. The walls in this room would have a natural wooden pipe configuration that would bring water from the lake in and then take it back out, creating an alluring design and also honoring the flow and feel, that a person was part of this scene only for a time and then passed on.

Jess put her sketchbook down. It was enough for today. For now, all she wanted in the world was to simply be. And that, she felt, was exactly what the lake wanted, too.

Chapter 7

SUDDENLY IT WAS FRIDAY. JESS WONDERED WHERE THE TIME HAD gone. She couldn't believe it was just earlier that week that she'd been profiled in 7×7. She almost had to double check her calendar to make sure that was the case. It felt like a lifetime ago.

She was well into her design of the new Jumbl campus. Moira had been incredulous at the idea of the interior water feature circuiting with the lake water. "Are you out of your mind? And how, exactly, do you think we are going to convince the SF Board of Supervisors to permit something like that?"

But Jess was nothing if not determined. After much convincing and even a little light bribing (Moira deserved a few more days of PTO, after all), she'd gotten Moira to at least agree to contact the board.

Charlie had been more enthusiastic. "That will be so amazing! I love it. Bring the lake inside. Perfect!" He'd been furiously researching plants native to the area and reaching out to various landscape architect contacts to consult on the space.

Jess was excited, really excited. Success with this project, others were never slow to remind her, could open an entirely new potential client base. More than that, though, the lake was special. Designing the campus in a way that captured that was a chance to honor this city that she so loved. She got to be the one to bring light to this part of the city, this quiet, unassuming green space. She could connect with its deeper spirit and bring others to connect to it, as well. Jess always felt the most inspired when she had found that flow, in this case by being chosen to channel the energy of the landscape. It was like a pathway into this whole new universe that, when she was at her best, she knew in her heart existed.

She was so immersed in her vision that she was startled to see the calendar invite pop up on her phone: "Lunch w Jack Stinson." Jess was doubly frustrated by the reminder. In the first place, she felt she'd been on the verge of some creative breakthrough. In the second, well, she wasn't exactly looking forward to the lunch.

She packed up her things: some sketches, notebooks, lists of vendors, budget documents. She was ready to go. And yet, she found herself dragging. She squared her shoulders resolutely. This was a professional lunch, nothing more. She hated feeling anxious about it, hated that Jack seemed to hold this power over her. Soon, she hoped, she'd get over this phase. With one last internal pep talk, she headed out.

At twelve sharp, she arrived at the restaurant to see him sitting at a table. He had gotten there early. She was impressed. She figured he'd be the type who was too important to be on time, let alone get there early.

Aaah, she stopped herself. She wished she didn't have to think like that. She felt betrayed by her psyche, which seemed, for some reason, hell bent on painting this nice, probably decent guy into this villain. Then again, she thought, maybe the ways her psyche was handling Jack Stinson were best left unexamined.

"Hi, good to see you." Jess forced a smile.

Jack stood up to greet her. "Hi, and likewise. I got here early to put our names in. I know how packed this place can be." Jack looked relaxed, casual. Jess noticed how the cut of his sweater highlighted the muscles in his arms. "I have to admit: I've been excited about this conversation all week."

Jess tried to stay casual. "Really? Well, I'm glad to hear it. Hope it lives up to the hype."

"I'm sure it will." He sat down and motioned for her to join. "I think it will be a great lunch regardless. I'm curious about the design process. Design is somewhat of a passion project."

Jess sat down. "Is it? I had no idea." She really hadn't. Actually, as she thought about it, she knew virtually nothing about him. She'd purposely refrained from Googling him.

"Yeah, definitely. I've always been intrigued by how to make the impossible seem more … possible. It's why I do the work that I do." His voice got louder, and his speech quickened. Jess could tell his interest was sincere.

"What work is that?" she asked, genuine curiosity replacing her guardedness.

"I work in solar, broadly. Solar paneling, of course, but what most interests me is the technology: how we can make the most efficient type of panel, what little tweaks here and there will lead to maximum output." Jack laughed and leaned back in his chair. "I swear, it's more interesting than I made it sound. Although that's probably not a high bar."

Jess felt the corners of her mouth go up. She was enjoying his company, despite herself. Maybe working with Jack wouldn't be so bad after all.

"I'm sure if I were to describe why I love design, I'd get a similar response. When you're into something, really into it, the most mundane things become fascinating. It's like a secret language that you have between you and your work that no one else can understand, and when you try to explain it, it always falls short."

Jack leaned in and tilted his head. "Yes, exactly." He was close to Jess now, and she could feel his energy. It was palpable, intense, and subtly shifting. That part that had felt hard before was moving back within him so that the softness that permeated it went more deeply, offering more room for her to move close.

"Hi, how are you both? Can I get you anything?" A waiter materialized beside them. Jess pulled away from Jack, relieved at the forced interruption from the intensity of her observation.

"You'll have to give us another minute or two, I'm afraid," Jess said. She and Jack had been so engaged in their conversation that they hadn't bothered to look at the menu. "But in the meantime, can I have an iced tea?"

"I'll have the same, please," Jack said. "Or if you have an Arnold Palmer, I'll take that."

"You got it. I'll be back in a couple minutes."

The waiter left, and it was just the two of them again. Some of Jess's previous anxiety started to return. She liked that Jack was interested in her work, but the more she shared with Jack, the more something inside her cautioned her to slow down. She worried that, if she didn't keep her guard up, something could happen that she wasn't sure she was ready for.

"Guess we'd better look at the menu. I don't want to get in trouble again." Jack's eyes twinkled mischievously. He determinedly put his head down and perused the menu.

"I get the sense that being in trouble wouldn't exactly be unfamiliar to you?" Jess questioned. She looked at the menu and chose an omelet with nettles. It was lunch time, but the omelets at Plow were legendary, and she liked the word "nettles," perhaps even more than she cared about how they tasted.

"I'm not sure what impression I've given you, Ms. Tyler, but I have never been anything but honorable." Jack looked dead serious. Jess looked him in the eye and saw that same mischievous twinkle. She shook her head as his face became even more mock serious.

"Oh, come on." She rolled her eyes as Jack laughed, returning to the menu. She had no idea what the past would have been like for this man: privileged, wealthy, growing up as invincible SF royalty. She could only imagine what kind of incidents a ne'er-do-well cocktail like that had created. The thought of it was intriguing but also sobering. It reminded her of all the people who Jack, she was sure, was accustomed to charming. What Jess had built was way too important to her to take even the slightest risk with him.

"Yes, well, I'm sure you'll have plenty of opportunities to confess your sins over these next few months. But in the meantime, let's get started on this design." Jess squared her shoulders and reached for her portfolio. Jack stiffened himself at the abrupt change, a puzzled look on his face as he tried to figure out the reason behind the noticeable shift. It was fine to let him wonder, Jess thought. They had work to do.

The waiter came back with their drinks, and they placed their orders. Jess took out some of her sketches and placed the rest of the portfolio back down.

"Okay, Project Jumbl," she started. "I'm sure we'll come up with a better name than that eventually, but it's a working title for now. Essentially the concept is centered around the lake. Or rather, the concept *is* the lake, with an acknowledgement that, although we are here, we are visitors partaking in something greater than ourselves. The design starts outside ..."

Jess flipped open to a page when Jack reached over to stop her.

"Jess, have I ... a second ago ... did I say something?" He looked so sincere, so baffled. It caught her off guard.

"No, Jack, you're all good. I just ..." she paused, not sure how to explain what had just happened herself. *I'm afraid of the effect you have on me? Something deep inside that I'd rather not explore too thoroughly is warning me against you, but I have no idea why and even the act of inquiry feels threatening?* "Look, we have a lot of work to do. A campus is no joke. And with now less than four months until deadline, the designs themselves should be at least 90 percent finalized by next week, if not sooner. I don't mean to come off as abrupt, but we need to tackle a lot and have only a short amount of time."

Jack sat back. She could tell that he felt there was something more but was wise enough not to push it. After all, everything she'd said was correct. They did have to get started on this project, and that took priority over all else, fascinating as the mechanics of solar panels might be.

"Alright, show me what you got." Jack was more reserved than before. Jess felt relieved at the change but also mildly disappointed. She had liked playful Jack, more than she wanted to admit.

"Okay, so as I was saying, this design is all about the lake." As Jess explained the concept, his eyes lit up. He seemed interested, fascinated. When she got to the main feature, the lake room with the water circulating throughout, he took a breath.

"Jess, this is amazing, sincerely. Stunning. It's fascinating to see what comes out of your mind." He leaned back. "I've been think-ing about some of the design elements, too, and while I wouldn't claim anything near your expertise, I was hoping we could incor-porate some of my ideas, if appropriate. For example, hammocks. Nothing says relaxed at the lake more to me than hammocks; plus, I think they'd be a feature that the tech world would appreciate, sort of like a lake version of a beanbag chair."

Jess stiffened. She immediately hated the suggestion. It was so ... tacky, the quintessential tech-bro move that she could tell would be an insult to the lake.

"Thanks, Jack. I'll take that into consideration." She plastered a smile onto her face. It was normal, she knew, for clients to interject ideas given that she was, at the end of the day, designing for their tastes. Part of the art of interior design consisted of graciously letting a client know when an idea was, to put it politely, not a great fit. Jess was used to this dance, but with Jack, it felt different. It wasn't necessarily that his idea wouldn't work—although Jess was pretty sure that was true—but her reaction had been too abrupt for her to ignore that any idea he offered would have felt offensive.

It wasn't his ideas, necessarily. It was him, in her process, and she didn't like it.

Jack picked up on the change, proving once more to be nothing if not perceptive. "Or not. Or that's a terrible idea because whoever thought of putting hammocks by a lake." He paused and became serious. Jess felt his energy shift, making it clear that he wanted to convey something important. "Listen, Jess, I don't know how to say this well, but I'm a good guy. Many people even consider me likeable. I feel like maybe I've come across some other way to you. I can do that; I know that. But trust me, I'm not interested in disrespecting your work. So, please, whatever I can do to make this process easier for you, I'm all ears."

Jess felt a rush through her body. He was so ... honest, refreshingly so, complimentary, true, but in a way that didn't feel contrived.

She looked at his eyes. "Okay. You might regret those words, but let's see. And I'll try, seriously try, to consider your proposal. I'm … I'm not used to having to let someone else in at this process. Or, I guess to be fully honest, there's some kind of dynamic happening between us that makes me feel like I need to speak up for myself. I'm not sure what it is."

She stopped talking then, worried that she'd been too transparent. To his credit, Jack didn't try to contradict her. "You know, I've been feeling like there's something, too. Although for me, it's been more of an overwhelming curiosity. I assure you, though, I deeply respect what you do. Your talent is undeniable. But if I'm making you uncomfortable, then I'll take a step back and Donathan … Well, Donathan will have to figure it out."

"No," Jess offered, softening at his words. "No need to do that. The timeline's tight enough without having to worry about finding a new client lead. Besides," Jess added, the words ringing more truthful than she imagined they would be, "I'm glad to have your help."

"And I'm glad to give it." He looked at her just then, the electricity between them palpable. As if sensing that Jess could tolerate only so much of this, he lightened the mood. "But, seriously, hammocks. In addition to their obvious lake appropriateness, there couldn't be anything more impermanent. That's your main thing, right? Impermanence? Well, hammocks. You put them up; you take them down. Really, Jess, the symbolism is undeniable."

A groan escaped from Jess's lips involuntarily. "Okay, while you make a halfway-decent point, I'm still going to veto the idea for now, with a promise to reconsider it later should they feel more fitting in the design, but only because it seems to mean something to you. Hammocks aren't necessarily what I first think of when I contemplate the meaning of life."

"Well, that," Jack countered, "simply means you need to reassess your priorities."

Jess laughed sincerely at that, almost coughing up the sip of water she'd just taken. "Alright," she continued after she'd recollected herself both from the water and the embarrassment she'd felt at almost choking, "we'll save the analyzing my priorities until after this project is complete; deal? Because for the next four months, my only priority will be finishing this monster."

"Sold, Tyler." Jack clapped his hands together, that glint in his eyes unwavering. "Incidentally, nice transition. I, as what's passing as your client, feel very important and duly buttered up."

"Exactly what I was going for." Jess pulled out some documents. "So, usually in this process I talk budget, but in this situation, I'll probably just have my team send it over to Donathan directly."

Jack nodded. "Makes sense. I'm sure he'll approve whatever you send, but you're right; that should probably stay in his wheelhouse."

"Good. Well, other than that, at this stage, I spend some time with the client. The bones of the design are finished, but I'd still like to get to know your tastes and find sources of inspiration. Things like going to different stores and seeing what you like. And in a case like this, going to the site and other parts of the city to see what calls your attention, what features you'd like to bring in, and what about them stands out to you."

"Sounds fun. I'm game." Jack leaned in again. "When do we start?"

"Well," Jess paused. He was closer to her now, and she found, in a way she was beginning to expect, that his closeness had the same effect as before. As much as she was nervous about spending more time with him, she might as well get this over with, she figured. Something like exposure therapy. Moreover, a quieter voice within herself said, she had to admit that spending time with him wasn't turning out to be all that bad. "To be honest, with the deadline Donathan has in mind, I don't think we have much time to spare. I know it's last minute, but if we could head to some shops after this, that would be ideal. If not, let's try for early next week."

"Okay, let me check my schedule." Jack pulled out his phone, scrolling to his calendar. "Nothing I can't move. Let me email my assistant."

Jack focused on writing the email. Jess let herself fully reflect about him. Despite her first impression, she was finding him to be kind and considerate. She knew that things had come easily for him, but he couldn't help that and seemed to be at least trying to make a positive impact with his solar company. In addition, he was a good friend, and that had to count for something.

"Done!" he said, putting his phone back in his pocket.

"For someone who runs his own company, you're very easy to get a hold of," Jess said, teasing.

"For things that are important to me," he smiled, "I always make the time."

"I hate to say it, Jess, but this place feels like a glorified Ikea." Jack was reclined on a grey armchair, his legs stretched out on the ottoman in front of him.

Jess looked up from her notebook. "Jack, around these parts, those might be fighting words, and you're hardly in ready position."

Jack's eyelids drooped lazily. "Don't underestimate me, Jessica. I can be surprisingly spry."

Jess made a disapproving noise. Inside, she was glad that his eyes were halfway closed. She had … felt something when he called her Jessica, something not unpleasant, and she was glad that she had a second to herself to regain her composure.

"I would never make the mistake of underestimating you, Jack." Her voice came out as a coo. She realized, to her horror, that what she said, and how she said it, could be construed as flirting. She rolled her shoulders, thankful that he still was half asleep, and fixed her gaze intently on her notebook. Flirtation was not the type of dynamic she wanted to approach Jack with, particularly not when they had several more months of working together ahead of them.

Jack cracked open one of his eyes. "Then you're more observant than most of the people I do business with. They mostly hear the name 'Stinson' and assume that I was gifted my company from my family. It's frustrating at times, but then again, the moment when they realize I might actually know what I'm doing is usually rewarding."

With no small amount of effort, Jack forced himself to sit up. "Seriously, though," he said, perusing over the item tag, "what sets a place like this apart from Ikea? Not trying to be disrespectful, but I swear I've seen couches there that look nearly identical and are probably a third of the price."

Jess assessed him. His energy felt open, less guarded than usual. She identified a genuine curiosity within him, which she found made her want to respond.

"We're at Cassina right now, which is at the higher end of mid-range. I wanted to take you here because, well, first of all, it's close to my office and convenient to the restaurant, but also, it's got a wide range of designers and styles, so I can get a sense of what your taste is." Jess sat down on a nearby chair.

"As far as quality goes," she continued, "full disclosure is that, in my opinion, there are some well-made items available at Ikea, and it could very well be that some of what we include in the final Jumbl design ends up being from there. But there are also some lower-grade products there that I wouldn't suggest. Bottom line is that, while it's a range, it's a range that skews lower."

She got up to size the chair again from afar. "By contrast, I'd feel comfortable with anything from here going in the design. I know that whatever we choose is going to be made from higher-end materials that will, in the end, last longer. Beyond that," she shrugged nonchalantly, "I personally like many of the designs."

Jack's expression was thoughtful. "Interesting. Pretty reasonable response. I thought a designer of your qualifications would shun something so pedestrian as Ikea."

"Don't underestimate me, Jack," Jess countered.

He laughed, and Jess couldn't help but notice his bright smile when he did so. "I guess that serves me right." He stood up and walked over to a Minotti table. "Won't happen again, Tyler. I only need to learn a lesson once. Usually," he added.

"Usually?" Jess inquired.

"Well, let's just say that, in the rare incidents I've needed to learn a lesson more than once, the lesson stays with me." The corners of Jack's lips turned up. Jess got the sense that he was reflecting on a few choice memories as he spoke.

"Hmm," Jess mused. "I think I'm equal parts curious and happy I don't know what you're talking about."

"Reasonable," Jack agreed. He pointed to the table. "This, by the way, is something I like. It's low to the ground and simple. I like that."

Jess joined him at the table. It was, she had to admit, the type of piece she might have picked out herself. She jotted down the style number in her notebook.

"Good choice." Internally, she congratulated herself on striking a tone that was supportive while not overly laudatory. She wasn't trying to boost Jack's ego, which she was sure was inflated enough. "I think it would go well with some of the accent pieces that were on that Pinterest board I showed you. Solid yet understated enough to go with the minimalist feel."

She forced herself to make eye contact with him and saw him looking at her with bemusement.

"See, that was easy, right? I think you'll find, Ms. Tyler, that it's a lot easier for you to like me than to dislike me, notwithstanding my pedestrian preference for hammocks." He gave her a smile before walking over to examine a set of stools.

Jess waited a beat before joining him. There was a way to his manner that allowed him to get away with far more than most, she noticed. She could tell that a part of her was shifting, some of her initial guardedness giving way. Perhaps most surprising of all, she was enjoying herself. He had a point—working together would be easier if they got along, and if there were a natural ease between the two of them, she might as well be open to it.

"Figures that a guy named after a beach would enjoy hammocks," Jess said. "I'll tell you what. I'll give some serious consideration to it, so long as it stops there and isn't the gateway to a conversation about a Tiki room."

Jack picked up a gold accent piece, a series of wires hung together to create an abstract design. "Couple things on that. First, now that you mention it, a Tiki room is a great idea, totally up Donathan's alley." He laughed at Jess's rolled eyes. "As to the other point, the beach is named after me, not the other way around."

"My mistake," Jess corrected. She made note of the chair, considering it as an option for one of the dining areas. "I could see how that would be hard, by the way, what you said earlier about people underestimating you. I get that. People must make a lot of assumptions about you based on that name."

"They sure do," he placed the accent piece down. "But you get used to it. I guess it ultimately made me more motivated to prove myself for who I am, which is not a bad thing."

Jess wondered how sincere his casual tone was. She suspected that there was more to the story than he was letting on and had to catch herself from asking more. She wasn't sure what the rules were here, in the middle of a furniture store, when they were only starting to know each other. She wasn't sure how personal it was appropriate to get. His energy was palpably different during this conversation, though, she noticed. Some of that inner hardness that had subsided a second ago was returning.

"It's interesting to look back retrospectively and see what twists and turns ultimately motivated us to become who we are, and to reflect on what's happening now that will shape who we are in the future," she said, making note of a pendant light that she thought would work well in the employee lounge area.

Jack walked over to her. "You speak as if you have experience. Mind if I ask? What twists and turns helped shape the version of Jess Tyler I'm getting to know now?"

Jess felt herself withdraw. This was getting personal, and even though she was finding Jack's presence more comfortable than she'd thought she would, she wasn't ready for the level of exposure that answering his question truthfully would require.

"Actually," she said, "it might be better if we save that for another time. We've barely made it through this store, and we probably need to hit up at least two more today before we call it quits."

Jack masked the disappointment on his face. "Another time, then," he replied, moving away from her. "Promise?"

"Sure," she replied coolly. "We can see about that."

Jack smirked at her noncommittal response. "Okay, Ms. Tyler," he continued, his smooth tone bringing him back to some of his original levity. "I love that light, by the way." He pointed to the pendant light Jess had just been regarding. "It would go great in an employee lounge."

Jess felt her lips purse as she put a star next to it in her notebook.

• • •

Jess poured herself a glass of wine when she got home that evening. After cutting up some strawberries, she wandered over to her bay window to set up a makeshift picnic before she returned to her computer to finish a few more hours of work. If she sat at a certain angle, she could see Alamo Square and, behind it, downtown. She positioned herself so that she could see the city and watch the sky shift behind it, the orange and pink of mid-sunset beginning their transition to the blue-blackness of night.

She felt blissfully calm. In the midst of the stress of the Jumbl project, of developing Anicca's image, of establishing herself as a presence in the small world of interior design, calm was a feeling she was awed to have.

The feeling, she knew, was because of Jack. She had sincerely enjoyed her time with him, having laughed harder this afternoon than she had in … she couldn't even remember how long. He was charming but a little mischievous. And right when the mischief was on the verge of crossing the line, that twinkle would come back into his eyes and reassure her that it was all in good fun. She could see why he was successful. He made people feel at ease.

She pulled a blanket up over her knees to get cozy. Jack ... Her mind wandered back to him. She couldn't figure him out. He intrigued her more than most people, not to mention the increasing undeniability of her attraction to him, which was inconvenient.

After Cassina, they'd visited a few other stores, and while their conversation had been decidedly more business-like, it had still felt vulnerable. Jess slowly ate a strawberry as she reflected on why, letting her thoughts percolate as she tasted the delicious juice.

Design was inherently personal, and for Jess, someone who had never felt like she "fit" until she found it, design was vulnerable. It was normal for a client to be involved in the creative process—that was true—but the way Jack was involved, showing a sincere interest, asking insightful, attentive questions ... It was like he understood that, for Jess, when she showed him her designs, she was showing him her soul.

She sipped on her wine and let her eyes wander towards the sun, which was steadily on its descent towards the SF cityscape. For just a moment, she let herself imagine what things would be like if it were different, if maybe she and Jack had met five years from now, when Anicca was more of an established player on the scene and Jess more known in the interior design world. She wondered what would have happened between the two of them, whether they ever would have been more than colleagues. The rapport that flowed naturally between them might have turned into something, maybe. It was possible that, if things were different, she and Jack might have had something, potentially something real, that could have, over time, led somewhere.

But then again, she thought, her eyes shifting downward to pick out another strawberry, Alex had probably thought the same thing.

The thought was a welcome reminder of exactly why she was glad that there was no chance of anything happening with Jack. She thought about Rebecca's words regarding the next few years for Jess's career and how she'd need to devote every second she could to building it.

Even without Rebecca's caution, Jess would have been wary of starting anything just then. She had had a good lesson in how one's dreams could be derailed because of a relationship—her mother. Head of her med school class at a time when women in med school were rare, she'd had a promising career ahead of her. Top hospitals from around the country were recruiting her. She ended up starting her residency in the oncology department of MD Anderson when, one day, she met Jess's father. They had dated for only a short time when her mother became pregnant with Bridget.

And the rest, as they say, is history.

Jess's mother had left her residency with the intention to return but never did. Jess's father was offered a position in Sacramento, and it made sense to take it. Besides, there were good hospitals in Sacramento too, they'd figured. But then her mother had become pregnant with Jess, and, well, one of them had to work to support the family and that certainly couldn't happen on a resident's salary and certainly not working the crazy hours that a resident is expected to work. And so, Jess's mother had settled into the life of a housewife. Happy, in many respects, but there were so many times that Jess dreamed for her mother, wished she had had the chance to have more, wondered if she wondered about what could have been.

Jess had another sip of her wine. That could never happen to her, would never happen to her. She didn't want to look back and wonder, *What if …* The promise she'd made to herself, to see her dreams through to their limits, didn't allow for distractions. Dating, or more accurately, relationships, was something that would only get in the way of her dreams.

Most of the time, she didn't exactly feel like she was missing out on much. She'd heard about the dating scene, and it frankly sounded awful, the end of romance. App after app and swipe after swipe so that, if you took the right picture and said the right quip in your profile, you could ultimately find out how expendable you were. Such a numbers game. And the pressure to come off cool and funny and chill and together and well-adjusted was … overwhelming.

Jess wasn't a complete novice to the dating world. She'd had a couple short relationships and even one that had lasted close to six months in college. But they'd been mediocre. She didn't mind sex, not at all. But it wasn't the earth-shattering, ego-destroying experience of True Connection that it was all cracked up to be. It was mostly awkward with a minute or two of pretty good, and then it was over. Jess was just as happy to spend her time daydreaming.

Her imagination, she had often been disappointed to find, was far better than most of reality.

Jack Stinson would almost certainly be no different. A nice guy, handsome, funny, probably irritatingly rich, the type of guy that most girls would completely go for, but, in the end, the idealized version would ultimately give way to the stark disappointment of reality, and Jess would end up wasting valuable time she could have spent nurturing her business.

The point of all this hard work was to reach something higher than that. Jess wanted to make her small mark on the world. That would take all the time and effort she had. She didn't have a Jack Stinson-sized amount of energy to spare. No, it was best to have fun, enjoy their time together, see if she could learn anything, and keep him as a professional contact and, perhaps, a friendly acquaintance. That was it, decided.

Jess set her wine glass down and hugged her knees to her chest, watching the final orange of the sun disappear behind Salesforce Tower. When she sat like this, she felt like a little kid again, in the best of ways, where all she had to do was sit and dream and let her mind show her all the ways it knew that this world could be possible. Curious, open, expansive—all she had to do was sit and be in awe.

Chapter 8

"Hey, lady of the hour!" Bridget waved her over to the spot she had saved next to her. They had made plans to take a yoga class with a hot new instructor before grabbing brunch. "You're such a big deal now that I made sure we had spots right up front." Bridget grinned.

"Ha ha, very funny," Jess said as she gave Bridget a hug. "Good to see you. Thanks for reminding me of my celebrity status. I brought my pen for autographs." Jess stuck her tongue out. It was childish, but it felt great to be silly and to relax around this person who knew her so well.

"Proud of you, sis. Not surprised, but proud all the same. I can't wait to hear more about what's been happening. If I'm still alive after this class, that is."

Jess groaned. "I know. A ninety-minute class at 9:30 a.m. on a Saturday—why did we do this to ourselves?"

"This teacher is supposed to be pretty tough too. We have to go somewhere they have waffles afterward."

"You got it. Even if they cost $30."

"Absolutely. Alright, here we go," Bridget said, pointing to the teacher who had just walked to the front of the studio. "See you on the other side."

• • •

Two and a half hours later, they were finally seated at their table. The yoga class had been killer. They were both sweaty and more than once had taken child's pose. They'd treated themselves by going to Brenda's, a French soul food style restaurant that was famous not only for its chicken and waffles, but also its notorious wait times. By the time they had ordered, they were ravenous.

"If our food doesn't come out soon, I'm going to eat my own arm." Bridget raised her arm to her open mouth.

"You know, I would say you were being dramatic, but at this point I'm not sure. There's hot sauce at the table. Maybe we can down it as a head start? Could be a nice treat."

"In a second, I might take you up on that. Seriously, where is our food? I'm going to—" Just then, they saw their waiter emerge from the kitchen, holding what looked like their order. "Oh, thank God." Bridget let her head rest against the wall.

"Here you go. Chicken and waffles for you, and gumbo and grits for you, with a flight of beignets on the side." The waiter placed the food down. "Can I get you anything else?

"No, thanks," Bridget said. Jess shook her head.

"Okay, enjoy." And with that, the waiter left.

Bridget and Jess both ate in silence for a solid minute before Bridget looked up.

"Okay, now that I'm starting to feel human again, I really do want to know. What's this week been like? Any new commissions? What's happened? Tell me all about it. I've been giving you space all week, and now I'm dying of curiosity."

"I know. Thank you for being so patient. This week has been …" Jess slowly savored her grits while she tried to think of what to say. "It's been … great. It really has. Surreal, a little, but less so than I thought it would be. Everyone's been congratulatory. A few new commissions have come in or at least the opportunities to pitch for them. I'm working on one already."

"Oooh, tell me all about it," Bridget said, dipping her waffle in syrup.

"It's for the new Jumbl campus. It's probably confidential, so don't tell anyone. Jumbl hasn't made the announcement that they're moving. But they are, to Lake Merced, and Donathan Lewis personally tapped me to do the design."

"Wow, Jess, congratulations! For the whole campus?"

"Yep, the whole thing," Jess replied, ripping off a piece of beignet. "It's a pretty extensive project. I love the location. Yeah, it's a great opportunity, except," Jess pursed her lips, "well, a couple things. First, the timeline is intimidating. They're opening up in four months, which is a ridiculous request that gives you a sense of the kind of—I don't know—either optimism or foolishness that Donathan possesses. Which brings us to the second thing: Donathan doesn't want to be involved with the process. He says he's no good at design and really picky and would make life miserable."

"Hmm, refreshingly hands-off for a CEO. Is that a good thing?" Bridget spread some butter on her biscuit.

"It's ... a neutral thing. He's hands off, but I'm still supposed to consult, except not with him, with his best friend, someone named Jack Stinson."

"Stinson? Like the beach?" Bridget took a sip of coffee to help the waffle down.

"Yes, exactly." Jess leaned in for emphasis. "Exactly like the beach. I guess Stinson was a real person, and Jack is his great-grandson or something, maybe further down the family tree than that. I'm not sure."

"Wow ... Hmm," Bridget's eyebrows lifted. "I guess I'd never thought about Stinson being a real person. I mean, I knew that Sutro was, and I think Bernal, too. I guess it makes sense that Stinson would be too, but ... So, what, are his clothes made of money?"

"Bridge," Jess laughed, slapping her arm playfully. "Jeez, no subtlety to you, huh?"

"Well, come on, I'm sure you've thought about it." Bridget's gaze narrowed. "You like him, don't you?"

"What? Where would you get that idea?"

"You do; you absolutely do!" Bridget clapped her hands together gleefully. "Oh, come on, Jess. You never, ever talk about guys. I barely even got two words out of you about that guy you dated in college. Even now, I kind of think his name was Mike, but I might be making that up. And now here you are, telling me about your commission with the big fancy tech company, and the thing that stands out to you most is that you are working with mysterious SF renaissance man Jack Stinson. I love it!"

Jess groaned. She was irritated by the possibility that Bridget was right. "Okay, okay. Jack is … He's good looking, okay? I admit it. And he's easy to talk to. But get real, Bridge. He's not the type of guy that you get serious about. And," she forcefully smeared some jam onto her biscuit, "my college boyfriend, if you can call him that, was named Matt."

Bridget sized up Jess with a knowing look that only an older sister could pull off. "We'll reminisce on Matt later. But, wow, 'not the type of guy you get serious about.' Does that mean you've thought about getting serious? This guy must have gotten to you. What does he do?"

"Um, not sure … Something involving solar?"

Bridget looked aghast. "You mean, you haven't Google stalked him yet?" She shook her head as she took her phone out. "*Such* an amateur. I'm looking him up right now."

"No, don't!" Jess exclaimed, reaching for Bridget's phone.

Bridget deftly moved it away. "Oh, it's happening. Jessica Rose Tyler, I did not just sweat my way through ninety minutes of chaturangas to not find out about my sister's new love interest. I haven't heard you talk about anyone in years, certainly not since you started at Unoa. We are absolutely Google stalking him, right this moment."

"Fine." Jess rested her head in her hands. There was no point fighting with Bridget when she was on a mission. And, Jess hated to admit, she was excited to see what they would find.

"Jack Stinson, Founder/CEO of ShineStar Inc. SF native. Great-grandson of Nathaniel Stinson." Bridget looked up from her phone. "Nathaniel Stinson. Yeah, so I guess that Stinson was a real dude." She kept scanning. "Hot," Bridget clicked over to an image search. "Really hot. Wow, Jess, this guy seems legit."

Jess leaned over, her curiosity overcoming her desire to remain cool. "What does that article say?"

Bridget leaned back. "I'll tell you if you give me a little room! Guess someone may be a little more interested than she lets on."

"Bridge, just read it," Jess said, exasperated.

Bridget smiled. She knew when she had reached the limit of what Jess could tolerate. "Okay, here we go. 'Hope Shines Through' is the name of the article. That's ambitious. Okay here it is saying that he grew up in SF, family is in real estate, went to Stanford for his MBA. So, *that* type." Bridget glanced knowingly at Jess. "Started his solar company six years ago, and it's really taken off. Oh, here's a quote from him: 'I've always found the sun, the entire sky, fascinating. To think of the power it has, a power so much greater than ourselves. Solar for me is really a small way of trying to understand some of that power, while at the same time acknowledging that there's some degree of mystery there, and realizing I wouldn't change that even if I could.'"

Bridget raised her eyebrows. "Connection to a greater reality? Into staring at the sky? Sounds like your kind of guy, Jess!"

She kept reading. "Here we go. So, okay, it seems like the reason for the name of the article is that he's got this new passion project to make solar more sustainable so that it can be used on tiny home structures to provide sustainability for people experiencing homelessness. That's decent of him. Here he's quoted again: 'For someone like me, I grew up with a lot and had a lot of opportunity. I worked hard, to be sure, but I had such a support structure around me that I knew that, even if I failed, I wouldn't really fail. Most people don't have that opportunity, and a lot of people suffer as a result. If it's within my means to make life a little easier, then I think it's important to do it.'" Bridget set the phone down and looked up imploringly at Jess. "Wow."

"Shoot." Jess shook her head.

"Hot, rich, fun guy with a good heart ... You are so totally screwed." Bridget leaned back. "But you know, I think that's a good thing. I think it's about time that you really fell for someone. And fell hard. It's ... one of the most important things about life. You'll grow."

Jess scowled at Bridget. "Says who, Ms. Too-Busy-To-Date-Until-I-Make-Partner? How am I supposed to date with a role model like *you*?"

Bridget scowled back. "Jess, come on." She got quiet. "You know I'm still recovering from my breakup with Jeff. That ... yeah, that hasn't been easy." Bridget straightened her shoulders. "But even still, I feel like I'm learning some lesson I'm supposed to learn from that, like some rite of passage. I feel different as a result. Sure, right now 'different' is showing up more like 'guarded' and 'shitty,' but I can already feel it shifting. Even now, I think I learned a lot about myself in the process, about what I don't want and don't need to settle for, but also, about what I have to offer. I think it will ultimately be a good thing." Bridget looked thoughtful. "Besides, that not-dating-until-I-make-partner thing is no joke. I've seriously been working like a dog, between the business development, the internal networking, and, oh yeah, by the way, still having to bill my normal amount of hours. Honestly, I should be billing for this brunch. Any chance you want to talk commercial litigation?"

Jess laughed. Leave it to Bridget to lift the mood, even when Bridget was in pain herself. Bridget always seemed so larger than life to Jess, the big sister who always achieved so much. It caught Jess off guard to see Bridget in moments of vulnerability. It reminded her that she was human.

"Mm, let me think about it." Jess closed her eyes and pretended to think. "Um, not even a little bit."

They both laughed.

"Bridge, you know where I'm at with Anicca. It's going to take everything I've got these next few years, maybe more than I've got, and I don't need any distractions. Anicca is my baby. I haven't dated because, well, it never really interested me or, I don't know, never fit me. Nothing has ever fit me as well as building Anicca has. It's ... it's like the best part of me manifested into reality, somehow, and I can't lose it."

"Aw, Jess," Bridget gently touched her arm. "I think all your parts are the best parts."

"Besides," Jess continued quickly, concerned that, if she slowed down, she'd start to tear up right there in the restaurant,

"I think we're getting ahead of ourselves by even assuming there's interest. I've only really hung out with Jack one time. I hear what you're saying. And I ... I know you're right. But I never wanted to look back at my life and think about what could have been. I mean, look at Mom ..."

Bridget nodded slowly, digesting Jess's word before continuing. "I mean, you're not wrong. It's hard for most people, particularly women, to get the career they want and everything else that we're told we should want too. But if you're saying what I think you're saying when you mention Mom, you're assuming a lot, Jess. And you can't be sure of how much of it is true." Bridget looked at her like she was trying to convey years of love into a single expression.

"Speaking of Mom, though," Bridget continued, moving her hand away from Jess's arm, "you better go visit her. She hasn't wanted to bother you, but Ashley has been having some trouble in school. I don't think too, too serious. But you should probably check in. The family has been wanting to give you a break because we know you're creating something amazing, but don't forget about us, k?"

Jess nodded. Bridget was right: she was due for a trip. She realized that she hadn't checked in with Ashley in weeks, maybe months. It was uncomfortable to think about how long.

"Okay, okay. And now, Bridget, I really need us to have brunch and talk about you. I'm so sick of talking about me! You have a lot going on, too, and I want to hear about it."

Bridget caught Jess up on the various travails of a senior associate soon to be a partner. Jess felt herself relax, comforted by Bridget's solid, funny, and patient presence. As they finished brunch, Jess felt happy.

Chapter 9

JESS RETURNED HOME AFTER A LONG AND PLEASANT DAY OUT. She'd finished brunch with Bridget, and the two of them had gone for a walk. Bridget had needed to leave early to do some work—she hadn't been kidding about that grueling path to partnership—but Jess had continued to meander. She'd made it all the way to Ocean Beach, through Golden Gate Park, and then climbed to the top of Land's End and looked out over the water. There was something so deeply soothing about the Pacific Ocean: constant, patient, present. Jess had stared at it, mesmerized, for close to an hour before heading home.

Jack was on her mind. She couldn't figure out their dynamic. It was presumptuous to assume that he had any interest. She had no reason to believe their relationship was anything more than professional. Jess was slightly irritated at herself for even entertaining the notion that there was something more. Even so, she did get a sense when she was around him that he was at least slightly curious about her. As someone who'd lived on the outside of "normal" for her whole life, Jess had had the opportunity to observe people closely. She could intuit certain things, and she suspected that Jack's courtesy extended beyond mere professionalism.

The problem was knowing what to do with it. The answer, it seemed, was nothing. She was receiving conflicting messages. On the one hand, relationships were a distraction at this point in her career. On the other, a relationship was something that could help her grow. The topic was already tiring to think about, and all she'd done was take a client stand-in furniture shopping.

That sobering realization brought Jess crashing back to reality. Bridget had talked about a relationship, even a heartbreak, as growth. Regardless, as far as Jess knew, there was no deadline on growing. Jess was growing plenty as it was. A relationship, and whatever growth came therefrom, could wait until Jess was less busy. And something bothered her about the traditional notion that you needed a relationship to fulfill something within yourself. It seemed so antiquated and disempowering. Jess wasn't sold.

She got home and checked her email, more to distract her mind than out of any real urgency. It was Saturday evening, after all.

Much to her surprise, she saw an email from Jack with the subject line *"Inspiration."* Intrigued, Jess opened it up.

Hi Jess, great seeing you yesterday and getting to know more about the Jumbl project and your design process more generally. Very much looking forward to learning more. Let me know when works for you to meet up again. Haven't been so inspired in a while.
~Jack

Jess was taken aback. His forthrightness stirred something in her. She had been expecting the aloof, playboy type, but what she kept receiving was someone who was sincere and kind. It was refreshing but unnerving at the same time.

Keep it cool, Jess, she thought to herself. *He just wants to know about design. You have something to offer right now that he finds interesting. Nothing more.*

She hit reply.

Hi Jack, thank you for the kind words. I had a pleasant time as well. I'll be completing drafts of designs and sourcing the first part of this coming week. Let's set up a site meeting to map things out as they would appear. What's your availability Wednesday?

~Jess

Jess shut her laptop and went over to her bay window. It was time to shift her focus from Jack to something more important—how she was going to finish that design. Wednesday was coming right up. She had some drafts completed but needed to flesh them out before their meeting, plus make some headway with the vendors. It was going to be a busy week.

She heard her phone ring, waking her from her reverie. It was Jack. Instinctively, she moved away from the phone like it was a bomb about to go off. Jack Stinson was calling her, in her own home, on a Saturday night. She couldn't imagine what was so urgent that he needed to talk it through at this hour and realized, to her horror, that anything so urgent was almost certainly not good. With a resigned exhale, she decided that it was better to know sooner rather than later. She picked up, cautiously.

"Hello?"

"Jess! Thank God you picked up. There's an emergency."

Jess's pulse raced. "What? What happened? Did something happen with the project?"

"No." Jack's voice was quick to interject. "I'm having a personal design emergency. I've been searching all up and down Google but still cannot find a clear definition of what it means when someone says 'clean, organic lines.' I really need your help!"

Jess shook her head. "Okay, Jack, first things first: do not, ever, call me up again when we have a huge project going on and say it's an emergency unless, I don't know, something is on fire, okay? Second, it's Saturday night, Jack. Are you really telling me you don't have better plans that a Google search?"

"Got it. Fire emergencies only." Jack sounded duly chastised. "But don't make fun, Jess. This is serious. 'Clean, organic lines.' Some people seem to think it means straight lines. Some seem to think it's more of an overall feeling. And I keep seeing a lot of beige in these pictures that remains unexplained. I can't make heads or tails of it."

Jess had to laugh. "You're probably in that conundrum because it's interior design mumbo jumbo, some phrase that was likely used on multiple HGTV shows that has become part of the lexicon. I hate to break it to you, but it doesn't mean much." Jess smiled.

"You're killing me, Tyler. Here I was, thinking my whole life of thinking 'organic' was a pesticide categorization was a fraud. I'm so glad we're talking. I wasn't sure how I was going to sleep tonight."

"Okay, stop it. That's quite enough," Jess said, laughing into the phone. "Ha, ha. So, you're good, then?"

"Well, as long as I have you on the phone, I might as well say hi. What have you been up to?"

Jess sank back against the window. It was flattering that he wanted to call under such an obvious guise. She decided to go with it. A guy like Jack, she reasoned, was so far from being a serious option that she might as well have fun, which, she realized, she did have when she was around him, more fun that she cared to admit.

"Oh, not much. Saw my sister and then sat by the beach. What about you?"

"Well, apart from my frustrated research into design terminology, I've had a busy day. Some crisis at work that's long and boring and not really a good story. But I think it's resolved."

Jess had to bite her tongue to refrain from asking more. She was nervous that, if she asked about his company, it would slip that she'd Googled him, which would have been unbelievably embarrassing. She changed the topic.

"I've been meaning to ask you, what's your relationship with Donathan? You two seem to know each other well, and yet you seem so different."

"Donathan? He's my oldest and best friend," Jack said. "We are different, in some ways, I guess in most ways, if you were to just meet us. But we're also the same, at our cores. We both understand what it's like to be on the outside."

Jess was legitimately curious now. "On the outside? But you both are so confident. I don't understand."

"I guess we come across that way now, but not always. Donathan and I always saw the world differently. We both had to deal with people's preconceived notions. Some of this I mentioned a little when I saw you yesterday, but yeah, being the namesake of someone who has a beach named after him comes with baggage. Kids saw the name before they saw me. Donathan had his own form of that. His dad is very prominent among the SF elite, and people were always trying to get to know him not because they really wanted to know him, but because they wanted to know what his father could do for them. It was a ton of pressure for him, too. I guess it's worked out because he's so successful now, but I think there's a lot about him that he keeps only to himself."

Jess felt her body ground naturally at his words, so sincere in their openness. She positioned herself in her favorite nook at the window. "I'm sorry, Jack. That sounds really tiring, never feeling like you can simply meet someone as yourself. I can see how that would be lonely."

"Yeah, it had its moments." Jack's voice was soft, raw. Jess intuited that these were the kind of topics that he didn't talk about with most people. She felt her own energy shift, expanding to receive his words with care. "I don't know that what I've been through is harder than anybody else's struggle, and it's certainly a lot easier than many. But it had an impact, and I guess Donathan and I bonded, in our way, over what it's like to always meet someone knowing that they already have an idea about you. It impacts you, moving through life that way, not that Donathan and I would have pieced that together at the time. I think we were both too interested in goofing around and getting into trouble. Donathan's a funny guy, way funnier than I am. I think it's served him well. Tough world he chose to break into, the big bad world of tech, and he's done phenomenally at it. I give him all the credit in the world."

"I get that. It's not easy to grow up not 'normal,' whatever that is," Jess reciprocated. "As an adult, I don't know if there really is a 'normal,' but when you're a kid, it certainly feels like there are 'normal' people and that, if you're not one of them, there's something wrong with you. It would be hard to feel different for something you couldn't change and probably didn't fully understand."

"Sounds like you have some personal knowledge?"

"In my way," Jess continued. She was surprised that she was talking to him in this way. But his honesty and trust prompted something similar in her. And she found that it was relieving to talk about it. "Not because of how other people treated me, like you and Donathan. So in that way, very different. But, yeah, I've always had an artist's soul, I guess you could call it. It sounds glamorous now, but it's not very fun when you've missed some important social cue because you were daydreaming. Kids think you're strange. But I always found the imaginal world fascinating, often more fascinating than the so-called real world."

They were silent then. Jess shifted uncomfortably in her seat. She closed her eyes and tried to even out her breaths, which had become stuck in her chest.

"I can relate," was all Jack said, but the way he said it spoke more than any words could have. He did understand, sincerely. A moment of genuine connection was happening between them. Jess felt the closeness, but it was too close, too much.

"Right," Jess said, stiffening up. "But I guess we've both found ways to make it work. So, there you go."

Jack chuckled at the abruptness of the change. "Okay, so it's like that, huh? Alright, Ms. Tyler, if that's how you want to play it. But I have to say, I'm enjoying getting to know you. These pockets of you, the real you, that slip out, they draw me in and make me want more."

Jess got up from her window. She was feeling too much from the conversation, a range of emotions coursing through her at once.

"Hmm. Well, thanks, I guess. It's been good to get to know you more, too." She bit her lip to keep from saying more. "Anyway, we should probably hang up. I responded to your email, by the way. How does Wednesday look for you to do an on-site?"

"Okay, okay, I can take a hint. Wednesday works great. Just name the time," Jack said. "And, Jess, I really mean it. I know you're still getting to know me, but you can talk to me. I don't want to hurt you."

"That's great to hear, Jack," she replied, her professional tone intentionally inharmonious to the emotions of the conversation. "I'll be in touch about the time. Good night."

She hung up the phone and looked out the window. Something was happening, and she wasn't sure what. It wasn't comfortable; that was clear. But she wasn't sure if that was because it was bad as much as it was because it was unfamiliar. On some deep level, she was worried she was getting in over her head. Something about this man made her feel exposed. He would be able to see her, really see her, if she let him, and as much as she wanted that, she was worried that she could end up getting very hurt.

But at the same time, she didn't see a way of stopping what was happening. It seemed to have a momentum of its own, this thing between them, and the Jumbl project necessitated her spending time with him. And that, she had to remember, was what this was all about. The Jumbl project was a make-it-or-break-it career opportunity. She couldn't forget that. Working with Jack was something that, unfortunately, came with the package.

She just hoped that she could make it through these next few months.

Chapter 10

Jess got to work early Monday, feeling refreshed. She had spent the day before enjoying simply being in San Francisco. She treated herself by sleeping in before going to the farmers' market and getting in a longer run. It had been cathartic, running past Crissy Field over the Golden Gate Bridge to take in the view before heading back. She usually didn't run over the bridge. It was too full of people and tourists trying to figure out how to ride a bike. But there was something about being lost in a crowd that had appealed to her, and the vibrancy of San Francisco nourished her soul. She knew she needed to incorporate some of that spirit into Jumbl.

She hadn't heard from Jack since that phone call Saturday night, which was fine with her. She had plenty to keep her occupied. Her internal deadline for the first draft of her designs was Friday, if she was going to be able to give her vendors enough lead time, which meant this week was going to be intense.

Jess sipped her coffee as she perused her morning emails. The reality of what she needed to accomplish that week was settling in.

She centered herself, preparing for the tasks ahead of her. She was drawing up her to-do list when Charlie walked in the front door.

"Hey, Charlie," she said.

He almost jumped out of his skin. "Jess! Oh my goodness, I did not expect to see you here this early." He set his coat at his desk and recollected his breath.

"Sorry." Jess walked over to place her hand on his shoulder. "Aw, Charlie, I didn't mean to spook you like that."

"It's okay, Jess," he replied, standing up to give her a hug. "But seriously, you look pretty bright-eyed and bushy-tailed for a Monday morning."

Jess shrugged. She went to pour Charlie a cup of coffee as a gesture of atonement. "That's good to hear, I guess. Although I can't tell if my expression is due to excitement or anxiety. Maybe both?" She handed him the mug.

"They say excitement is physiologically the same as anxious," Charlie mused, taking the mug from her with a nod of gratitude. "I think I heard that on *Oprah* or something."

"Well, if Oprah said it, it must be true," Jess laughed. She placed her hands on the back of a nearby chair and sighed. "Charlie, Charlie, we got a lot to do this week, don't we?"

"We certainly do. And starting at 10 a.m. for you, you have a consultation call with a landscape architect. I put it on your calendar, but I want to make sure you received it because I scheduled it over the weekend."

Jess saw the invite on her calendar and groaned. "Ugh, okay. I was hoping to use today to make some progress on my designs."

"That certainly would be nice, wouldn't it?" His tone conveying mock optimism. "But, honey, I think that plan is gonna have to change. We have another meeting this afternoon with textiles, and then tomorrow one with some furniture reps. I think Moira may be handling that. You'll have to ask her when she gets in."

Jess scrunched her face like she'd smelled something rotten. "Remind me why we agreed to do this again?"

"Because we have latent masochistic tendencies?" Charlie offered.

"Oh, right, that." Jess plopped herself down on the couch in the foyer. "Are you allowed to say that word, by the way? I kind of assumed that someone who always said 'goodness' instead of taking the Lord's name in vain was prohibited from talking about masochism."

Charlie raised his eyebrows at her. "That, Jess, just goes to show how much you don't know. All that light has to have a darkness to balance it out."

Jess considered his words. "Touché. But, seriously, how are we going to get this done?" She placed her head in her hands. Her brightness of just ten minutes before was dissipating.

"I don't know, like we always do." Charlie joined her on the couch. "You've been through harder things than this, Jess. I mean, it couldn't have been easy starting this whole place up."

Jess peeked one of her eyes out at him. "Yeah, I guess that's true." She sat up in her chair to look more directly at him. As she did, she was reminded of why she'd hired him. It had been in the flurry of starting Anicca, and Charlie had come in fresh out of school with almost no experience under his belt, apart from a few summer internships. But he was talented. His portfolio showed that he had a great sensibility, a solid style that blended familiar, homey aesthetics with a modern edge. He had virtually no professional contacts in the SF area, having just moved from Atlanta, and his sensibility was more country than the SF crowd wanted. But Jess noticed right away that he was kind and thoughtful. To Jess, when she was starting her firm, having good people by her side was the most important thing. Design aesthetic could be enhanced, but having people she could trust on her team was invaluable.

"Thanks for saying that, Charlie. You're right. There have been so many times these past two years when I wondered what I was doing or whether I could even do it, and yet, here we are. Maybe this will be the same."

"Absolutely." Charlie patted her shoulder in a bright gesture. "That's the spirit our fearless leader needs. Plus, you got the dream team of me and Moira. We got you."

"Thanks, Charlie." Jess felt a warmth spread across her chest. It was nice to remember, sometimes, that as impossible as things seemed, she wasn't alone.

"So, what's going on with you and Jack Stinson?"

Jess felt her eyes widen. "What? What do you mean, what's going on?"

"Oh, honey," Charlie said, shaking his head at her, "who do you think you're kidding? It's obvious that there's chemistry."

Jess stood up, indignant. "Obvious? I wouldn't say obvious. I mean, maybe there's ... I don't know ... *something*. But obvious? It's ... We're ... we're working together and ..."

Charlie leveled her with his eyes. Jess stopped talking, mouth still open, with the horrible realization that every word that came out in her awkward attempt to deny his suggestion was only making things worse.

"Okay, fine, I think he's attractive, okay? But that doesn't mean anything."

Charlie rolled his eyes at her. "Attractive? Jess, that only means you got eyes in your head. That boy is objectively hot, and clearly into you, by the way. Dropping all his meetings every time you summon him around."

"Hmm, do you think?" Jess tried her best to sound unaffected by his words.

Charlie's expression was unmoved.

"Okay, fine," Jess said. "Okay, yes, I've thought about it, too. Maybe something's there, I don't know, but he's practically a client, and the last thing I need right now is to have something interfere with this project, which, by the way, is going to kick our asses these next few months, not to mention I could be making this up completely and spending time thinking about someone who, it turns out, is not even interested. I mean, if I would even want that! Which I'm not even sure I do and maybe am sure that I don't." The words came tumbling out of her, the initial embarrassment at being called out overcome by the release of having someone to talk things through with.

Charlie took a slow sip of his coffee. "You're not making it up completely, Jess. As for the rest, well, I don't know how to help you there, honey. All I know is you're clearly mixed up about it."

"Ugh, I don't want to be." Jess shook her head. "I'd like to just ignore everything and wait for it to all bubble over in a day or two."

"Oh, honey," Charlie laughed. "I think you got about a snowball's chance in Hades of that happening. But what's the conflict? So what? You're into him; he's into you. See how it goes for a bit. It's not the end of the world."

"Easy for you to say, Charlie."

"It's true, Jess! You're so in your head about it all that you're forgetting that everything could turn out just fine."

"Thanks," she mustered up a smile. "I really appreciate that, Charlie. Sometimes, I don't know what I'd do without you and Moira."

"I hope you'll remember that around bonus time," Moira said, emerging from seemingly nowhere to join the conversation.

Charlie jumped again. "Oh my goodness, can you two knock or something? You made me spill my coffee!"

Moira pulled out some tissues from her purse. "Not my fault, Charlie. You're right in the foyer. There's literally no other way I can come into this office. Bigger picture, you need to calm down. Take me up on the lunchtime yoga offer, okay?" She looked at Jess.

"Yes, tomorrow is furniture day: a few major players plus virtual consults with some local artists. We have a lot to do."

"Indeed." Jess thought for a minute. With all these meetings, she was struggling to imagine how she could also create client-ready designs, even draft designs to not-the-real client. She might have to push her on-site with Jack until Thursday, which, considering how raw her emotions still were following her conversation with Charlie, was welcome news. "Okay, we better get started. I've started some mock-ups, but I need both of you to look at them and give your opinions and propose edits as you see fit. I'm going to turn back to these exteriors to prep for my meeting with the landscape architect. Let's plan to reconvene at lunchtime to see where we're at."

"Roger. Permission to attend yoga at lunch?" Moira asked, saluting Jess mockingly.

Jess scowled. "Permission granted. Only you could mock your boss literally a minute after asking for a bigger bonus."

Moira laughed. "I guess that's true. But that's why you love me! Besides, I finally have Charlie committed to yoga and need to hold him to it. I mean, look at him."

Charlie looked up from cleaning the couch. "I could still back out of that yoga class anytime," he challenged.

Jess lifted her brows. "You both ... Okay, let's meet at eleven thirty, have a quick check-in, and then you two can get centered before our textile meeting."

They both agreed, thanked her, and went to their desks. Jess settled back into her office and closed the door. She texted

Jack: *First part of week tied up in more meetings than anticipated. Move the on-site to Thursday or Friday?* She pressed send. She felt some relief at the delay in seeing him, but also something that felt vaguely like disappointment. She shook her head. The fact that she was disappointed at all was only further proof that any delay in interacting with Jack was for the best.

A few minutes later, her phone buzzed with a text from Jack. *Thursday's no good. Work crisis I mentioned. Friday morning?*

Jess was surprised at the abruptness of the response. It was so unlike the tone that he'd had Saturday. She forced herself not to dwell on it. After all, she was the one who had drawn clear professional boundaries, and her initial text that morning had been all business. Regardless, it was a letdown.

Sounds good. 9?

See you then.

Jess put her phone away. This was what she wanted, she tried to convince herself. She knew that it was best if things stayed professional between them, and yet ... some small part of her was saddened at the transition away from the friendlier dynamic that they had been creating. She needed to refocus, she told herself. The friendly flirtation that had been developing was dangerous. That energy was nothing but a distraction, not in line with what she wanted for herself, not now. For now, she needed to focus on her career. She squared her shoulders and set her attention back to her designs.

It was better this way, really.

Chapter 11

THAT WAS THE LAST TIME SHE COMMUNICATED WITH JACK UNTIL Friday. The week had been so busy that she'd barely had time to slow down, what with the seemingly endless meetings with various vendors, reviewing the contracts that came from those meetings, working with makers to design some of the bespoke furniture pieces, and somehow completing a draft set of designs to show.

To say Jess was ready for the weekend would be an understatement.

She called for an Uber straight to the lake, having spent the morning in her apartment laying out the designs and preparing what to say about them. That was something she usually preferred to do in her office, keeping her home her space to simply be, but she'd gotten home so late the night before that she opted for the extra half hour of sleep in the morning rather than make the commute.

She rested her head on the window of the Uber. As the car made its way down 7th Avenue to Laguna Honda, the sight of

Sutro Tower made her smile. It was such a classic response of the few people she'd now told about Jack. Everyone knew that Sutro had been a real person, but Stinson? It must have been a forgotten part of the city's history.

Jack ... Her eyes shifted downward, the realization sinking in that she was about to see him. In the almost week since they'd had a real conversation, she'd experienced a range of emotions, from denying that there was any attraction, to warming up to it, to being disappointed in herself for even considering it, to now it having been so long that she wondered if her initial doubts hadn't been spot on in the first place. It was like she'd already experienced a relationship's worth of emotions about something that hadn't even come close to beginning yet.

Jess shook her head to herself. This, of course, was why she didn't get involved in the whole romantic scene in the first place—too much trouble.

No, she'd been right all along. Even if Jack had ever had something more than professional feelings towards her, which was unlikely, they had clearly been fleeting. Jess was grateful for that, really. Now they could focus on finishing the task at hand.

Which was all she wanted. She was sure of it.

She arrived early to the site to set up. She'd been so busy that she'd barely had time to return to the building since that initial meeting with Donathan and Jack. Their meeting today would be her visualizing the designs as they'd be in the space for the first time.

It was exhilarating. Charlie had been kind enough to meet her at the campus and had brought croissants and coffee. He had refrained from being too smug about Jack, instead focusing on setting up and talking through the designs before he left to head back to the office. Jess glanced at the time and saw that she had a few minutes to spare before Jack arrived. Jess decided to take advantage of the gorgeous day by seeking some inspiration from the surrounding nature.

The lake was stunning. The windy day meant its surface water rippled, moving like waves. Jess found a tree to tuck behind as shelter for the wind and watched, hypnotized, as the water rose and fell in something that almost felt like a pattern but was so unpredictable that she couldn't be sure. She inhaled the refreshing air and felt alive. The brisk wind, the green nature all around, and here she was, on the brink of something big. She breathed in deeply to soak in the feeling. She relished in the beauty of simply existing.

She took another breath before turning around and gasping. Jack had materialized about ten feet away from her.

"Sorry! I was trying not to surprise you again, and I completely failed. Wow, I must look really creepy, just standing here and watching you. I stopped by the building but didn't see you so decided to take a walk. I just now arrived here and was going to say hi but then you turned around, and now it looks like I've been here staring at you. Not a great look." He placed one of his hands behind his head and intentionally avoided eye contact. Jess consciously deepened her breathing, some of her startled nerves settling, and looked up at him.

"It's okay. I mean, okay, you're right; it could come off as creepy. And I'm not totally sure I believe the 'just walking by' defense. But I'm willing to suspend disbelief and chalk it up to bad timing. Again." She extended her hand and intentionally softened her shoulders to relax herself. "Hi, by the way."

"Thank you for your charitable benefit of the doubt. Hi back." He shook her hand. His deep brown eyes met hers. The hint of green showed through once more, highlighted by the sunlight reflecting on the water. It puzzled her, how different she felt around him. Her entire body pulsed, sensing some unrealized connection. It was as if their time not communicating had, unfortunately, only served to heighten her response when seeing him again.

Or maybe, she reasoned, it was just that he'd caught her off guard. She hadn't been expecting their reunion to be like this. She'd been expecting it to be indoors, with several laptops and coffee and, well, not this awkward turn of events.

Jack released her hand. "I have an idea. I'm going to walk back to the building now. And then I'm going to stand outside and check my cell phone for about seventy-five seconds, you know, per proper waiting protocol. And then I'm going to knock on the door to the building, where you will open it because that's where you've been this whole time. And then we'll start fresh with our meeting."

Jess appreciated the playfulness in his tone. "Sounds like a good plan. Yeah, I mean, because that's where I've been this morning."

"Yeah, exactly. And so … okay, well, then I'll see you in about ninety-three seconds, give or take."

"Perfect. Go team." Jess half-heartedly pumped her fist. She saw Jack's lips curve up, his eyes dancing before he headed back to the building.

After he left, Jess took a real breath. That had been ... something. Jess was relieved to know that Jack Stinson, esteemed SF poster-boy, could be awkward as hell sometimes. Extreme awkwardness was a feeling she knew all too well. It was odd, though, that he could be that way. Jess wondered why. It was almost as if was nervous to see her as well, except she didn't understand why that would be. She'd just convinced herself that any interest he'd had was short-lived, and yet his behavior told her she'd been on his mind.

Jess shook her head and decided that this train of thought was probably best not to dwell on too much before she spent her day in a meeting with the man. She collected herself and made her way back to the building.

Ninety-five seconds later, Jack knocked.

"You're late," she smiled as she opened the door. She was struck again at how good he looked. He wore a cool grey sweater and dark denim jeans that flattered his chocolate brown hair and toned physique. He looked better than he had at their lunch meeting, and a small voice inside Jess wondered if he'd dressed up for her.

"My apologies. How incredibly rude of me." He walked in and looked around mischievously. "How are you this morning? No surprises so far, I hope." A glint in his eye and his upturned mouth put her at ease. His energy today was back to being expansive and inviting, and some of that comfort that she naturally felt with him was returning. Unfortunately, so too was some of that uneasy feeling. She couldn't wait to not feel so attracted to him anymore. Things would be so much easier then.

"No, nothing memorable," she teased. The energy between them was electrified by their shared conspiracy, the secret of what had happened outside combined with the promise not to mention it. "So," she reached for a mug and handed it to him, pointing in the direction of the carafes, "should we grab some coffee and talk design?"

"Right. Let's get down to business." He took the mug. "How have you been, by the way?"

"Good, busy. Busy getting ready for this meeting. Yourself?"

"I can't wait to see what you've come up with. Me? Also busy. Work crisis all week. Mostly resolved now, but …" he paused and looked at her intently, "I'm sorry I haven't been in touch."

Jess started slightly. She was surprised to find that some part of her had needed to hear that, some part that had been hurt by the lack of contact that lay underneath the bigger part of her that insisted she was just fine. "Oh, it's no big deal. Please." She began to pour herself a cup of coffee, intentionally focused on the task.

Jack looked at her quizzically. Instead of responding, Jess let there be silence as she filled the rest of her cup. She knew she was being cold, but she couldn't help it. It was hard enough trying to remain nonchalant despite her intrigue. She flashed back to her brunch with Bridget and how easily Bridget had picked up on her interest in Jack. She hoped she wasn't that obvious now. Silence, as awkward as it was, was preferable to the alternative.

"Alright, Jess. Okay, I get it." His brows furrowed. He seemed to understand, intuitively, that Jess needed to keep her distance. "What do you have in mind for the place?"

Jess forced herself to ignore the nagging sensation inside her that was conscious of hurting him with her aloofness. She opened her laptop and launched her design program, turning her thoughts to the descriptions of the designs that she'd practiced. It was grounding to have something concrete to turn their attention to. That was why they were here, after all, to talk design, and any hurt she'd caused would be, she hoped, short-lived.

A few hours later, they were winding down the meeting. They had made headway, more or less reaching an agreement on the various components of the design, and now they were both ready for a break. There was one last area to explore: the roof deck with the communal garden that Jess had in mind. It would be nice to finish the tour there.

"Okay, one more area. Can you handle it?" Jess pointed to the direction of the stairs.

"Absolutely," Jack stiffened his jaw. "Please, I grew up on the mean streets of San Francisco. I can handle anything."

Jess eyed him suspiciously. "You know, I *want* to believe that you're joking, but to be honest, I'm a little terrified to find out about the trouble that you and Donathan and your associated crew got into. So rather than ask you to explain, I'm going to take you at your word and simply assume that you can probably handle a roof deck."

"I appreciate your faith in me, even if it's based on a colorful understanding of my misspent youth. Lead the way." He followed her up the stairs and took in the beginnings of the roof garden.

"So, over here will be benches and general seating. You can see in my designs that I've framed the view of the lake using indigenous woods while keeping the aesthetic subtle enough so that the lake continues to stand out. But over here," she walked him over to a corner of the deck, "here is the real heart of the space. It's a communal garden where there will be tools so that people can participate during their breaks. The idea is that it will be a meditative area to come to, a place to take a break from computer screens and let the mind dream."

Jack nodded approvingly. "Yeah, I can really see that, a place to relax in between writing code. I don't know how anyone can do that for hours a day to begin with. I like technology but prefer having something tangible, that I can get my hands on."

"Like a nice, hot, steamy solar panel?" Jess laughed.

"Exactly. With all of its sexy cords and wires."

Jess feigned fanning herself off. "Too much, too much! This is a place of work!" She glanced back at the lake, consciously avoiding his eyes. The admonishment that this was work was just as much to be playful as it was to remind herself. Yet, still, she sensed a flirtatious energy between them. They'd both been so careful to keep it professional all day, which had proven increasingly challenging given the natural ease she felt with Jack. His energy beckoned her to come closer; she sensed herself expand around him. And now, something about being here on the roof, overlooking the lake, it made her feel more carefree than she had when they were inside.

"Jess, do me a favor." Jess caught Jack's eyes. They were open, the richness of their coloring inviting her in even further. "Let me show you around this city."

Jess shook her head. "It's okay, Jack." She tried to brush him off. "I'm sure you have too much on your plate to be my personal tour guide. I've lived here for almost a decade now and know my way around well enough."

"No, seriously," he pushed past her objections. "You keep talking about how you want SF itself to play a role in this design. Well, who better than an SF native to show you around? You might even have fun. Believe it or not, I've been known to be enjoyable to spend time with."

"For a good time, call Jack?" Jess arched her eyebrows.

"Some might say ..." Jack became quieter. "I think you'd enjoy yourself." Jess got the sense that he was talking about more than a trip around San Francisco, more to do with the growing tension between the two of them.

The sincerity of his request moved Jess to respond in kind. "Okay," she said, her voice low. "When do you want to go?"

Jack looked up. Jess's heart softened at the hopefulness in his expression. "Good, I'm glad. How about Sunday?"

Jess agreed to the plan. After deciding to start at 11 a.m. Sunday at the Transamerica Building, they wrapped up at the site and parted ways. Some of the tension that existed between them had eased, soothed by the certainty of seeing each other in a few days. It meant that this, whatever it was, didn't have to be resolved right away.

And maybe, Jess hoped, Charlie was right. Maybe the pressure to have things figured out was too much. Maybe she could simply allow it to exist however it was supposed to be.

Chapter 12

"ARE YOU SURE DONATHAN'S A KITSCHY TYPE OF GUY?"

Jess looked over to see Moira holding an "I left my heart in San Francisco" anatomical figure, with the place where the heart should be replaced with a picture of the city outline.

"Hmm, that might be a touch too far. I think we're going for 'fun' and 'delightfully local' without veering into 'cringe.'" Jess glanced around the store. "Although, the longer I look at this place, I'm not sure we can find that here."

Moira laughed. "Who would have thought that something this touristy would be this far down Polk Street? I thought this kind of thing was reserved for Fisherman's Wharf."

"Never underestimate the city, I guess." Jess placed a visor sporting a puff paint version of the Golden Gate Bridge down. "Thanks for coming out on a Saturday. I know it's a pain."

"Don't mention it," Moira said. "I was part of the crack team that convinced you to take on this project. I guess it's only fair that I shoulder the burden, too."

"Well, when you put it that way ..." Jess was touched by Moira's loyalty. Moira was different than Charlie, harder around the edges, but Jess knew that she could count on her no matter what. She was incredibly talented, able to look into a room and tell, almost instinctively, what it needed. She had vision, and beyond that, she was organized, responsible, and capable of serious contract negotiation.

Jess had been amazed that Moira had joined her team. Someone with Moira's talents could have gone to any firm she wanted, certainly one more established than Anicca. Moira, though, had always believed not only in Jess's potential, but also her values. She understood, along with Jess, that the objects with which we surround ourselves reflect, on some level, a deeper understanding of the way we view the world. She had been excited to move design forward at Anicca and was willing to accept a lower pay rate than what she was worth for the chance to be part of something she believed in.

"How did it go yesterday?" Moira asked. "Was Jack pleased with the designs?"

Jess automatically blushed at the mention of Jack's name. She purposefully picked up a book on the hidden stairways of San Francisco to hide her expression. Whatever was, or wasn't, happening with Jack was something she didn't feel ready to share with Moira.

"I think so," Jess said after regaining her composure. "I mean, he basically approved everything, although he keeps insisting we incorporate more hammocks. I can't tell if I find it amusing or if it's driving me crazy."

Moira rolled her eyes. "Ah, one of *those* clients. Or, I guess, substitute client. Did you get any more scoop on what's up with him and Donathan, incidentally?"

"Not really." Jess casually flipped through the book. "I mean, little things, here and there. They seem to have grown up together and bonded through some shared experience of dealing with others' judgment."

"Wow, he shared all that with you?" Moira gestured towards the stairway book. "Also, that book is great, and if you don't have it, you should."

"Noted." Jess made her way to the cash register, intentionally avoiding Moira's comment on Jack. "Let me pay for this, and then let's please go somewhere else."

Moira regarded her studiously. "Jess, what's going on? Is there something you're not telling me about Jack?"

"*What?*" Jess emphasized the shock on her face, hoping she didn't come off as overacting. "No, of course not! Things just come up when we talk. I've been interacting with him here and there because of this project, and talking about this project naturally leads to talking about Donathan, and, I guess, he's mentioned some things."

Moira's expression was unchanged. "Right. I'm going to take you at face value, Jess, because I know you, and I know that the only thing that matters to you maybe more than life itself is Anicca, and I know that you wouldn't do anything to jeopardize that."

"Exactly," Jess said before she turned to the cashier to pay for the book. She tried to hide the hurt that Moira's words had caused.

She didn't know why she was having this reaction. She'd had these thoughts herself, a thousand times, but hearing Moira say them out loud stung.

They were quiet as they left the store. Eventually, Moira spoke. "When are you seeing him again?"

Inside, Jess cringed. The news that she was spending the day with Jack touring San Francisco a mere two minutes after denying that there was anything more than a professional acquaintance was hard to square. Even so, she didn't want to lie to Moira. Their relationship meant more to her than that. Instead, she braced herself.

"We're supposed to get together tomorrow," she squeaked out.

"On a Sunday? Did you not get all the designs approved yesterday?"

"No, I did, but …" she considered the best way to frame it, "he's got this thing about being a native San Franciscan. It's important to him that we incorporate the spirit of the city into the design, so he's taking me to a few places tomorrow that are particularly special to him, you know, so that the design can pay homage to them somehow."

"Hmm," Moira's tone was cool. "Be careful, Jess. There's a lot at stake here. Jack's fun and charming, but keep it professional, okay?"

Jess paused their walk to turn to Moira, shaking her head. "Yeah, Moira, I got it. Okay, believe me, the last person you need to remind that this project is a big deal is me. I think about it every waking second of my life and probably some dreaming seconds too. And what I definitely don't need to add to my stress right now is you opining on how I live my life!"

Moira took a step backward. "Whoa, Jess. I'm just looking out for you and trying to make sure you don't risk everything and be sorry for it later. But fine. It's your life. You do whatever you want."

The words hung, unresolved, as they turned and continued walking. Jess felt terrible. She had never been particularly skilled at conflict; if anything, it was something that she'd avoid at all costs if possible. That it was conflict with Moira made it even worse. They'd known each other only a few years—a short time, in the grand scheme of things—but, in that time, they'd been through a lot. They were more than colleagues; they were friends. Even though Moira could be harsh, Jess knew that she was always coming from a good place.

"Look, Moira, I'm sorry I reacted that way. I think we're all on a short fuse here with everything going on."

Thankfully, Moira accepted the olive branch. "Apology accepted. And I'm sorry, too. I didn't mean to go off on you like that. I just worry about the business, and not only because I'm personally invested, but because I know what it means to you."

"I know you do," Jess told her. "I don't want to do anything to jeopardize that. Please believe me on at least that."

"That I can believe," Moira replied, some of her compassion emerging through her voice.

They continued to a few more shops after that, each minding the tacit agreement not to speak any further about Jack. There was plenty to talk about besides, including the intimidating topic of additional pitches and hiring more staff, which was at once both a dream and a nightmare to consider. But the impact of their conversation hung with them when they said goodbye. Even though they had both moved on from being upset, the reality behind Moira's concern, and the resonance it found with Jess's own, stuck around.

A small part of Jess worried that it was already too late, that try as she might, there was some electricity surrounding her and Jack that was moving beyond her power to control. She had been able to keep things professional to date, but their interactions had been so limited. They were barely noteworthy at all, and yet she felt something being created that exceeded what she consciously understood. She was so susceptible to energy. It compelled her being and was the basis for her being a designer, but she felt, in this instance, at its whim. She looked out her bay window when she got home that evening, staring at the sky and hoping, offering her trust to it, and asking whatever force was operating here to please, please not let her do anything she would regret.

Chapter 13

"Welcome, Ms. Tyler, to a once-in-a-lifetime event: a custom tour of San Francisco from a city legend himself, Jonathan 'Jack' Stinson." Jack waved to Jess as she approached the Transamerica Building. His brown eyes were enhanced by the brightness of his smile. He was, it was clear, excited to see her.

Jess felt a pang of remorse in response. When they'd parted company Friday, she'd been, well, if not looking forward to their day together, at least anticipating it with some amount of enthusiasm. Following her conversation with Moira, though, those doubts that had been growing progressively quieter had been awakened. She wasn't sure what she was getting herself into.

She'd almost canceled, come up with some excuse that she had too much to work on. It wouldn't have been a lie, really. She had spent several hours revising her drafts the night before and was planning to do the same after her time with Jack. But face time with a client, or at least a reasonable stand-in for a client, was a requirement of the job. She had to get to know their tastes, and if, indeed, Jack wanted some of what he showed her incorporated into the design, there was simply no way of getting around their day together. Moreover, canceling last minute would have been rude, and she didn't want to do that to Jack. For all the flip-flopping of emotions he had inadvertently caused within her, he had never been anything but kind to her.

"Hi!" She mustered up some animation. They embraced in an awkward half hug that coupled perfectly with the in-between energy in which their dynamic resided. "I haven't been to the Financial District in a while. There's a different energy here. Even on the weekend, it *feels* busy, like wherever you are is certainly not where you are supposed to be, and wherever you're supposed to be is somewhere you were late to five minutes ago."

Jack's delight registered on his face. "You know, that's a great way to put it. Come to think of it, maybe I should move my company somewhere else, like Marin or something. Get some nice granola vibes to chill my employees out so that we can focus on natural energy."

"I think it may have been a while since you were in Marin," Jess countered. "I think these days it's less free love and hippies and more multi-thousand-dollar mountain bike weekend warrior types."

"You're breaking my heart here, Jess! And ruining the reputation of my legacy beach!"

"Sorry!" Jess laughed. "Don't worry. I'm sure there's still plenty of patchouli oil if you know where to go."

"You know, Jess, you could work on your condolences." The enjoyment in Jack's expression reassured Jess that their banter was all in good fun. "Come on, let's get going. There are a lot of places I want to show you. I'll have to warn you that I can get carried away with the SF history. If you need a break, let me know, and I'll get it. I can be a little intense when I'm excited about something, and I'm very excited to do this with you today."

The increasingly familiar energy Jess felt within her when she was near him stirred now. Jess noted with some chagrin that the nerves she had felt coming here simply dissipated when she was around him. It was equal parts liberating and disorienting to experience.

"I'm sure it will be fine, Jack. I love SF, too, in my own way. I'm looking forward to seeing it through your eyes." Jess looked away. That had come off more intimately than she would have liked. She couldn't help it. His passion moved something inside of her. This was personal, she realized, Jack showing her the city, his city. It meant something to him, and he was letting Jess see that.

To his credit, Jack let the comment slide and gracefully began the tour. "I wanted to start at the Transamerica Pyramid, not because I'm particularly drawn to the Financial District, but because I like the *idea* of this building, what it represents. When they first put this building in, people hated it, said it was hideous. Now it's one of the landmarks of the SF skyline.

"I like thinking about that. You know, that often happens with new architecture. There's a period of twenty or so odd years where people adjust to the change and hate it in the meantime. And then the change settles, and people feel more comfortable and mostly ignore it. And then more time passes, and the building becomes a beloved classic. But the building is just a building. It's our perceptions that change. We all think our perceptions are permanent, but they're not. The building outlasts those perceptions. It makes its own way in the world and, in the end, wins, fighting the good fight. Now we couldn't imagine the SF skyline without this building."

Jess let her eyes scan up the building. She was intrigued by the way Jack spoke about it. His philosophy resonated with that part of Jess that, too, found such solace in the concept of impermanence. "I like that idea, the wish to create something beyond ourselves, that will outlast us. And I know we both understand the experience of not fitting in but continuing to be true to who we are until others learn to accept us."

"Yes, exactly," Jack spoke softly. "Thanks for agreeing to do this, Jess. I've been looking forward to this since we said goodbye Friday." He was near her, and she could feel the warmth of him. His energy was expansive, perhaps the most expansive it had ever been.

It left her flustered. "Yes, I think we'll come up with some great inspiration to add to the design," Jess said, purposely sidestepping the force behind his words.

Jack raised his eyebrows, looking at her as though he couldn't figure her out. "Me too," he replied.

They walked up Montgomery Street. Jess felt the awkwardness of the moment but figured it was inevitable. She couldn't figure him out. In some ways, he was so direct, but then, frustratingly, he would drop these hints, these intonations that everything he said meant something deeper, but his words always left enough room for her to question, for her to worry that, if she assumed any deeper meaning, she would be proven wrong. What did it mean that he was "excited"? Did "excited" mean "I'm attracted to you and hoping that this day will become more than professional"? Or did it mean only "I'm excited because I love walking and you seem like a nice person"?

Jess decided to let it go. "So, what's next on the tour?"

"Well, this is part of it right here," Jack said, picking up on her implicit request to move on. "We're passing by Columbus Avenue, which we'll come to on our way back, but we're making our way up to Coit Tower, the top of Telegraph Hill. But this intersection," they stopped at the corner of Bush and Montgomery, "Do you remember how the Gold Rush started?"

"I remember the legend, hard not to, growing up in gold country. Some guy fooled people by raising a piece of gold in the air and claiming he struck it rich and then that started the Gold Rush. Everyone wanted a piece of the pie."

"Right, except turns out, he was a fraud, and there was no pie." Jack pointed up Montgomery. "This is the street that he supposedly ran down with the gold. This is, according to urban legend, where it all started."

Jess's eyes widened. "What? Right here? Wow. That is ... so strangely cool."

"Yeah, this whole area has a rich history. It's all art galleries and fashionable boutiques now, but it used to be the epicenter of sin, not only in SF but, according to some religious figures, the world." The two kept walking, now approaching Pacific Street. "This was the old Barbary Coast area of San Francisco. Utter, utter depravity. Things I won't describe, but it suffices to say, anything sexual or otherwise bizarre that you'd want to find, you'd find it here, even things no one in their right mind would want to find. Pacific Street was colloquially named Terrific Street as an act or irony because it was so depraved.

"Tons of interesting history," Jack gestured to the builds around them. "Everywhere you look. Multiple ships, entire ships, have been found buried below these streets, essentially intact. There's a bar that has one in the basement that you can take an elevator down to see. Some of the alleys are named after those ships, like one alley down there called Balance Street, named after The Balance. Also, the first club that allowed mixed race couples to dance together was in this area. It was called the 'So Different' club, and as you can imagine, it received more than its fair share of threats and actual violence." He paused. "Not as much of that has gone away these days as I'd have liked."

Jess was struck by the sobriety of his words. "Is that why you do what you do?"

"You mean solar panels?" He tilted his head.

"Well, yes, but more specifically, the work you are doing on housing: to provide housing alternatives for people in need." Jess realized as she said it that he'd never actually told her about that. She had only known about it through Bridget's Google search. An unfortunate slip of the tongue that must have happened because she was so caught up in the present, enamored of the city and the walk and of his unexpected knowledge. She hoped it went unnoticed.

"Oh, yeah. Well, kind of. That's not really about race, though. I believe that all people deserve basic rights. Sustainable solar panels are a small contribution to that, if they can help people have some form of stable housing. It's the type of thing that's hard to brag about, though, because it feels so basic. After all, what else better am I doing, is anyone doing, than trying to make sure that all people have some form of essential dignity?" He closed his eyes. "Sorry, this isn't exactly the light mood I was hoping for today."

"No, it's fine." It really was. She liked seeing this side of him, the passionate, soulful side. "I think it's great, what you're doing. You call it basic, and maybe it should be, but most people don't help out in that way. I don't, for example, although maybe I should."

"You could, you know, there's definitely a need for sustainable, economic design. It's … Yeah, anyway, I didn't take you around the city to proselytize, but if you were ever interested, your skills could certainly be used."

"Let me think about it," Jess said. "I have so much going on with the business right now and don't want to commit to something unless I can do it, but … you're right. There is something about giving back. And if I can, I want to."

Jack smiled. "No pressure. It's a big commitment to make, or at least, it can become that way."

They kept walking, but something was changing. In a way, this conversation felt more intimate than when they had talked before, even more than when they had talked about themselves in a more obviously personal way, connecting about their childhoods. What Jack had said had exposed a side of him that was honest and vulnerable. And Jess was finding that those insights, those moments of connection, made her feel closer to him, like she wanted to share more of herself with him in turn.

The conversation continued as they made their way to Columbus. Jack insisted that they grab lunch from Molinari's, a traditional Italian delicatessen that had been one of the features defining the North Beach area as the Italian part of town. He was full of interesting trivia. North Beach had been the area of the Beat Generation, and they had fun each choosing a favorite quote at Jack Kerouac alley after passing by the famous City Lights Bookstore, founded by Lawrence Ferlinghetti, the person whose publishing of beat poetry in paperback made the work accessible. It was a revolutionary act at the time, paperback having been heretofore reserved for decidedly nonliterary works like pulp fiction. Ferlinghetti's choice of the medium had been an act of egalitarianism as much as it had been a practical consideration, that it was simply cheaper to print in paperback. Jess marveled at how something that the culture now took so much for granted could be so radical at the time. She loved seeing the aftereffects of change like that, a reminder of all things transient.

They started the climb up Green Street, paying attention to the unique architecture that resulted from a combination of zoning restrictions, creativity, and bribery. It was fascinating, seeing the city in this new way. It felt like a secret: terraces constructed over alleyways illegally and then being grandfathered in, a whole world that had been created around the Italian immigration that resulted from the Gold Rush, where everybody knew everybody else, including all your secrets, and accepted you anyway.

"Now I'm going to show you one of my favorite parts of the city," Jack said, as they approached the corner of Green Street and Montgomery Street. They came up on a street named "Calhoun" that appeared to be nothing more than a dead end leading to a concrete wall.

"A wall? Perhaps a testament to the inevitability of human frustration in a cold, uncaring world?" Jess asked, faking seriousness. She felt playful, light, and excited for whatever it was that made this place so special to Jack.

"Exactly," Jack joked back. "Except ..." As they walked out to the end of the street, it curved, revealing an unobstructed and expansive view of the bay. It was beautiful. The bay, Yerba Buena Island, the Embarcadero, and the Ferry Building—all set against a clear blue sky with the sun shining down. Jess closed her eyes and took a deep breath, letting the unrestrained energy that surrounded her permeate her being. Jack watched her, intrigued.

"I see what you mean," Jess said, with her eyes still closed. It was a testament to how at ease she felt that she was able to be so in her process with him nearby. "I can't believe how clear this view is. I'm surprised this place isn't more popular."

"As to the popularity, I don't understand, either, well apart from the fact that the trek up Green Street is likely enough to discourage quite a number of people. But the view—it's not an accident. Do you notice how the edge of this hill abruptly drops off at the edge of the concrete wall?" Jack summoned her over to peer over the edge where, indeed, the drop was sudden, almost perpendicular. Jess nodded her head.

"That, Ms. Tyler, is the work of George and Harry Gray, the infamous Gray Brothers. They ran a quarry here and had no qualms, either imposed by law or by conscience, about blowing up Telegraph Hill." Jess gasped. "No, seriously," he continued. "No permits, nothing. If you lived on Telegraph Hill, you could be reading in your living room when, suddenly, an explosion would cause half of your house to collapse. When the city finally started to get involved, the Gray Brothers had the nerve to argue that, if they successfully blew up Telegraph Hill, the residents of Russian Hill would have a clear view to the bay."

Jess laughed. "*What?* Wow. I'll have to try that tactic next time I'm encountering some pushback from the Board of Supervisors."

"You should; tell them it's based on precedent." Jack turned to look back at the bay. "A pretty sordid tale, but it ultimately resulted in a view like this. Not that I'm saying it's worth it, by any means. But we all have a history, blemishes that end up making us who we are. San Francisco is no different. I love it for that."

"Me too." Jess was thoughtful. "It's why I moved here, I think. Sure, sure, growing up in Sacramento, moving to San Francisco was always the thing you did if you wanted to make your dreams a reality. But more than that, I remember coming here as a kid and just being enchanted, the natural beauty of it all, and the history. I remember feeling the energy of the streets and the buildings, like they were tuned into this different reality that was fun and exciting. Kind of like how in Toy Story, the toys come alive at night. It felt like all the different parts of the city had their own language that came alive when no one noticed. And I think a lot of my work here is about noticing it and capturing that feeling, or at least those parts of it that the city will let me see." She paused for a beat. "That it lets me understand."

They were silent, looking at the water. Jess felt comfortable, though, in that silence, reflecting on their paths and this city and the here and now. The reservations Jess had felt about how this day would go were gone, a carefree lightness in their stead. Being around Jack comforted her, and she sensed, by his ease in the silence, that he felt the same way.

"Shall we continue on?" Jack asked. "We're almost at Coit Tower, and I've been thinking about these sandwiches for close to an hour."

Jess nodded. "Sounds good."

• • •

By about 3:00 p.m., they were winding down their tour. Jess had had a wonderful time. The view from Coit Tower had been breathtaking. She'd been there before, of course, but this time it had felt different. She really noticed the wind on her face, the warmth of the sun. Learning so much about the history of the area, how the side overlooking the bay had once been considered the less desirable side, how the Irish lived in a culture war with the Italians on the other side—it had all been so fascinating, and she had been truly present in the experience. Seeing the city with new eyes made her feel like a kid again.

She liked that Jack knew so much. He clearly loved his hometown, and there was something she admired about that. Her day with him had taught her more about him too, that he seemed to be a genuinely good person, at least to those who were close to him. He deeply cared about Donathan, had been there for him through some hard times, as had Donathan for him. It was like they were brothers more than friends. Jack, having grown up an only child, treasured that relationship more than most.

He had planned the whole day so that all she'd had to do was enjoy herself, and she was relishing in being able to let go. The stress of running her own business and being responsible for not only herself, but the livelihood of two other people, had worn on her more than she'd consciously known. Being here with Jack on this day, where all she had to do was listen and walk and learn and be charmed, relaxed her in a way she hadn't felt in … She didn't even remember how long. Too long.

She and Jack had made their way back to her neighborhood, Alamo Square. Jess knew the history was rich here but hadn't known how rich. Jack told her about the origins of Bill Graham, the now-ubiquitous music promoter who had acquired the Fillmore, previously named Majestic Hall. Jack pointed out how you could still see the old name as you walked up Fillmore towards Geary. As they turned the corner on Geary, Jack let her know that the now inconspicuous post office on the corner had once been the recruiting headquarters for The Peoples Temple, the religious cult behind the Jonestown suicide.

"You mean, don't drink the Kool-Aid Jonestown?" Jess asked, incredulous that this nondescript structure was associated with something so macabre.

"That's right. Kool-Aid laced with cyanide. Now just a part of history."

"Wow," Jess paused. "I guess you can never take a building at face value."

"Everything is more complicated than it seems."

Jess looked at the building with new respect, letting the complex and rich energy of its history flow within her. So much life had happened there: hope and tragedy and sorrow.

Their conversation flowed effortlessly while they found their way back to Alamo Square. As they approached, she found herself sad that their tour was ending. She'd had a great time and didn't want it to end. At the same time, she felt herself on dangerous ground. The words of Alex, the interviewer, how Jack wasn't someone that you expected to commit, suddenly flashed back into her mind. But her delight from the day allowed her to push them aside. He'd been so kind to her all day long. And she wasn't Alex; she was her own person. If she wanted to say thank you, she was going to.

She turned to him. "I have an idea. Let's go grab a picnic from Faletti's and set up in Alamo Square so we can watch the sunset over the Painted Ladies. It will be the quintessential San Francisco evening to cap off the quintessential San Francisco day."

Her enthusiasm was contagious, and Jack responded in kind. "That would be great. Does that mean you've had a good time?" His eyebrows raised hopefully.

"It's been a great day, Jack. I've had a wonderful time. I mean, I'm not *exactly* sure how I'll incorporate any of it into my design. But certainly, the feeling of the city has to be there. So many people have come to this city drawn by the belief that something more was possible. I want to honor that."

"Thanks. I'm glad you liked it. I've had a great time, too, really great." He looked down, his expression charmingly bashful. "To be honest, I'm happy that it's not ending just yet."

"Me too," she said with a small nod. She couldn't bring herself to say anything more. She felt exposed enough saying what she had. She was happy the day wasn't over yet. They'd picnic and watch the sunset and then say goodbye. Then they'd return to the real world the next day as professional colleagues or, maybe, Jess thought, maybe now becoming friends.

"Friends" was a title she could live with. "Friends" felt neutral, at least neutral enough. "Friends" didn't involve jeopardizing her career or the comfortable life she was building for herself. And "friends" was a wonderful thing, wasn't it? Who didn't need more friends? San Francisco, for all its surface welcoming, could be a lonely place. The transience of the city meant that it was hard to find people who stuck around, and with Jess as busy as she was, she hardly had time to meet any friends these days.

They created a picnic with their findings from Faletti's—salami and various cheeses and crackers and dried fruits—and opened some canned wine to go with it. Drinking openly was prohibited in Alamo Square, so they'd opted to get canned wine and brown bag it. It was hardly classy, but it was cathartic: joyous and fun and uncomplicated. Jess missed feeling this way. In her increasingly fast-paced life, she had forgotten the bliss of being in the present. Jess felt young again. Or maybe, Jess thought, she felt her actual age rather than ten years older.

They spoke more as they picnicked. Jess learned that a knowledge of SF history was basically Jack's family birthright; his family had been behind the scenes on huge projects involving the city's preservation. Jess had blushed as Jack regaled her of stories of his and Donathan's youth: how they'd snuck into concerts at The Fillmore or the Boom Boom Room and pretended to be part of the crew so they didn't have to pay; how they'd gotten into trouble at school when Jack and Donathan had coordinated a ditch day via an extensive "locker flyering" campaign, only to be ratted out when one kid had turned them in for fear that missing school would impact his chances of passing an AP exam; but more than that, how they'd also been there for each other, how when either of them was having a hard time, they would head over to Golden Gate Park or the Sunset Reservoir and take a break from it all; how having each other in their lives had helped them get through some dark periods and emerge with a deep bond.

Jack had learned more about Jess, too: about her sister Bridget, the attorney, who lived in San Francisco and who probably worked too hard but who had always protected and encouraged her; her other sister Ashley, still in high school, who Jess knew less well but was looking forward to knowing more as she grew up. Ashley seemed to be a dreamer, like Jess, and was having some trouble in school, perhaps as a result. Jess shared about how she meant to go home more often but how the business had a life of its own and how that made making the time to go home seem so impossible. Jess shared memories of growing up in Sacramento, of going to the train museum, where the building looked so big Jess could hardly believe it. She spoke of time spent at the Capitol Mall, where it was green and peaceful and calm, and she would look up at the sky and feel the bigness of the world.

Jess smiled as she described the last image of the Mall. She closed her eyes and let herself fall backwards into the grass. The day's walk and the sun and the wine was a heady combination, and she felt like she wanted to relax and stare into the sky and think about how big it was again. She placed her hands over her eyes to block some of the sun, which was beginning its journey into the night. She let herself peek through and saw Jack looking down at her, smiling.

On a whim—something she never could have justified had she not been feeling so free—she pulled on his shirt to bring him to lie down next to her. He complied with her request, easing himself to lie down so that they were close, their arms touching, looking up at the sky and experiencing the heat between them. Jack propped himself up on his elbow and stroked her cheek with his other hand. His eyes met hers.

The tension between them grew intense. Jess felt her pulse quicken. Her body answered the implicit question that lay between them. Did she want this? Did she want more?

Yes, yes, she did. She'd wanted this since she'd first met him, at the photoshoot. She'd wanted this since she'd been told they would be working together. She'd wanted this since she'd seen him on Friday, since he'd called her the Saturday before, since she'd woken up that morning, and since she'd gone to bed the night before. The anticipation was dizzying. She wanted this despite all the reasons her head worried would take her off track, despite the concern about what it all meant or didn't mean and what happened next or didn't happen.

Her eyes met his, and she gave a slight nod. He kissed her, a passionate kiss, the heat coming from his very core and moving through his chest into his lips as they met hers, soft and warm and feverish. He was fully present in his kiss. She closed her eyes and let herself receive the intensity of his passion, the sensation she felt in her chest and stomach and even lower. She let her lips meet his, kiss for kiss, second for second. Her tongue found its way into his mouth almost without her knowledge. Her reason had been completely taken over by her desire and her feeling of needing this, just this, right now. Right now was all that mattered. Her body pressed against his. Her breathing quickened to match his. Her skin felt alive, tingly, reborn after having been neglected for far too long.

All that mattered was this moment. All that *existed* was this moment, here, with him. The probing, searching kisses that found answers to questions she didn't know she had, his body and her body and the heat that was created between the two, the very smell of him, so strong, like a cedar mixed with something else that could only be Jack—Jess wanted this, badly, with all of her. She needed this more than she could consciously understand. It was deep, this craving. It was all-consuming. It had the power to completely take over.

But that was exactly the problem. It could take over, everything. She could lose everything.

Memories of her conversation with Moira, of her warning from Rebecca, and of her own doubts came flooding back into her mind. She pulled away, sitting up and distancing herself from Jack.

"Jack, I—" she started to say, only to find that she had no idea how to explain what was happening, to possibly make clear something she didn't understand herself.

Jack sat up next to her, confused and worried. "Is everything okay? Jess, I ... Did I do something wrong? I thought you wanted ... Are you okay?" Jack reached out his arm to her shoulder.

Jess placed a hand on the grass to steady herself. "I ... I'm fine, Jack. I just ..." She forced her face into a neutral expression, gently removing his hand. "Listen, I don't know what to say other than that I don't think this is a good idea. We're working together. I value my career very much and have no desire to jeopardize everything I've created. I'm sorry if I sent you any mixed signals. I didn't mean to. I've had a wonderful day, but I think we should end it here."

Forever passed between the two of them. Jess was coming back to herself more and more, and some of the reality of the situation was setting in. She looked up at Jack but found his expression inscrutable.

"Okay," he said. "Okay, if that's what you want. But, Jess, I'm not sure what you think this is; I have no idea what it is myself. But I like you, the more and more I get to know you. I'd never want you to do something you didn't want to do. But a moment ago, it seemed like you were right there with me, and I wonder if maybe you do want this, as much as I do, but are convincing yourself you don't. I know it's fast. It's fast for me too. But maybe that's for a reason, and at the very least, I ask you to consider what that reason might be."

He placed his hand on his forehead and exhaled. Jess thought about responding but couldn't. She didn't know what to say and was worried she would say too much or something she didn't mean. And more than that, it was taking all her concentration to remain composed. She couldn't spare any energy for speech.

She felt removed from her body. From a distance, she felt herself pack up the picnic. She knew, on some level, that she needed to respond, but right now, she needed to take action, even as small of an action as putting away the crackers. Jack moved to help, packing along next to her in an awkward silence. In a minute, everything was cleared up, no evidence of anything that had transpired there remaining.

Jess turned to him. "I'm going to head home now. I live just a couple blocks away. Thanks again for today. I did hear you what you said, and I'm not ignoring you. I just … I have a lot to think about. And I need time to do it." Jack nodded, understanding. "I'll send you over the latest drafts of the design tomorrow, and we can go from there."

She stood up to leave, as did Jack. "Goodbye, Jess," Jack said. "I want to say so much more, but I …" He stepped closer, his eyes probing hers fervently, conveying more than he could say with words. "Think about it, Jess. I … hope to hear from you soon."

With one final look, Jess turned to walk home.

Chapter 14

Jess remained in a state of disbelief when she got home. She poured herself a glass of water and went to sit at her bay window. Try as she might to relax, she couldn't. She wanted to move but had no idea where to. Her discomfort emanated from within, the type that couldn't be easily undone. Even looking at the sky, normally so soothing, wasn't helping. Her thoughts were racing, flashbacks to the kiss, wondering if it had really happened, wondering what it all meant if it did and where, if anything, they would go from there.

And the one thing that she tried not to think about: where it would have gone if she hadn't stopped it.

The thoughts were too big for only her to hold. She needed to talk to someone. She picked up her phone and dialed Bridget's number.

Bridget picked up immediately. "Hey, Jess, everything okay?"

"Hey Bridge, yes, um, yes, I think so. Or maybe not. I'm not sure." Jess was surprised at how dazed she sounded even now on the phone, like she was watching someone else talk through her body. She shook her head and tried, unsuccessfully, to snap out of it.

"Jess, what's going on? You're worrying me. Have you been hurt?" Bridget spoke with an urgency that a now distant part of Jess was responding to. If Bridget sounded alarmed, then Jess must sound worse than she thought. The realization, coupled with the soothing familiarity of her sister's voice, slowly began to bring Jess back. She wasn't okay, far from it. But she was calmer and more able to be present in her body.

"No, Bridge, it's nothing like that. It's ... Oh I don't know. Jack and I, we just kissed, and it was wonderful for a second, and then it wasn't, and then I ran away, and now I'm home and I ... I ..." Tears poured from Jess's eyes, tears of release of some of the tension in her chest, tears of grief over what had happened or, perhaps, over what hadn't, tears of feeling vulnerable and raw and exposed and at the same time being able to talk to a person in her life who made her feel so loved.

"Aw, Jess. You must be so overwhelmed." Bridget's kindness was like a balm, soothing and softening the tension in her chest. This was the right thing, talking to Bridget. It was going to be okay. Jess could feel that. She had no idea how, but it was.

She told Bridget everything: about the day that she and Jack had spent together and how wonderful it had been; about how there were times she felt really close to him, like they could be friends, but then there were times that she felt terrified, like the life that she'd imagined for herself was spinning out of control and she didn't know how to stop it; and about the kiss, how she had felt so caught in the present that it had sort of happened and how she had liked it but had no idea what it meant and was worried that she'd messed everything up.

"And now I don't know what to do," Jess said through her tears. "The thing is … Oh, I don't even know what the thing is. It's complicated. I'm working with him. And this project matters to me, really matters."

"I know, Jess," Bridget tried to soothe her. "You've worked so hard to build Anicca."

"Exactly!" Jess reached for the box of tissues that she, thankfully, had had the foresight to bring over. "Anicca is everything to me. It *is* me, the only place I've ever really felt like I could be me. And now I'm afraid that I'm screwing something up."

"You're afraid being with him means the end of Anicca? I'm not sure that's fair, Jess."

"Isn't it, though? Already I catch myself thinking about him, and nothing has even happened! Or, I guess, before a couple hours ago, nothing had." She released a fresh wave of tears. "I hate this feeling, that I'm getting something wrong or that I will get something wrong. I feel so lost. I haven't felt this way for years, since before I found design. I used to feel this way all the time."

Jess paused as she processed her own words. She was saying something important. There had been a time when she felt lost, all the time. As much as she was happy to not feel that way anymore, she was immensely sad to remember what it had felt like. Anicca had given her a sense of purpose. It had even, it occurred to her, become her identity. She wondered how much of her fear was about losing Anicca and how much of it was fear of what that meant, that she might return to that lonely place again.

"Jess, do you like this guy?" Bridget questioned.

Jess hesitated. "It's not that simple, Bridge. It's not only about me liking him. It's about … oh I don't know, what liking him means for me and my career and my future."

"Well, I guess in one sense it's not that simple. But in another, it is, right? You like this guy. He seems like a decent enough dude. Maybe that's all you need to know. I get not wanting to start something while the project is going on, although I certainly don't know that you *have* to wait. Relationships start at the workplace all the time, and if there's something there, there's something there. It's not necessarily a bad thing. It could be the best thing. I—" Bridget cut herself short.

Jess noticed Bridget's trepidation. "What is it? Tell me."

"Okay … The thing is, I think maybe you're more afraid of this than you should be. I think you got the message, maybe from Mom or somewhere else, that relationships mean the end of your dreams. And I think maybe you owe it to yourself to challenge some of that narrative because I don't think it's the truth, and because I want to see you happy."

Bridget paused to give Jess a chance to respond. "But Anicca makes me happy."

"Yes, but it might not be the only thing, and it might not give you happiness that lasts." Bridget spoke with a sense of urgency. "I've always believed in you, Jess, even when you didn't believe in yourself. Remember that time in high school when you had convinced yourself that your final art project was garbage, and I had to stop you from throwing it away?"

"Yes," Jess croaked. "You pulled it from the trash and helped me glue it back together."

"Right," Bridget went on. "You had put your entire sense of value into that project, and then when you were worried it wasn't good enough, you spiraled. And guess what? It was phenomenal, like always, because you made it, Jess, and you're amazing."

"Thanks, Bridge." The words barely escaped Jess's lips.

"Look, somehow along the way, you got this idea that you're only as good as what you create, and I guess I don't hate that because I think that has helped you follow your dreams professionally. But I also want you to be more than that, to feel happy in all parts of your life. You have a big heart, one of the biggest I know, and I want to see you share it with someone else. Jack may be the one, or he might be just some guy. But it worries me, thinking that you are afraid to let yourself explore because you're afraid it means the end of everything you've worked towards. I wish you had more confidence in yourself than that."

Jess was silent, stunned at what Bridget had said. "Wow, Bridge, I'm not sure what to say. I have to think about what you're saying. It's a lot."

"Okay," Bridget said. "Look, it sounds like you've been through the wringer today emotionally, and maybe it wasn't the best time for me to share that with you. But, then again, maybe it was, because maybe now, when you're open like this, you'll hear it."

"I heard you, Bridge. I only wish it made more sense. I understand half of what you're saying, but the other half is trying to reach a part of my brain that's not working right now."

Jess heard Bridget sigh. "I get it, Jess. For right now, let yourself be confused. You won't always be. And if you ever want to talk more about what I said, you can. I love you."

"Love you, too."

They said goodnight and hung up. Jess tried to process Bridget's words but kept coming up short. Design, and, by extension, Anicca, was who she was. She couldn't figure out how it could be any other way. Before design, she felt out of place. After? She had a place. It was that simple.

But Bridget was certainly correct that Jess was beyond emotionally drained. With resignation, she got up to prepare herself for bed, grimacing at the thought of the work she'd been supposed to do that night but couldn't and the mess it would leave her in tomorrow. No part of Jess felt inspired right now, and all she could hope was that she could get up early and feel better, if not completely then at least more like herself. She usually did, after she'd had time to let herself be.

She hoped this time was no different.

Chapter 15

DESPITE HER EFFORTS TO REST, JESS FELT OFF THE NEXT MORN-
ing. She went running that morning in an attempt to feel normal
and to prove to herself that everything else was normal, too, but it
had the opposite effect. She felt tired, slow. There was a heaviness
in her heart and mind that wasn't going away on its own. She was
going to have to address it.

At some point.

Meanwhile, Jess was doing everything she could to make
sure that "some point" didn't come for a while.

She arrived at work early, in hopes of catching up on the
work that she'd been unable to do the night before. After making
a pot of coffee, she went to her office and shut the door. It was
all she could do to focus right now. Moira and Charlie arriving
and inevitably asking questions about her weekend was too much
to handle, particularly when Moira knew she'd spent that Sunday
with Jack. The self that avoided her own staff wasn't her best self,
but it was, at this point in time, the best she could do.

She checked her emails: status updates on the furniture, confirmations on the timeline, proposed revisions to a contract. Jess rued the days when all of this was someone else's problem. Alas, those days were long gone, and since her daze was not leaving her feeling particularly creative, she settled into those more mundane aspects of her work.

As she came to the end of her new messages, she noticed that she had not received one from Jack. She checked her phone for what must have been the tenth time that morning. No text messages either. She wasn't sure what to make of that.

She hadn't exactly been expecting him to message her. After the way she'd left things, she hardly could have. It might even have been off-putting if he had texted, overwhelming her when she needed time to think. But still, it stung. She knew it didn't make sense, but a part of her had wanted to hear from him, at least to know that he was thinking about her.

She ignored that part, pushing it down so that she could focus on clearing out her inbox. Although not as soul fulfilling as when she was designing, this was an increasingly important part of her work. They had three months left to complete the project, and the order of painting, furniture arrival, installation, and decoration had to flow flawlessly to make it work.

She ran through her to-do list. Her designs should be finalized this week, and then it was simply a process of implementation. After today, most of her week would involve being on-site, either at a vendor or at the Jumbl campus. Another busy week, but she was happy for it.

Her to-do list, though, coupled with the thought of being back at Jumbl naturally brought her mind back to Jack. In theory, he should be involved in some capacity at this stage, even if only to get a sense of how an installation would look once it was in the space itself. But Jess couldn't bring herself to reach out to him. It was unprofessional—she knew it—but she needed a break from Jack. She needed to figure out what, if anything, she wanted out of their ... well, relationship was the closest word for it, she supposed, and she couldn't think while he was around. Moreover, she reasoned, he had already approved the draft designs. Having him there wasn't necessary, strictly speaking, and could only slow down the process. There wasn't time budgeted in for that.

More than that, or at least equal to it, she wanted to give it a little more time, to see if he would reach out.

She heard a knock at her door and, with some reluctance, got up from her chair to open it. It was Moira, holding a cup of coffee.

Jess attempted a smile. "Hi Moira, how are you this morning?"

"I'm fine," Moira said. She handed Jess the coffee. "You okay, though? You have been shut in your office all morning, and I'm worried that something is wrong."

Jess turned to face her. She wasn't sure how candid she could be. Even though the tension between them from the weekend had subsided, Jess was wary of mentioning that her current malaise stemmed from a half-realized make-out session with Jack Stinson. "I'm fine. A little tired, maybe, and nervous about how we're going to pull this off, but fine."

"Mind if I join you for a bit?" Moira asked. She gestured to a nearby chair.

"Sure," Jess reluctantly agreed, figuring that whatever conversation Moira wanted to have might as well happen sooner rather than later.

"Okay." Moira shut Jess's door and took a seat. "Listen, I wanted to talk about what happened Saturday. I know we spoke about it then, and I was hoping it was resolved, but I'm wondering if your being in here all day is because maybe it's not."

Jess had to give Moira credit for addressing the topic directly. Moira's directness could be challenging at times, but it also meant that conflict didn't usually fester. Moira considered having difficult conversations to be a way of preserving the relationship and not letting resentment build.

"It's not, Moira," Jess replied gently. "We're good." She considered how she could possibly explain what was going on for her. "You're right that I'm feeling off, but not because of what happened between us. The thing is, though, it's about me and Jack, and I'm not sure how much you and I can talk about that."

Moira considered that. "Okay, it didn't go so smoothly Saturday. But I do trust you, Jess, and if you want to talk, I'll try to be supportive."

"Thanks," Jess said. "I guess it would be nice to talk, if it's not upsetting."

"Let's try it out," Moira said gently.

"Okay," Jess sighed. "I do think there's some chemistry between me and Jack, but I know it's not what Anicca needs, and I want Anicca to succeed more than anything else. I guess, if I think about it, some of what I'm feeling is sadness that I have to make this choice."

Moira nodded slowly. "I understand that, Jess. We've all had to make sacrifices to get Anicca where it's at, you more than anyone else. It gets old, after a while."

"It does," Jess agreed.

"Did something happen between you two yesterday?" Moira inquired. "I know you were supposed to do his whole tour-of-the-city thing."

"Right." Jess took a deliberate sip of her coffee, unsure of how much to disclose. With some resignation, she decided that honesty was best in the long run. "We kissed. It was brief. I kinda freaked out after, and we haven't spoken since."

Moira's expression was stoic. After what seemed like an interminable pause, she spoke. "I'm not sure what to say, Jess. I want to be supportive, but I think pursuing anything with him is the wrong decision. He could be a distraction when we don't need any distractions; we need miracles. And he could be hard for our reputation. People could start saying you only got the Jumbl project because you were dating him."

Moira's tone was calmer than it had been before; Jess could tell she was making an effort to remain even. Nevertheless, her words touched all those fears that Jess carried inside of herself and had been fighting to push aside.

She took a breath before speaking. "I get it, Moira. I said I ended it. We're on the same page that Anicca is the most important thing. It's just hard."

Moira's expression was kind. Jess could tell that she really did understand, in her way. They had been through this since the beginning, and Jess had seen time and time again how Moira put Anicca above all else.

"It is," Moira agreed. They were quiet, the mix of emotions settling between them, the sweet pain of having to make a hard choice and wishing with all your heart that you didn't have to.

"Do you really think people would assume that, by the way? That we only got the commission because of something romantic between me and Jack?"

"I think there's a good chance." Moira shook her head. "I know it wouldn't be true, but that often doesn't matter. There are a lot of people who would kill for that commission, and jealousy can prompt people to be unkind."

Jess considered that. "Thanks, Moira. I hate talking about this stuff. I'm not used to it."

"You'll make the right choice, Jess."

Jess pushed on, eager not to linger on Moira's words. "Let's talk about this week, shall we?"

Moira didn't push Jess. "Yes, let's run through it. I have one or all of us scheduled for on-sites basically every day this week. The plus side of that is that we'll have a good idea of how the site will come together by Friday. The downside of that is that we might be dead by Friday. I'll draw up a schedule for you. Jumbl aside, I want to make sure you've called back some of the other potential commissions. I have listed the Hyatt group; I guess they want to open a new hotel near Lands End. A few private individuals have reached out that we need to decide what to do with. And this Friday, I have you slated to attend a gala at the Aquarium of the Bay, in preparation for your RFP proposal."

Jess took some notes. "No rest for the weary, huh? Alright, thanks. If you could create a list of the commissions, I'll make sure to call. I almost forgot about that Aquarium of the Bay thing. I'll have to get a dress, I guess. Okay, thanks."

"You got it."

Moira left, closing the door quietly behind her. Jess reflected on what Moira had said, that she would make the right choice. Moira had meant those words to be comforting, but they landed as hollow. Jess was losing more and more confidence that she would make the right choice or that she even knew what the right choice was. She needed a break from everything, a place to clear her head.

She texted her mom. *Good time to visit this weekend? Could come Saturday, leave Sunday.*

Jess immediately felt less anxious. It was slightly irresponsible, she knew, to go out of town when she had so much going on, but Jess wanted to be home, away from everything, with nothing to do but be comforted by her mom. She'd make up for the lost time somehow.

She turned her attention back to the lengthy to-do list. Jess was ready for the weekend already.

Chapter 16

"ALMOST READY, JESS?"

Jess looked up from her computer at the sound of Charlie's voice.

"For what?" she asked. It was a little after 6 p.m. that Friday, and Jess couldn't imagine what vendor would have possibly requested a meeting at that time.

Charlie pushed her office door open. "Don't you have that Aquarium of the Bay gala? I saw it on your calendar."

Jess blanched. "Shoot. Thanks for the reminder, Charlie. I honestly would have forgotten until I got a ping on my phone ten minutes before it started."

Charlie took a seat by Jess's desk. "No problem." He looked at her with concern. "You okay? It's not very like you, to forget something that big, and I know you have a lot on your plate."

Meeting Charlie's expression brought the beginnings of tears to Jess's eyes, which she had to fight back. "To be honest, Charlie,

I've been better. This project is really tiring, and I knew it would be, but knowing something in theory and living something in reality are two entirely different things, I'm discovering."

"Very true." Charlie's eyes were understanding. Jess was struck by how, despite his youth and the many ways in which he came off as naïve, he possessed a certain depth. "In a lot of ways, these past couple weeks are the worst of it. You had to hustle to get both the design finished and the team lined up. Now, it's execution."

Jess nodded. "I guess that's right. And hoping everything goes smoothly, which may be harder, in its way, having to depend on others to do their parts of the project."

Charlie laughed. "Honey, you were never the best at that, but you have a good team, and Moira will whip anybody who steps out of line into shape."

"I think you're right about that again, Charlie."

"Always," he continued. "But, Jess, is it really all about the project? Jack hasn't been around much this week."

Jess felt a pang at the sound of his name. "Yes, well, there's that too. I've been avoiding him all week. Last weekend things kind of got out of hand, and, well, I've needed some space. I've contacted him when I had to, of course," Jess added quickly. "Like if I needed approval or something. But nothing more than that. I thought having the week would give me time to think, but the truth is I've been so busy with this project that I haven't been able to make any progress on that. At least I'm going home this weekend. I need to get out of the city."

"That's good." Charlie looked at her thoughtfully. "Jess, when it comes to Jack, do whatever feels right. Everything will work out, in the end."

Jess snorted. "I don't think Moira shares that opinion."

"Moira is … Moira. She thinks she knows what's best for everyone, but she's human like the rest of us."

"Then how come she doesn't seem like it?"

"I could say the same about you, honey! But seriously, everything will work out. Speaking of which, you better get your ass home and change if you want to be on time to that gala. I want you looking fierce for those fish, Jess."

Jess laughed. "Thanks, Charlie," she said, as she packed her things to head home.

• • •

Jess used her time on the way to the aquarium to center her thoughts. The gala tonight was to celebrate its twenty-fifth anniversary, and she, along with several other up-and-coming designers, had been invited to view the space in the event context before they pitched their design proposals. The aquarium, once an innovation in design, was now badly in need of a facelift. Its presence in the heart of Fisherman's Wharf would always guarantee it a throng of tourists, but it had started to lose out on repeat clientele, who preferred the newer and much flashier California Academy of Sciences.

The opportunity to pitch was exciting. The winning designer would gain not only a big commission—the aquarium was sparing no expense—but also the prestige of having their work associated with what the aquarium was clear was to be nothing less than the most innovative design. The aquarium was purposely tapping designers who did not typically work in the museum and public spaces arena, with the express goal that designers who worked in different spaces would bring something unique to the redesign.

While Jess was honored to be asked, her feelings were ... well, mixed. There was something about the aquarium that felt nostalgic to her. True, there were some elements that could use a pick-me-up. But Jess loved the feel of it as it was. She remembered coming there as a kid, standing under the signature fish tank tube and staring, mesmerized, at all the fish. Their colors were so vibrant, blues and yellows that she had only been able to picture in her imagination brought to life. She had loved seeing the colors move and sway in a dance that spoke of some secret communication happening between the fish. It was like they vibrated to some way of being that was underneath conscious experience, that understood a kind of magic that humans had lost. Jess had spent long periods of time as a kid there, holding completely still and hoping that, if she were still enough, the fish would forget she was there and reveal their language to her.

Jess sighed as she thought about tonight. Exciting as the aquarium redesign was, it represented a change of part of her youth. All things change, and with that change comes loss. She understood that. After all, the concept of impermanence was one of the hallmarks of her design aesthetic, one of the things that made Lake Merced so awe-inspiring to her. Even so, a part of her longed for something that lasted, longed for a place where she could breathe in the comfort of knowing that some things stayed the same, longed to release into the stillness of it all.

Jess opened her closet and pulled out the dress she'd chosen for tonight. She'd called in emergency assistance from Bridget to go shopping with her, and Bridget, loyal as she was, had managed to squeeze helping Jess into her busy schedule. She smiled as she remembered the conversation with Bridget.

"What do you wear to an event like this?" she had wondered. "Something that captures the honored-to-be-invited yet ambivalent-about-this-commission because you're-messing-with-my-childhood but thank-you-anyway kind of sentimentality?"

"Oh my God," Bridget had retorted. "You're acting like you've been invited to redesign San Quentin. Honestly, Jess, wear something red, put on some gold earrings, and call it a day."

Bridget's ability to be inherently practical in all things was one of the many reasons why Bridget was the attorney and Jess was the designer.

Jess slid on her dress, applied her makeup, and ordered her Uber. The dress she had chosen was racier than she was used to, but Bridget had been adamant that Jess looked great and that, at this type of function, the dress was upscale and appropriate. Perhaps more importantly, Jess felt confident in it. And if she felt confident when she felt sexy, Bridget insisted, there was no harm in that at all.

She got the ping that her Uber had arrived. With one final look in the mirror, she squared her shoulders and went to meet it.

• • •

It was quite the scene at the aquarium. Jess had expected a big event, but the massive turnout took her by surprise. It was only the Aquarium of the Bay after all, and Jess had thought it would be a more subdued affair. It turned out, though, that she was not the only one to have nostalgia about the place. Some of the SF elite were donors, and buzz had been created about the redesign. Plus, the view right out onto the bay, with its postcard-ready sea lions and majestic Golden Gate Bridge, was something spectacular to witness in the evening. Jess was indebted to Bridget for insisting that she dress up. Her dress felt more than appropriate in this atmosphere, not too much at all.

Jess dropped her coat off at the coat check and stepped into the main room. As she scanned the room to get a sense of her bearings, she saw Rebecca, engaged in conversation with two other people she didn't know. Jess went over to introduce herself.

"Sorry to barge in, but I had to say hi." Jess waved her hand in a kind, welcoming gesture.

"Jess, you look fantastic! How are you?" Rebecca hugged her quickly, balancing her wine glass in the other hand, before turning back to the others. "Gentlemen, this right here is Jessica Tyler, one of my former protegees who decided to fly the coup and now is soaring. Jess was profiled in 7×7 recently as one of the new wave of designers. But, of course, and I'm sure Jess would agree, it's all due to having an unbelievable mentor such as myself."

Jess shook her head. It was good to see Rebecca. "It's true, it's true. She's joking, but not completely. Rebecca was a fantastic mentor." She extended her hand out. "Jessica Tyler, Anicca Designs."

"Todd Philips, Gallant Ventures." The brown-haired man on the left shook her hand. "And this is my business partner, Sam Wu."

Jess shook his hand. "Pleasure to meet you."

"So, are you part of this redesign concept Rebecca mentioned?" Sam asked.

"Well, I've been invited to pitch. I assume Unoa has too?"

Rebecca nodded. "Indeed. Seems like an interesting opportunity. There's so much you could do with a space like this."

Todd took a sip from his drink. "Tell me, Jess, are you feeling inspired?"

Jess looked around. "You know, I'm not sure yet. I know that sounds like a cop-out answer, but I really can't design a space until I've gotten a feel for it. I need to spend some time wandering around to get a sense of what would work best."

Rebecca stepped in. "Jess is telling you the truth, gentlemen. She's always been like that, even when she was at Unoa. I'd wonder, wonder, wonder what, if anything, she was doing because there'd be no work product and just a lot of daydreaming. And then one day she'd sit down and spend an afternoon at the computer and bang out the design. Jess has … her own way of doing the work."

Jess beamed at the compliment.

Sam's eyebrows lifted. "What is it that you're looking for, then, when you're seemingly not doing anything?"

"Oh, it's more like I'm waiting for the space to speak to me. That sounds enigmatic, I'm sure, and I'm not trying to be. But really there's an energy behind every space, and I let myself be open to it until it finds me. I'm sorry, I … I can't explain it better than that."

Sam's eyes were thoughtful. "No, I get it. It's like you're trying to find the Chi of the place. My grandmother would sit for hours in her garden until she figured out where a plant wanted to be planted. That's how she'd say it. It 'wanted' to be planted, like it had a will of its own."

Jess smiled. "Yes, something like that." She looked around again. "Which, actually, I hate to cut this short, but I've been so busy that I don't know when I'll be able to come back before the pitches are due. I need to sneak away to take advantage of my time in this space. I hope you'll excuse me."

Rebecca placed her hand on her shoulder. "Do your thing, Jess." Then she whispered so only Jess could hear, "This would be an incredible opportunity for you. I hope you know that."

Jess exchanged business cards with Todd and Sam, gave a quick hug to Rebecca, and left the conversation.

She walked around. She wished she could close her eyes; she'd get a better sense of the energy that way. But the room was full of people, and she'd learned the hard way as a child that doing that would prompt funny stares. She'd have to settle for feeling in her body as much as she could with her eyes open.

As she moved through the aquarium, she let some of the energy settle into her chest. Jess had learned that truly experiencing a space meant using all her senses, not only sight but also the smell, the sound, the feeling that being there would elicit.

The walls hummed as she moved through the aquarium. She felt the sensation first in her chest, a knot that she had only been half aware of finding a release she didn't know she needed. The release soon moved from her chest lower, into her abdomen, first the front and then circling round to the back, bringing with it the sensation of her shoulders softening and her energy shifting downwards, into her feet, feeling the connection to the earth.

Her body became attuned to the energy within the walls. Everything around her felt alive. Part of that was easily explained by the fact that fish and other aquatic life lived within these walls, but it was something more. The building carried not only the energy of life moving through it currently, but of the life that had moved through it before, life that had come and gone. This building held secrets, held time, represented the relatively permanent amongst the impermanent as well as the knowledge that it too would change.

This whole place was an offering, to those who could receive it. Jess remembered how it had been to visit when she was small, how deeply it had comforted her soul. Her internal energy took on a dreamy quality, ethereal yet grounded, receptive, like the water that surrounded her. She let herself meander according to her feeling and found herself, to no surprise, at the fish tank tube.

Jess audibly gasped as she turned the corner and saw the tube. It really was amazing. It could be hard to return to places as an adult that were special to you when you were a kid. Oftentimes, the memory of them is so much larger than the reality. But sometimes they live up to your memory, and when they do, they are spectacular. This place was one of those special ones, that lived up to the memory and that was majestic all over again.

Jess walked silently, observing, noticing. A manta ray swam overhead and approached her, curious, with its soft white beak. Jess smiled in response, a ritual of deep respect. Orange garibaldi danced next to soupfin sharks, brazen in the way they commanded their environment, and Jess was caught in the rhythm, a rhythm beyond time, beyond consciousness, a vibration that existed underneath what humans conceived as "reality," that moved to a different and, perhaps more true, truth.

Jess remembered how it had been when she was a kid, to see all those vibrant colors moving in a pattern that she couldn't begin to understand, to feel the energy that these were beings in the water and that they were communicating to each other. She remembered learning once that some fish use electric pulses to speak to each other and pressed her hands against the tank when no one was looking, to experience that pulse. Jess was always amazed at how much was there if you paused to notice. She felt lucky to be one of the ones that did.

She closed her eyes. It was private enough now, with no one around, that she could sneak in, just for a second, that feeling. She let her awareness settle on her senses, the energy vibrating on her skin, her heart rate soothing as she matched its vibration. The building was speaking to her. She didn't know how, but she knew that whatever her design would be would honor this feeling and also honor that this place was meant to be transient, to be passed through, honor the precious sacredness of participating in this energy and then letting it go.

She heard a voice. "Jess?"

Oh no. Not that voice. "Um, hi." She opened her eyes reluctantly and saw Jack standing there. A part of her had wondered whether if she kept them closed, maybe she could pretend this wasn't happening.

"Hey, there, I didn't mean to disturb you. I remember how much you don't like being caught off guard. We have to stop meeting that way." Jack took a step closer. "I wondered if you'd be here. You look … wow you look fantastic. That dress is great on you." His eyes took her in appreciatively, immediately reminding Jess of their last interaction.

Jess broke eye contact. She felt that deep calm that she'd had a minute ago, immersed in the energy of the aquarium, subside. It was replaced with that energy that she now associated with him, a push-pull in her stomach, beckoning her to move closer while at the same time insisting that she move away.

And yet, the effect he had on her was different, somehow. She felt those parts of her that rose up to protect her still present but softer, muted, like they were coming to know him, that they wanted to trust him.

"I had no idea you'd be here. Why … are you here, exactly?"

Jack shrugged. "I'm, or rather my family, is a donor. Have been for years. This is exactly the SF-legacy type work that the Stinson crew is all about. Is it … good to see me?"

"I'm ... I think so." Jess titled her head. She hadn't expected to see him there, and his presence, while not necessarily unwelcome, was unsettling. "Jack, I'm sorry for how things ended on Sunday. It wasn't a great look and certainly not a kind way to end a day that had been very sweet and that you'd taken the time to create."

"It's okay, Jess. It's okay." His words were comforting, sincere. No judgment, just understanding, like he understood more than she did. And instead of feeling threatened by that, she felt some relief, like at least one of them understood what was going on. "You don't need to apologize. I hadn't intended for Sunday to go to that place, although I have to say I was hoping it would. I ..."

A couple guests came to the area of the fish tank but stopped, awkwardly, as they realized that they were interrupting a serious conversation.

Jack's eyes met Jess's. "Jess, I've been thinking about you all week, wondering when I'd get to see you again. There's so much more I want to say, so much more that I want to hear. But this isn't the place, not for what I want to talk about. Come on, let's get out of here. I want to show you something really special, tour of San Francisco encore. I don't want to push anything you don't want, but I ... I think you want this, too."

Jess found herself nodding. She did; she did want this. Something about this man made her want more, always more. Besides, she could perfectly justify talking to him. The "adult" thing to do would be to have a conversation with the guy, after running out Sunday and then not contacting him all week. Plus, she could only avoid seeing him for so long considering the Jumbl project, so it made sense to get the conversation over with. But her desire to talk to him was more than logical, she knew that. Jess had missed him. Being in this place, so full of childhood memories, was starting to bring Charlie's words back to her. Maybe life was simpler than she thought, maybe it would all be okay, and maybe she should listen, once in a while, to how she felt.

"Okay," was all she could say. "Okay."

Jack's forehead softened. "Great. Let's get out of here, then. I know just the place."

Chapter 17

It was refreshing to be out in the fresh air. In the confines of the aquarium, so close to Jack, Jess had felt that merging of their energies that was becoming more and more familiar. It wasn't unpleasant necessarily, but it made it hard for Jess to think straight. Outside, getting her bearings again, she was becoming aware of how much unspoken lay between them. Here she was, with Jack, for the first time since ... the last time. Memories of the last time flooded her mind. She knew she should say something, but she had no idea what.

Fortunately, Jack spoke. "I can't wait to show you this place. You'll love it."

Jess breathed more deeply, relieved that Jack had broken the tension. "No pressure, right?"

Jack shook his head. "None at all because it's simply not possible for you to feel another way. Tell you what, though. If you tell me you don't like it, I'll decide you were lying and tell myself you loved it anyway. I'm not above occasional self-deception."

"Oh my God," Jess rolled her eyes. "Do you seriously hear yourself sometimes?"

"I try not to," Jack said. "Gets in the way of my confidence."

"Clearly." Jess felt the corners of her mouth turn up. She was having fun. She knew she and Jack had a lot to talk about, but it was deeply grounding to also know that they could still be friends despite it all.

"So, are you excited?" Jack asked. His question contained a certain innocence, a hopefulness in his tone. This quality of his, she began to notice, made her feel safer. He lacked guile, at least with her, which, Jess suspected, was because she brought that out within him, like she too made him feel safe.

Jess nodded thoughtfully. "You know, I think I am."

"Good, because it's a little bit of a walk …" His forehead creased with some concern. "Now that I think about it, with your heels on, maybe I should order an Uber."

Jess was touched by his consideration. "Thanks, but it's okay. Lucky for you, I brought some flats in my purse. I can wear them, but you have to hold my heels."

"Sounds like a fair deal, Tyler. Your wish is my command."

Jess decided not to analyze any deeper meaning that might be hidden in those words. It was unfair. He was talking about holding her shoes. Only he could make something so boring seem fun and mischievous, even a little sexy.

The two walked on for some time, to Fort Mason and then past. Jack hadn't been kidding about wherever they were going being some distance away. Jess half regretted that she hadn't taken him up on the offer of an Uber. But they had more than enough conversation to last the entire walk. Some tension Jess had been carrying all week released on talking to him. She hadn't realized how much she'd missed him. It didn't make sense. She had only known him a short time. Yet, Jess felt at ease, happy, to be discussing the mundane of her week with him.

She caught him up on the Jumbl project. That was normal, of course, given that he was, for all intents and purposes, her client. But it was different than how she usually spoke to a client. The conversation was more collaborative, less formal. She was able to bounce ideas off him and could admit that she was worried about the tight timeline. Jack listened patiently, offering what counsel he could, but also letting her talk without needing to fix it. It was calming, talking to him about work. Jess realized that she didn't have anyone that she really did this with, how usually all her anxieties and concerns would have to stay hers. Even with Moira and Charlie, whom she loved dearly and who were friends in many ways, she had to hold back. She was the boss, after all, and as much as they were close personally, there was also an inherent boundary that simply existed whether she wanted it to or not. Talking to Jack felt good, better than good. It felt soothing, letting go of a huge weight.

Jack told her about his work as well. The crisis that had been happening the week before was close to resolved. Jack had been gathering funding for a new type of portable solar technology. ShineStar had made a breakthrough in solid state battery technology, leading to a battery that was capable of holding a much larger charge. Although the new battery could be used for many types of structures, many of which Jack was having no trouble funding, he had been met with a lukewarm response from investors for the tiny-home market. Part of this was because the tiny homes Jack's company was prototyping were designed with cost efficiency in mind, given that the target demographic was people who would otherwise have trouble affording housing.

"What it all comes down to is, how do you get people to care about people who aren't themselves? Everyone's on board for green technology when the profit's there. But no one seems to care when the profit line is not so clear.

"The bottom line is that we needed to show why this venture is profitable. My team was, luckily, able to come up with some convincing statistics, and we have a first round of funding. But it was touch and go, there, and if we don't deliver on these admittedly ambitious figures, there might not be a second round. At the end of the day, it's all about where the money goes." He gestured to indicate a right turn. "It's always about the money. At least it's an easy system to understand, even if it's a system that is broken."

Jess wasn't sure what to say. Sorry? That was hollow and, more importantly, not how she actually felt. What she felt was something closer to empathy, for how he was feeling and for all that he was carrying. When you truly cared about something, truly, then nothing short of perfection would be enough. That was a feeling Jess could definitely relate to.

But it wasn't a feeling she could easily speak to. That kind of intensity cut close to the quick, and this setting, walking along Marina Boulevard around runners and cyclists and people generally winding down after a long week at work, wasn't amenable to that kind of vulnerability. Instead of speaking, Jess placed her hand on his shoulder, cautiously, hoping it would express all the things she couldn't figure out how to say. He looked at her hand as if it were a life raft calling him back to the present. He removed her hand from his shoulder but, instead of releasing it, continued to hold on so that now they were walking hand in hand, intimate, close.

The remarkable thing was that Jess didn't hate it. Jess wasn't sure what was best for her anymore when it came to Jack. This game she was trying to play, being close but not too close, being professional while ignoring the potential for more, was getting out of hand. She wasn't sure what the rules were anymore.

And she was becoming less and less clear on what the prize was. Not ever getting hurt at all costs? But if the cost meant never letting anyone get close to her, then that was sounding less appealing. Life had to be about more than that.

"Alright, we're here. Or close enough." Jack had taken them to a parking lot outside of the San Francisco Yacht Club.

Jess's brows raised. "Are we … going yachting? I mean, you'll have to forgive me because I haven't had much occasion to yacht before, but I was to understand that that was more of a daytime thing."

Jack shook his head. "Very funny, Ms. Tyler. But no, where we're going is a little walk past this. The ground gets a little dicey, so we'll take it slow." Jack took her hand and turned her to face him, his expression serious. "Also, Jess, and this is important for you to know," he paused for dramatic effect, "yachting easily transitions into a nighttime activity."

Jess groaned and playfully jabbed his shoulder. "You are impossible. Am I even surprised that you know about yachting? Christ, your family probably owns a yacht here."

"Well, I wasn't going to say, but yes, a couple. One that's dedicated for business functions. But the other is for personal use. We should go sometime, maybe check out the Farallons, if you've never been," Jack suggested, referencing the island chain off the coast of San Francisco.

"Yeah, sometime." By this point, Jess felt she should hardly be surprised at finding out just how wealthy Jack's family was, but it was jarring nonetheless. She wasn't sure how she felt about the dynamic that it potentially created. She certainly didn't want to come across as being interested in him *because* of his money, if that's what she was—interested. Which, it seemed, was becoming more and more clear to be the case.

Jack noticed her hesitation. "Money is not the most comfortable topic for me either. It's certainly nice to have but leads a lot of people to come to conclusions about you or to get to know you for the wrong reasons. The trappings aside, I'm a regular guy who wants to do good by the people he cares about. Anyway," he stopped walking, "here we are."

The sky had darkened, and it was hard to see with only the light reflecting off the moon to guide them. Even so, Jess could make out some rocks and structures that looked like they had tubes coming out of them.

"What is this place?" she asked, moving slowly over to one of the rocks.

Jack followed her. "This is the wave organ. It's something that was originally created as part of the Exploratorium but now is here available for all. I'll show you how it works. Come with me." Jack helped her over a couple of rocks until they came to a pipe. "Okay, now listen."

Jess placed her ear to the pipe. It was like the bay came alive. The pipes amplified the naturally occurring sounds of the bay. Jess listened to the roar, like the echo of thunder, belying the wildness that was underneath her feet. Jess's body responded to the amplified sounds, and she closed her eyes to feel the electric energy light up her chest and forehead before moving to her crown. Jess was fascinated by the experience. She normally tuned into energy through sight and touch; it was a treat to enter through sound.

Jess gasped. "That is so cool!" Her eyes widened as she motioned to Jack. "Here, you try!"

Jack put his hear to the pipe, smiling. "Yep, exactly like I remember." He listened for a beat longer before stepping away. "At least some things stay the same."

"I'm going to try another one!" Jess was having fun. She felt free, here in her formal dress, having escaped from a decidedly adult function, to come and play at the bay. She started to move towards another pipe but felt unsteady, unable to see with the increasingly dark sky. She instinctively reached out for Jack's hand, and he helped guide her, using his phone as a flashlight to create a path for them.

"Oh, here's one!" Jess put her ear to another pipe. The sound was different from the previous one, more like a murmur, hollow and low. She put her ear on another and discovered yet another sound, a drumbeat rumbling, clashing, making its own sweet music with indifference as to who heard.

Jess felt light, giddy. She breathed in some of the sea air and moved towards another pipe. Suddenly, though, she stumbled. Her left foot was caught between two rocks, making her lose her balance.

Instantly, Jack was there, catching her. "Jess, are you okay?" He sounded worried, almost panicked.

"Yes, I'm fine. I'm fine." The concern in his face touched her. It was an overreaction, she thought, but still … He cared about her. She placed her arms around his neck. "I'm so lucky you were there." She hadn't intended to hug him, but a combination of her carefree mood and the adrenaline from her fall had pushed her towards him. Now that she was there, it felt so good to stay.

Jack embraced her tightly, his relief that she was okay palpable in his touch. "Always, Jess," she heard him mumble. "I'll always be here for you." His words were barely audible, but the impact landed on them both. It was as if saying the words incarnated a truth that had been lingering between them. They had a connection that didn't make sense given the amount of time they'd known each other. Regardless, they were drawn to each other, connected by something more than reason. Jess slowly tilted her head up, her eyes questioning, wanting to know if he had meant what he said.

Jack's lips took hers, answering her question through the force of their presence. Her lips responded to his, warm, soft, matching her movements, responding to them one by one in some instinctual dance that they fell into from a deep place of rightness. His kisses were passionate. She could feel his need as it came from deep within his belly, from within his soul, to meet her. There were no questions here, only answers—only yes, and yes, and yes.

Jack picked her up, lifting her as if she weighed no more than a feather, and placed her on a rock to sit so that now they were at the same height. Without words, with only the intensity of their need, their lips met again, even more passionate than before. The tension that had been building between them was here, powerfully here. No use fighting it anymore, only surrendering. And surrendering felt so good.

Jess wanted this, needed this. She moved her hands along his back, shaking, vulnerable with the extent of her need. In response to a question she didn't know she'd asked, Jack moved her hands to hold him more tightly. Yes, he wanted her here. She held him more forcefully. Yes, she wanted to be here, too.

A groan released from deep within Jack, full of wanting. He placed his hand next to her and moved in closer to the rock, standing so that his hips were pressed against her. She could feel his desire, the fullness of him. It sparked something from within Jess that wanted more, that wanted to meet him in his fullness. Her breath quickened. Jack took his other hand and placed it at the back of her head, pulling her gently closer to him, taking her mouth more deeply. His tongue found hers and pulled her closer. They moved in a dance, his tongue finding hers and hers responding in kind, welcoming him in, needing him to be there.

It was heady, like a drug: the high of being completely, utterly, absorbed by someone, of leaning into one's desires, of being in the present and feeling that the present was all there was, that there had never been anything but the present, would never be anything but the present, the hereness of it, the heat of it.

They kissed again, and again, greedy with kisses. There could never be enough. Their rhythm continued, lip for lip, stroke for stroke. The heat built within Jess. She wanted more. All she could see was Jack. All she could think was Jack. She needed him, now.

Jess took Jack's hands and moved them lower on her body, still kissing him. Suddenly, Jack pulled away, shaking his head.

"Jess, Jess, I've wanted to do that for so long." He kissed her palm and stayed close, barely finding the breath for the words so that they came out ragged, as a pant, desire coursing through each syllable. "I want to go further, but I need to know that you want that, too, not like last time."

Jess breathed deeply, steadying herself, coming to grips with what was happening. Here she was, in the middle of the SF bay, in public, with Jack, making out like a couple teenagers, except better than teenagers, much better.

The burst of reality was sobering. Jess sat upright, moving slightly away from Jack. She caught her breath. "I'm not sure what to say. I think I want this, but I don't know what that means. I need time." The words came out before Jess had time to think about them. Did she need time? She seemed to think so, at least part of her did. But now that she'd said the words, she found them comforting. Yes, time. Time to do what, exactly, she didn't know. But time had to be the answer.

"I don't know what you're asking for," she continued. "And I ... To be honest, I worry about whether what you're asking for is more than I can give. And more than that, I worry that what you're asking for is less than I want."

"Jess, what do you want? Just let me know. I want something with you, but we can go at your pace. Just promise me you won't run again." He kissed her cheek, his lips continuing to make their way down her neck with soft, powerful, reassuring kisses.

The dizzying sensation started to overtake her again. She forgot what she had said she wanted. Oh right, time. Beyond that she had no idea. She lifted his chin and pressed her lips against his, not running, staying right there.

She pulled away and looked at him intently. "I won't run, Jack. I need to figure out what I want, though. This whole situation has me questioning so much. I wasn't planning on you, or anything like you. And it's hard for me to think when you're around." She pushed herself off the rock and steadied herself. "I just need time."

Jack paused. "I understand, but Jess, last week, after we kissed and you disappeared ...I don't want to go through that again. How much time do you think you'll need?"

Jess looked at him, catching the pain in his features through the moonlight. "I'm sorry, Jack," she said, still coming back from her daze. "It wasn't kind of me to do that to you." She exhaled. "All of this is so overwhelming. I want to tell you how much time I need, but I don't know. Hopefully not too much. Whatever is happening between us is bringing up a lot for me. I can't put a timeline on knowing myself."

Jack looked down, his jaw set. "Okay, Jess. I would never want you to feel pressured or rushed. I just hope, for the sake of my sanity, that you find your answers soon."

She nodded. She wasn't sure how to feel. Some part of her was pleased to have Jack's presence in her life. Another part was upset that her life had finally gained some structure and now was being so thrown off course. And yet another part wished it didn't have to be so complicated, that she could meet someone and it would be fine, or not meet someone and it would be fine, and that relationships and dating and societal norms and expectations didn't exist. So many emotions were moving through her that she was awed.

They silently made their way back from the wave organ, down the path back to the yacht club and the parking lot. Jack ordered an Uber for her. They stopped under a light in the lot to wait, the silence tense as they both tried to understand what the hell had just happened.

Jack turned to her. "Jess, it's taking everything I can do not to kiss you right now. I want to respect you—I do respect you—but I also want you, in that dress, right here."

Jess's body responded involuntarily, desire coming dangerously close to replacing reason again. She shook her head to maintain her steadiness. "I want that, too, Jack. But kissing, the chemistry, that's the easy part. The hard part is the everything else."

"I know. I know." The Uber turned into the parking lot and headed towards them. Jack grabbed Jess's hand, urgently. "Jess, I … I don't know what you think of me or maybe even what you've heard of me. But I'm a good guy. And this, what I feel for you, I want to pursue it. You think that you don't want this, but I think you're scared. You and me, we both see the world the same way, and I think if you really think about what you want, what you want is someone who understands the world like you do. Please don't let fear make you give up on the chance for something great."

The Uber pulled up. Jess was silent, taking in his words. She didn't know what to say. She wondered whether he was right. She'd been so worried about what everything meant for Anicca that she hadn't thought more deeply about the attraction, why she was drawn to him.

She opened the door to the Uber. "Goodnight, Jack. I'm glad I ran into you tonight. I have … a lot to think about. I … Goodnight." She sat down and closed the door without waiting for his reply. She had enough on her mind already without needing to worry about what he had to say.

Chapter 18

Jess watched the rhythm of her breath as she ran through Golden Gate Park. The steady inhale and exhale, in sync with her footsteps on the pavement, helped ground her. Pine, cypress, and eucalyptus trees surrounded her, and Jess could feel the life within them. She let the energy pour into her body, relishing this moment of perfection in its impermanent glory. Everything, at least for right now, was okay.

Jess had planned her run for early that morning to give herself time to make it to her scheduled train to Sacramento. After she had gotten home the night before, however, she'd had trouble falling asleep, with the result being that she'd only had a few hours of rest. So, she'd chosen the relatively flat path from her apartment through the Panhandle to Golden Gate Park rather than the intimidating hills that stood between her and Crissy Field on her usual route. It was her gesture of kindness to herself amid the emotional hangover from the night before.

The night before … It felt like a dream: she and Jack, in the middle of the bay, the moonlight reflecting off the water, the chemistry flowing between them. But the flashbacks from the night were so vivid that Jess knew it had been no dream. The feeling of the evening was palpable. What it all meant, though, was less clear.

Jess turned her mind back to the present, her and the park and the music from her iPhone. She ran through her favorite parts of Golden Gate Park: near the Conservatory of Flowers, the botanical gardens, the duck pond. She saw people setting up at the "Church of 8 Wheels," the longstanding roller skate event put on in the mornings at the park, famous for its funky music and eccentric costumes as much as for its amazing skaters.

The residual charge of Jack's touch coursed through her body, and running helped release it. Later today, on the train to Sacramento, she'd have plenty of time to think things through. This morning, though, she needed her processing to be physical. Her body needed to catch up to what had happened in order for her mind to begin to understand it.

Jess kept running, fueled by the music and the thrill it brought of feeling alive. Running had always been there for her, helping through so many periods of her youth when she had been anxious and depressed. Running, and the connection it gave her to her other dear friend, the sky, had been the only way she'd made it through before she'd found design, which had given structure to her barely assembled sense of self. And running was here for her now. Before she knew it, she'd made it to the end of the park, all the way to Ocean Beach. She hadn't intended to run that far, hadn't even thought she had it in her after the rough sleep she'd had, but now that she was here, it felt wonderful. Her lungs felt full, expanded from her run and able to take in the fresh sea air.

For all its problems, San Francisco still stunned her in its beauty. She walked along the beach. She didn't have too much time before her train to Sacramento, but it was so peaceful here that she knew she couldn't leave just yet.

She relaxed more deeply. The ocean, the sun, her breath, and her body were all that mattered. The rest was all clutter, entertaining clutter, possibly-worth-looking-into clutter, but clutter all the same. The intensity of whatever was going on with Jack felt smaller here. The vastness of the ocean put it all in perspective. She watched as the waves changed colors, from deep blue further back in the ocean to a lighter blue that became white at the crest of each wave. So many shades of the same color, each speaking in its own timeless language. The movement of the waves calmed her nerves, as if whispering a message to her: *"There, there. There, there. Nothing to worry about. Things ebb and things flow, and things stay the same. Surrender to it, the nature of change."*

That message reminded Jess of why she had been called to the Wabisabi aesthetic when she'd first encountered it. It had intuitively made sense to her, the idea that impermanence was part of life. The aesthetic embraced that truth rather than treat it as taboo. Design school was the first time Jess had encountered that idea expressed externally, and it was validating. She could lean into that honest look on life, allow it to give her the necessary perspective. She had sorely needed that then, when her feelings of being lost seemed never-ending. The acceptance of impermanence reoriented her so that she was able to see her whimsical, artistic soul as a blessing rather than a curse, as the gift she'd been given in this lifetime. Her path was not to figure out how to make herself fit where she didn't, she'd realized. Her path was to find her own way.

Here, on the beach, looking at the waves, the same ease of surrender began to take place again. The waves were so energetic, creating an uproar as they emerged, fighting, from the water to reach so, so high, impossibly high, and then fell back again into the vast ocean—so much battle to create something that ultimately passed.

Jess took another breath of the ocean air, letting the salty scent fill her lungs. The ocean was telling her that whatever was going on with Jack would either happen or it wouldn't. She was bigger than it. It wasn't worth all this emotional turmoil. Her life meant more than this chapter. She would build something with her business, and then it would change. That was the nature of it. It was meant to change; its purpose was to change. So, let it. The problem came when she fought the change, because then she was asking something to act outside of its essential nature. It was a battle that she would lose, every single time. Whereas if she could listen to the subtle pull of transformation, if she surrendered to its omnipresence, she would unlock some deep magic that existed, some universal pattern of which she could only ever understand a part, but understanding that part was a tremendous thing.

Jess closed her eyes to experience her surroundings with her other senses. The sound of the ocean, of people laughing, of the birds flying by; the feel of the sun against her skin and the wind against her body; the smell of the salt and the seaweed and the brine; all here, all present, for this magical moment only—she was lucky to have even that moment. It was enough.

With a final inhale, Jess opened her eyes. She smiled, thanked the ocean for having reminded her of the bigger picture, and made her way back home.

The perfection of Jess's time at the beach was quickly made chaotic by the reality of having to make a train that departed from Richmond, California, on the other side of the bay, in a little over ninety minutes. Jess sprinted home, quickly packed an overnight bag, and headed to BART. It was a crash back to reality—nothing like SF public transit to bring you back into the real world—but Jess was grateful, in a way, for the distraction. Rushing to the Amtrak train kept her mind from racing about Jack. BART arrived just in time for Jess to make the train to Sacramento, which was about to depart. She'd have to buy her ticket on board. She realized she hadn't had time to get anything to eat and hoped that there'd be something palatable, or at least palatable enough, available for purchase in the dining car.

She chose a seat by the window, placed her bag overhead, and settled in after a quick text to her mom letting her know her ETA. As the train took off, Jess opened her laptop and plugged into the train's Wi-Fi system. She knew this train ride well, enough to know that she preferred to get any work done in the beginning of the ride so that she could daydream when they started going through the Capitol Corridor, with its vibrant scenery of the bay. Jess answered a few emails that she hadn't had time to get to before leaving the office in a rush the night before.

It was hard to believe that everything that had happened since she'd last opened her laptop, that at this time yesterday, she'd been immersed in design and having a lively discussion with Moira about the best way to subtly incorporate the green of the lake into the office reception area without it being too obvious. Taste mattered, after all, and being vaguely reminiscent of a lake was the goal, not being made to feel like you were standing knee-deep in the lake water. Moira had suggested adding blue and green at various points in the wall, in discrete spots so that, standing in the room, you didn't immediately notice them but instead felt softly soothed in the way the lake made you feel. It had been a good idea but one that prompted a redesign of certain aspects, which made an already tight timeline even tighter. Nothing about a project ever went smoothly. Jess was seasoned enough by now to know that and always factored in contingencies into her timelines and budgets, but that didn't mean she ever looked forward to the bumps in the road. On a project like this—especially a project like this—where the timing was tight and the stakes were high, those bumps were even harder to stomach.

She sent off a few emails and updated a few designs before closing her laptop. The train was approaching the Capitol Corridor, and Jess was looking forward to the ride. She was more stressed than she realized by the Jumbl project, which was saying something because she had realized she was pretty stressed. The break-neck pace of it all hadn't allowed much time for second-guessing about the overall aesthetic, which in a way was good because time to ruminate could cause anxiety in and of itself.

Jess couldn't help but be nervous, though. This was a bigger project than she'd ever taken on, certainly since starting Anicca but even counting her time at Unoa. Besides, at Unoa, she'd always been part of a bigger team. Even though her style had been mostly to work independently, there was something reassuring about knowing that someone would put you in check if your design was completely impracticable. Moira and Charlie, much as she loved them, were junior to her. They wouldn't necessarily have the experience to tell if something were a nonstarter, and beyond that, they wouldn't have necessarily told her even if they thought so. The culture at Anicca was egalitarian, but there was something to be said about the authority that her role inherently gave her and the lack of being sure of yourself that came with being junior to someone, a combination that resulted in tending to favor silence over voicing a negative opinion if there was any doubt.

No, as much as this project was a team effort, it nevertheless was hers in a way that only she could understand. The comforting part was that being independent, a trait that naturally resulted from growing up on the outside, was something she was familiar with. But it was a default mode that was starting to wear tired, an old sweater that felt great to wear but that you'd bought when you were two inches shorter and had since gone through a growth spurt. It fit, mostly, but maybe it was time to try on something new.

Her thoughts eventually turned to Jack, in particular what, if anything, she would say to her mom. Her mom would inevitably ask if Jess was dating. It wouldn't technically be a lie to say no. She and Jack were undefined and hadn't exactly been on any dates, *per se,* but it would feel disingenuous regardless, keeping what would feel like a secret from Diane. Plus, practically speaking, there was always the risk that Bridget would spill the beans. No, it was better to be honest if the question came up.

Moreover, a part of Jess wanted to tell Diane. She could use a mom right now. All of this was weighing so heavily on her chest that she felt physically dragged down by it. She couldn't fully wrap her head around it. It didn't make sense that she'd be this preoccupied over a few kisses. She sensed that something deeper was going on, that some way of seeing the world, and herself within the world, was being called into question.

And a part of her was scared, of the obvious, of course: the impact on her career and life trajectory. But there was something else, something lingering, that terrified her. If she fell for Jack, she would fall hard and fast—dependency, her great fear, something her mother knew too much about.

She'd never had the courage to ask what it had meant for Diane to give up her life's ambitions to raise children. The inherently awkward position of embodying the reason for her mother's sacrifice was enough to give Jess pause. Jess wasn't sure how it would feel if she found out she was right, that if her mother could do it all over again, she'd have pursued her medical career and put off having children until whenever, if ever, it "made sense"—as if there's a time it ever "makes sense" for a woman trying to juggle it all. Potentially worse than that was the possibility that Diane, in an effort to spare Jess's feelings, would give the acceptable answer, that of course she'd make the same choices, and then the heaviness of the lie would sit between them, enormous, instilling a divide that hadn't been there before and that would now always be there, hanging between them and making them both complicit in keeping up the narratives we tell ourselves to push ourselves to go on.

Jess shook her head and stared out the window. They were at her favorite part, just where the beach to the left let out onto the bay, miles and miles and miles of water that transcended into the sky. This was too big, what was going on for her. She needed to understand more. It would be good to be home.

Chapter 19

THE TRAIN PULLED UP TO THE AMTRAK STATION IN DOWNTOWN Sacramento. Jess grabbed her bag and hopped out. She was still hungry; the dining car had been woefully unsatisfying. Maybe she could convince her mom to stop by The Squeeze Inn on the way home for a burger. It was hardly the healthiest choice, but this trip home was all about comfort, and the Squeeze, famous for the amount of cheese it piled onto its burgers, would hit the spot.

"Jess, over here!" Her mom was waving at her, clearly overjoyed to see her. It touched Jess to know that her presence could make her mom so happy. It was powerful to know that someone found joy simply in her being around.

Jess gave Diane a hug before seeing her sister, Ashley, in the car. "Hey, Mom, good to see you." She tapped on the window and waved at Ashley, who waved back. "You too, Ash. Thanks for coming to get me!"

"Of course! So, so good to see you. Aw, Jess," Diane hugged her again. "I missed you."

"Missed you, too." Jess put her bag in the trunk and hopped in the car. "What's up, Ash? Haven't caught up with you in a while."

"Not much. Just, you know, high school, I guess." Ashley was quieter than Jess remembered. She recalled Bridget saying Ashley had been having some trouble in school. She hoped it was a phase and that nothing more serious was going on. If she could, she'd try to talk to Ashley. If anyone knew about not having a great time in high school, it was Jess, and if that knowledge could help her sister, she was happy to share.

"Yep, high school. The worst." Jess smiled meaningfully at Ashley, who cautiously returned her smile.

Jess turned back to her mom. "Mom, can we stop at The Squeeze on the way home?"

Diane lowered her head at her. "Oh Jess, some things never change. Fine, but only because this is a special occasion. I always feel miserable after that much cheese." She paused and then added, "It's a pretty fun way to get miserable, though."

Jess squeezed Diane's knee. "We'll both be miserable together, then. Can't wait!"

Diane laughed. "I really have missed you, Jess." Jess nodded in response. It was good to be home.

• • •

They had a full day, stopping by the Capitol Mall after getting their burgers to have a picnic. Then after settling in at home, Jess took Ashley to Target to take advantage of how much easier it was to shop for essentials in the suburbs. Jess bought a lot, too much, and wasn't sure how she'd take it all home on the train. But the sheer bigness of the store in comparison to what she was used to back in the city made holding herself back impossible.

It was fun, just her and Ashley. Ashley didn't disclose everything that was quite going on at school, but some of it, at least, was feeling her friendships transition. Many of Ashley's friends were starting to date, and Ashley felt pressured to do the same. She really didn't want to, though, and thought the whole idea of, in her words, "changing yourself so that some guy asks you on a date" was ridiculous. Jess felt in a strange position to give advice, considering she was in the middle of her own dating ambivalence. So, instead, she just listened, which turned out to be exactly what Ashley needed. They'd come home feeling closer to each other, well worth buying an extra $50 in toothpaste just because the deal was so good. She and Ashley promised to try to see each other soon or at least talk on the phone more often.

The evening was winding down, though, and Jess still hadn't had a chance to talk to her mom. She was in her room, the same one from childhood, changing into her pajamas, trying to figure out what to say. She'd felt so sure on the train ride up that talking about her mom's choice to leave medicine was a conversation she needed to have, but now that she was here, now that things had been going so well between the two of them, she was starting to question whether it was worth the trouble of opening this pandora's box. Back home in Sacramento, Jack, everything in San Francisco, felt so far away.

Someone knocked on her door. "Jess?" It was her mother's voice. Jess opened the door to see Diane with a bag of chocolate chips in her hand. "Any interest in making chocolate chip cookies."

Jess felt touched by her mother's gesture. She recalled countless times where they'd made cookies together when she was a kid, both in times of celebration and on one of those many days that Jess had needed cheering up. It had become a ritual of theirs, a time of bonding that had brought them together in more ways than words could.

"That sounds great," Jess said. She put some slippers on and followed Diane to the kitchen.

"I'm sorry your father couldn't be here this weekend," Diane said. She put two sticks of butter in a bowl and handed it to Jess. "He's had to travel so much since this new promotion. We're all adjusting. I know he was really upset to have missed you."

Jess creamed the butter in the bowl. "It's okay. I'll see him soon." Jess was used to her dad being gone away on business. He worked as a consultant, which meant frequent travel. Even before his recent promotion, which required him to be away 80 percent of the time, he had been gone more often than not. It was something they had all gotten used to as a family, but it had meant that Jess had never been close with her father. It was Diane who she remembered being around when she was a kid, being there when Jess was having a hard time. Jess wondered how it was, dealing with the day-to-day of raising three children alone—one of the many sacrifices her mother had had to make, one of the things that terrified Jess about letting her guard down with Jack.

As the familiar anxiety surrounding Jack came back to Jess, so too did the knowledge that the conversation with her mother would have to take place after all. The reality of Jess's life back in the city would be waiting for her the next day, and she'd promised Jack some clarity. Tempting as it would be, she could not avoid putting off her processing forever.

"Mom," Jess started, hesitantly, as Diane measured out some sugar, "you don't have to answer this if you don't want, but … do you ever wonder what life would have been like if you hadn't met Dad?"

Diane tilted her head curiously. "Aw, honey, are you asking because you're upset that Dad is traveling?"

"No, it's not that." Jess wasn't sure how to phrase what she wanted to say. She took a deep breath and let the words come tumbling out. "I've just been thinking about things lately, thinking about you, and how if you'd never met Dad, you probably would have gone further in medicine. You worked so hard for that career, and then you had to step away to raise us. I wonder if maybe you would have been happier if you'd gotten to live your dream."

There it was, hanging between them. Now that the words were out, Jess wasn't sure how she felt, perhaps both relieved and anxious that she'd started the conversation. She noticed Diane pause in the middle of opening the vanilla extract and wondered if she'd gone too far.

"Oh," was all Diane said at first. She poured a teaspoon of extract into the bowl. "Jess, honey, is that what you really think?"

"Kind of," Jess squirmed.

Diane placed her hand on Jess's, which had, Jess realized, stopped stirring. "Jess, I hope you know that you can always talk to me about these things. You can talk to me about anything, even if it's hard."

Diane squeezed Jess's hand before continuing. "It's a complicated question, Jess. It's not that I've never wondered what my life would have been like if I'd never met your father and gotten pregnant. Of course, I have." She measured out a teaspoon of baking soda. "But any life that involves me not having you and your sisters, I can't imagine that. You all mean so much to me, and I believe with every fiber of my being that I was meant to have you."

Jess looked up to see the beginnings of tears in Diane's eyes. "Aw, Mom, I love you."

"Love you, too, Jess." Diane wiped the moisture away before reaching for some flour. "The easy, and truthful, answer is that I know that life has taken me where I was supposed to go. I think it's natural to look back on huge choices, life-altering choices, and wonder what the other path would have looked like. And certainly, things haven't been perfect with your father. It's been hard, with him being gone so much, and there were a few years there, particularly when you all were little, where I really thought we wouldn't make it."

She paused to measure out two-and-a-quarter cups of flour. "Marriage is really hard, Jess, interacting with another person and going through life not only on your terms anymore. Your father and I have had to keep learning each other as we've grown and changed. And there have been challenging times. I think any couple that's being honest would admit to that. But we've had more times that have been good, many more times. For all that he's been gone, we've made efforts to stay connected to each other. And we've built this family together."

Jess gently mixed the flour together with the other ingredients. "I don't understand, though," she said. "You had this whole career ahead of you, this whole life ahead of you. Don't you ever miss the idea of being a doctor?"

"The idea of it, sure," Diane agreed. "But only the idea of it. I wanted to be a doctor so I could help change the world. Then when I started my residency, I saw that so much of our healthcare system is broken. There was so much bureaucracy around helping people. What would the insurance companies say? How much money did a person have? All these things that shouldn't matter but did matter. I suffered a real crisis of faith in those years. The way I thought I was going to make an impact wasn't turning out to be what I thought it was. It was a hard time."

She stopped speaking, her eyes distant, as if a part of her had traveled back to what it had been like then. With an exhale, she continued, as if describing a dream, "Meeting your father was so different; *he* was so different from the life I had mapped out for myself. He was charming and funny. He's really very funny." She smiled, shaking her head. It made Jess happy to feel like her mom was remembering things he had said and that doing so was bringing her joy. "That sense of humor has helped us get through some tough spots. You're right that I hadn't been planning on getting pregnant with Bridget, and I'd be lying if I said I didn't have mixed feelings about it."

She shook her head. "Jeez, I hope this is okay to talk about. One of the many incredibly challenging things about being a parent is not knowing what the rules are or how much you're supposed to share with your children."

"It's fine, Mom," Jess replied. "I want to know."

"Okay, but let me know if it's too much." Diane poured some chocolate chips into the dough. "When I first learned that I was pregnant with Bridget, I was overjoyed, but I was also sad, at least initially, for all the reasons that you surmise. Becoming a mother didn't necessarily *have* to mean the end of my career, but it did mean that having the career I wanted would be infinitely more difficult, especially the first few years." She pulled some cookie sheets out of a cabinet. "I can't imagine working a resident's hours while raising a newborn. I don't think I would have slept for years.

"But then I really thought about it. I had wanted to be a doctor to help make the world a better place. Now I had this opportunity to love one tiny creature as much as I possibly could. My heart was so full of love with this new baby, Bridget, that I felt like bringing that amount of love into the world would make it a better place, too.

"It wasn't the life that I thought I was going to have. And certainly, there's a lot more prestige in announcing you're a doctor than in announcing you're a mother—the difference in how society viewed me was one of the most challenging things to adjust to. But being a mother was ultimately the way that life found for me to express my purpose. It's a blessing, Jess, to be such an integral part of shaping a whole being."

Diane leaned against the kitchen counter and closed her eyes. Jess picked up on her energy, then, the intensity of that feeling emanating from her mother and into Jess, conveying a love that Jess found deeply soothing.

Diane continued, her eyes still closed. "There was a time, after Bridget was born and before I was pregnant with you, where your dad and I seriously talked about me going back to medicine. I really thought about it and even had reached out to some connections at the hospital about resuming my residency. But I did some serious soul searching, much like what it seems you are doing now, and realized that I was happy with the choice I'd made."

She opened her eyes to look at Jess. "Your father and I, we chose to have both you and Ashley. We *chose* to have the life we have now. So, when you ask me do I regret it? Of course, I look back. Of course, I've had moments where I wonder. But I can't see my life being happier if I had gone that route. There is nothing that makes me happier than seeing my daughters happy. I don't know if that was a feeling I ever could have had, could ever have even understood, if I'd never become a mother. That was the path for me, Jess. You'll find yours. Maybe yours is the same; maybe it's not. The only thing I would want, though, is for you to feel like all paths are possible, so that you choose the one you end up choosing because you really want it and not because you feel like it says something about you to choose something else."

Jess considered what Diane was saying. She was surprised at the answer. The truth of how her mother felt was much more nuanced than the narrative that Jess had carried all these years. Diane didn't feel guilty or resentful about the choices she'd made.

On the contrary, she was content. The notion that Jess had held close, of life being simple and career being the most important thing, was being challenged in ways both big and small, seemingly every day. Jess didn't know what to make of it. It was a change in the plotline that she'd have to spend some time unpacking.

"Thanks, Mom. I appreciate your honesty. I'm sure it wasn't easy, but it means a lot to hear. Shall we get these cookies in the oven?'

"Absolutely. And after that," Diane's tone was playful, "let's have some wine and watch the sunset. I know how much you love the sunset, Jess, and, after that conversation, I think wine may be a requirement. Plus, I want to hear all about this big social media project."

Jess smiled at the transition. "Okay. Hope you're ready for a doozy."

"Always. And Jess, I love you."

"I love you, too, Mom."

They finished baking the cookies in the quiet comfort only possible with someone you have known for years. A weight that Jess was holding had been released. Some part of Jess had needed to know that her mother was happy. She'd been carrying the heaviness of that doubt for some time. Out on the porch, with wine and conversation and the sunset, Jess felt happy.

A couple hours later, they said goodnight. Jess went to her bedroom and checked her phone. There was a message from Jack, sent a few hours prior: *Having a good trip home?*

Emboldened by the heady combination of emotional release and wine, Jess replied: *Hey, trip home was great. Are you free tomorrow evening?*

She pressed send. Tomorrow evening, she and Jack would talk. Jess only hoped that, by then, she would figure out what to say.

Chapter 20

JESS ARRIVED BACK IN HER APARTMENT THE NEXT DAY. IT HAD been a bittersweet goodbye. She had missed her mom and Ashley, and she could tell that it meant something to them to have her there. She made plans for Ashley to come visit her in the city after the Jumbl project finished. Diane would drive Ashley to San Francisco, which solved the other challenge: how to get her loot from her suburban Target experience back home. And it also would give her a chance to see her mom again, which was something she had missed more than she realized.

But Jess had little time to reflect. Jack had responded to her text confirming that he was free that night, and Jess had, without fully considering it, suggested he come to her place at five. At the time, she had figured that having him come to her place would be the easiest thing, giving her time to unpack and do a little work before the week ahead. Now, reality was sinking in. In a little less than ten minutes, Jack Stinson would be in her apartment. To talk.

She debated sending a text and suggesting they meet at a nearby restaurant instead. She ultimately decided against it. It was too close to the time they were supposed to meet. Plus, she'd delayed doing work so she could clean her apartment and run to Faletti's for wine and charcuterie, unsure of what exactly one serves during these conversations and figuring that charcuterie was appropriately mature.

Beyond that, Jess wanted Jack to be there, in her space. Her conversation with Diane had made her further question her perspective on things. She liked being around Jack, and she was opening up to the idea of having him more in her life. The priorities that had so far guided her life had been important to her when she was younger, but she felt like they were shifting.

At 5:03 p.m., the doorbell rang. Jess rose, unsteady on her feet, and went to the door. "Who is it?" she asked, immediately regretting what had felt like a compulsion to come across as aloof. She hoped she felt more relaxed soon.

"Um, it's Jack. You've met me a couple times." She opened the door to find him standing there. The reality of how attracted she was to him sank into her again, especially now, in this context, in her apartment. The tension between them was thick, like the heat that had been created between the two of them on the bay was now concentrated, fitting just within the size of this doorway, almost unbearable.

"You know, Jack," he continued, his voice getting heavier as he took a step forward. "We're working on this Jumbl project together. And I think you like me, quite a bit actually, but you're afraid of what that means, and so you invited me over here so we could talk about it." Another step and now he was close. She could feel him, his heat radiating into her body, intoxicating. "Ringing any bells?"

Her voice caught. Her desire for him was a tangible thing, caught within her throat, making it hard to speak. She swallowed. "Right ... I think I remember you. It's good to see you, Jack."

He took a step closer, his face now next to hers. "I hope you mean that. I haven't stopped thinking about you since Friday, this little Jess loop replaying in my mind. It's been driving me crazy."

He placed his hand on her cheek. She touched his hand with hers, the heat of it against her cheek, her eyes closed. Jack was here, really here. His smell, his heat, his passion ... Something carnal in her opened up as she remembered Friday, her body immediately recalling how it had felt, on that rock, his hands on her, her body alive.

"Oh yeah? What's the memory?" She opened her eyes softly and glanced up at him, locking her eyes with his. It was just the two of them now, only had ever been the two of them, only this moment.

Jack pushed the door behind him shut, never taking his eyes from hers. "The memory ..." He kissed her cheek. Her eyes fluttered closed as her breath caught. Yes, she needed this. Badly, she needed this. He kept kissing her, gentle kisses, down her neck, avoiding her lips, speaking in between kisses. "The memory always stops when I get to right here." He stopped, his lips now hovering right above hers. "I'm going to kiss you now."

His words stirred something deep and primal within her. Some place inside that she hadn't even known existed was being brought to life, and from that place, words came out. "What are you waiting for?"

His mouth took hers, answering her challenge with actions, claiming its territory, confirming her permission with urgency. "Is this what you wanted?" he asked in between kisses, and she answered with passionate kisses, movement after movement in sync, each finding each other and communicating in a way that was preverbal, pure instinct, some part of Jess that lived beneath her brain taking over and moving her to match him, move for move and rhythm for rhythm.

He looked at her, his eyes wild, his need palpable. "I want you, Jess, all of you. Tell me that you want me, too." His words were feverish. All of her shoulds and whys and maybe-nots seemed so far away right now, replaced only with wanting. This was right. This was what she needed. Nothing else mattered.

"Yes, Jack." The words came out as a release, a surrender to the desire of it all. "Yes," she repeated. It was spectacular, no longer needing to hold back, able to say and act and feel how she wanted to feel without it needing to mean more, without it needing to mean anything. Her body melted into his, his kisses meeting her vulnerability, comforting it, creating a container where everything was safe and right and perfect. The boundaries of herself, all that had kept her protected and guarded, were being undone, and he was there, meeting all her parts and holding them together with soft, fierce, steady kisses, showing her with each kiss that this was right, that he was here, that she could be here, too.

He placed her arms around his shoulders and lifted her up, her legs around his hips. "Bedroom," he managed to say in between kisses.

"Over there," she pointed, and he carried her, never taking his lips off hers, into the room and placed her on the bed.

"God, Jess, you have no idea how much I want this. I've never wanted anything this much. What are you doing to me?" She answered only by pulling him closer, kissing him and moving her hands to his torso. Her hands found the bottom of his shirt and pulled up. She needed to see him, all of him. The wait had been intolerable in a way that she fully felt now, each moment of delay interminable. He complied, lifting his shirt overhead and revealing a defined torso, smooth skin along sculpted muscle.

"Damn," Jess's eyes widened as she took her hands to his abdomen.

He laughed. "I've been hitting the gym pretty hard recently. Found myself having all this frustration that needed working out, ever since I met you, it seems."

Her eyes met his again. Behind the humor was something else, something real. She meant something to him. She meant a lot to him. That was clear now. His kisses felt present because he was giving her himself. That realization flooded into her body and changed everything. Jess slowly started kissing his chest, blind need being combined now with feeling. With these kisses, she was saying all that she couldn't say, because she didn't have the words, because she wasn't ready to admit things to herself. These kisses were the answers she couldn't give.

This was different than it had been before, with the few other people Jess had been with. She was actually *here* right now, not distracted, not impatient. She wanted this, wanted him, and that realization brought a new release within her, some untouched part of her being finding a respite she hadn't known it craved.

She kissed lower, her lips on his belly, her tongue swirling along his skin. He groaned, deeply, as he suddenly sat up. "I can't take it, Jess. I … This is too much. I need this too much. Let me see you."

She nodded, and his hand moved to her shirt, pulling it up overhead, his lips kissing her chest as he removed her bra. He paused to look at her. "My God, Jess, you are beautiful. In my fantasies, you were beautiful, but the reality is so much better." His lips moved again to her chest as his kisses continued, each one soft like a prayer, the fullness of his presence showing up with every kiss. His mouth moved down to her breast as his tongue started licking and biting in an intoxicating combination that moved things within Jess that she hadn't known were possible. Her breath quickened with every gesture of his tongue, every nip of his teeth. She placed her hands on his head to pull him closer, even closer, exploding with the need for him to be close, dizzy with her want for him. His mouth moved to her other nipple, massaging and nipping that one into aliveness. She hadn't known she could be touched like this, hadn't known touch like this was even possible. She closed her eyes and let her head roll back, surrendering to it all.

"Jack, I want you. I want you," she panted. He answered by moving his mouth lower, hovering now at the top of her yoga pants. Her fingers started to pull them down, and he finished removing them from her legs.

"No underwear? God, as if I could want you more." Jack moved his mouth close. She instinctively tightened. She felt exposed, inviting him down *there*. He moved up to kiss her lips. "Relax, Jess. I got you. I want to make you feel good. You have absolutely nothing to be ashamed about." He whispered in her ear, "Even in my fantasies—and there were many—it was never this good."

The sincerity of his words soothed Jess's fear, replacing it with desire. He gave her a deep reassuring kiss as he traced his mouth down against her body, moving slowly and steadily to the epicenter of her need. He got to her thighs and started kissing and then moved closer, ebbing closer and closer but never getting to the center until she thought she would explode with anticipation. He was easing her in, building her up, waiting until she really wanted, needed, him to be there. It was a torturous game, one in which he had all the power, but it was power she wanted to give him, the power to give her exactly what she needed. Finally, inexorably, his lips went to her clit and sucked. She exploded, her back arching up as she felt herself get wet. He kept his licking, nibbling, sucking in a steady rhythm that was seeking, searching, taking his time. This was all he had to do in the world: pleasure her. He was so clearly into it that Jess felt herself free enough to relax, to receive.

Her breath quickened, getting heavier, faster, pulsing, wanting. He pushed her thighs open with his hands as he continued his search, moving all around until he found a spot that made her go wild, that when he licked it, she came undone. And then he stayed, licking, in a steady, rhythmic flow that built her up, built her up, built her up until she was right on the edge. When she thought she couldn't take it anymore, he gently slipped his finger inside and she came, in a flash, pouring herself over the edge as she came undone around his hand, her muscles tightening, contracting and releasing into her orgasm.

Jack slowly removed his finger and kissed her softly down there before coming back up, again to touch her. She looked at him, raw, disbelieving that someone could make her feel like that. She started kissing him, ready to go on, finding the taste of her on his lips unbelievably hot. She unbuckled his pants and he complied, pulling his pants down and taking his underwear off.

"I … I suppose I should, you know, for you," Jess said cautiously, gesturing at his erection. How she could still feel so shy after being so exposed was incredible. Jess saw the fullness of him, big and ready and waiting, and her hand started moving down, almost involuntarily, to touch him.

His hand stopped hers. "No, Jess, wait. Slow down. Not … not today. I need you too much." His mouth took hers again as he rolled her on her back, moving on top of her. "If you touch me, I'll go over the edge, and I want more tonight. I want you, all of you. I want to be inside of you. Do you want that?" Jess nodded, her eyes meeting his. Jack sat up and looked at her, intently. "No, Jess, I want to hear you say it."

Jess was undone. Her need made the words come out urgently. "Yes, Jack. Yes, I want you." He reached inside his jeans for a condom and put it on, kissing her while he did so, the raw desire pulling the two of them closer.

He hovered above her, ready. "I'm going to fuck you now." And with that, she felt the long, slow glide as he entered her. Jess gasped at the size of him, filling her all the way. Her body expanded to meet him. And then he began, moving slowly, methodically, in and out while he kissed her, claimed her, his rhythm quickening as she adjusted to his size. Her muscles relaxed as she eased into his presence. He was claiming parts of her beyond her control, and she was tired of fighting it. This was a man who wanted her to surrender, and from deep inside of her, a part of her responded that desperately wanted that, too.

He kissed her, fiercely, as he continued his rhythm, building her up again, her body still ringing from the ferocity of her first orgasm. His pace became quicker, the two of them now in sync. Bodies took over as something moved between them that neither of them could explain, something cocreated, some movement that they felt rather than understood as the two of them grew closer, quicker.

"Jess, I'm close, I'm so fucking close." Jess realized with his words that she was too. His rhythm naturally slowed to give her time to meet him. She took her hand and started touching herself, her eyes finding his, pleading with him to continue, as his rhythm again built. He kept moving as she touched, her body becoming something foreign to her, the Jess she knew replaced with something primal now, only need.

She looked at him. "Jack, Jack," she said, "I'm ready." He moved quicker now, stronger, until he sent her over the edge and she cried out, riding into her release.

"Fuck, Jess," he said, his rhythm continuing to quicken as the sensation of her orgasm moved him to find his own.

The two of them lay there afterward, him still inside her, his lips slowly finding hers, the kisses now punctuation to the sentences that had come before. After a minute, he slowly, patiently, rolled himself off her, giving her time to adjust to his exit. He removed the condom and threw it in the trash and then lay on his side, his breath still recovering.

He pulled her close, resting her head on his chest, as they both looked up into the ceiling. "What are you doing to me, Jess? That was the best I ever had, Jess. Did you know it could be like that?"

Jess could only shake her head, nestling into the safety of being in his nook and smelling him, feeling his warm skin. "No, Jack. I had no idea."

He tilted her chin up and kissed her, sweetly and softly, before letting her lie back down into him. It felt right, this moment. She was here. He was here. It was everything.

Chapter 21

THEY STAYED LIKE THAT FOR A TIME, KISSING AND CARESSING, drifting in and out of a relaxed half sleep. Jess felt peaceful. She was amazed that she could feel this way around a man she was still getting to know. His energy soothed her, flowing from his chest into hers where it mingled before spreading and calming down her torso and relaxing through her legs. She wanted to stay like that, intertwined with him, forever, to forget everything else. As her rational mind came back online, though, her euphoria was replaced with the reality that they had yet to talk and that, lovely as it sounded to procrastinate, she needed to let him know what she was thinking.

She sat up. Jack grumbled as he peeked his eyes open, roused from a restful sleep.

"Jack?" He pretended to close his eyes, so she playfully tapped on his shoulder. "Wake up, fake sleepyhead."

"No, never," he turned over to the other side and snored loudly for dramatic effect.

"Oh my God," Jess ripped the covers off him, struck again by the gloriousness of seeing him naked in her bed, her resolve to push through with the conversation momentarily weakening. With significant strength, she reminded herself of the task at hand. "You are the worst fake sleeper. All you need now is for the bubbles to come out of your mouth like one of those old cartoon characters."

Jack formed his hand into a bubble shape and mimicked bubbles escaping, using his other hand to form the shape of a sleeping cap overhead.

Jess tapped him again, laughing. "Knock it off. We have to talk, and you know it. Help me out here."

Jack sighed and turned to face her. "I guess you're right." He sat up, giving her a quick kiss as his hand brushed her cheek. "But I think we start with me listening. I've told you how I feel. What's less clear is what's going on with you."

Jess inhaled. It was a fair point, and she knew it. But in her mind, "talking" was more of a concept, something that you did because you were mature and responsible. The reality that now it meant words coming out of her mouth, words that reflected some coherent story around what she was feeling ... that was a new, unwelcome spin on the concept.

"Right. That makes sense. So, how do I feel ..." She caught her heart racing and consciously slowed herself down. "I feel a lot of things. That this is going too fast. I'm worried that maybe this is going nowhere. I'm worried that you say things that you don't mean. And even though you think you've been clear, you haven't been *that* clear, at least about what you want beyond something physical, or even *if* you want something beyond physical. And I'm worried that, at this stage of my career, a relationship, which by the way I feel presumptuous even saying, would throw me off track."

Jack considered her words. "I hear a lot about what you think, Jess. But I still don't know how you feel about me."

She hesitated. "I … I like spending time with you."

Jack took her hand in his. "I like that, too, Jess. I'm not someone who wants a lot of things, but the things I do want, I go after. Something about you, ever since I first saw you, I wanted you. And then when Donathan asked me to do him this favor … well, I would have done it anyway, but I also wanted the chance to get to know you more. I'm like that. I instinctively know things, and they don't have to make sense. But the more I've gotten to know you, the more I see that really it does make sense. We're pretty similar, once you get past the surface."

Jess looked up to meet his eyes, finding reassurance in their sincerity. He was right, she thought, their natural comfort, the ease of their conversation. Once she looked past their superficial differences, she could see they both shared a dreaminess, a belief that a better world was more possible, and a desire to fight for it. "What does that mean? Does that mean you want to date exclusively?"

"It means that whatever you're ready for, I'm ready for. If you're ready to date exclusively, I want that. I'm not the type that likes to date multiple people anyway, at least not when I'm serious about someone. Before that, it's fair game."

Jess thought about that. "It's so strange because when I met you, though, you were dating Alex."

He shrugged his shoulders. "We went on a couple of dates. I wouldn't say we were dating. What can I say? Alex is a great girl, and I think she will really make someone happy. But we didn't fit, not in the way you and I do. So we went on a couple of dates and then parted ways. You can't begrudge me too much for that."

"No, that makes sense." Jess pulled the covers up. This conversation made her want to hide, more exposed even than when they had been having sex. "I guess you should know that I haven't done much of this, dating."

Jack's eyes were soft and understanding. "How much is not much?"

"A date here and there, not more than a handful, mostly when Bridget gives me a hard time for not living my twenties to their fullest."

"Anyone special?"

"Not really. I dated this one person in college for a few months but … ." Jess was sure her cheeks were red. "This is so embarrassing." She covered her eyes with her hands. "Revealing my paltry dating history, if you can even call it that, to my half-client half-romantic interest who just saw me naked for the first time."

"Jess …" Jack gently lifted one of her hands away from her eyes. "You have nothing to be embarrassed about. If anything, it's helpful to know this. You've been kind of hard to read, and this helps give me some context." He moved her hand to kiss her palm. "As far as half-client status, I admit there's some potential awkwardness there, but I don't think it has to be a big deal unless we let it. I'd like to tell Donathan, but I won't if you're not ready. And

I promise not to let anything that happens with us jeopardize the project. I know how important it is to you."

Jess felt the stiffness in her shoulders loosen. It was incredible how much he understood without her needing to explain. "Thanks, Jack. You can tell Donathan. He's your closest friend, and it's not really fair that I get to talk to Bridget, and that I'll probably have to tell Moira and Charlie, but you can't talk to anyone. Speaking of which, I have no idea what to say to them."

Jack nipped her earbud. "You sound so excited. Should I be taking this personally?"

"No, it's nothing about you." Jess put her arms around him. "It's the idea of you. It's … my own shit. Yeah, okay fine, I'll just say we're dating."

Jack kissed her deeply. "Maybe, just maybe, consider that they'll be happy for you. I'm a pretty great catch after all." She kissed him then rather than answering. Kissing was easier than words, she was finding, in so many contexts.

"What are you going to tell Donathan?" Jess asked after a minute or so, coming off far less casually than she had hoped to.

Jack leaned back. Jess saw him tense, as if bracing himself, endearing in the way it reflected his nerves about what he was going to say. "I'd like to say that we're dating, exclusively, to answer your question, if you're ready for that."

Jess nodded. "I think so. Exclusive, you and me. Okay." Jess paused, thinking through what it meant. "Does that mean you're my boyfriend?" The word felt strange coming off her tongue, more juvenile than she'd intended it. Or maybe it was just that it had been a while since she'd thought of that concept as applied to herself.

Jack leaned up to give her a kiss, his lips reassuring her in ways that words alone could not. "How about we don't have to decide anything more right now? I know this is all new, and I'm fine with going slow as long as you're honest with me about where you're at and as long as you don't disappear again." He kissed her again. It was nice, this feeling. Jess could get used to it.

She spoke in between kisses. "Okay, I like that idea." Her stomach growled. It was now close to 8:00 p.m., and she realized she hadn't eaten dinner. Having just come back home, though, the only thing she had was that charcuterie from Faletti's. "Um, are you hungry? I have some charcuterie …" Her voice trailed off as a mischievous grin appeared on his face.

"Did you buy us some meats and cheeses for our big talk? Aw, Jess." He pulled her in for a kiss. "I think I'm going to like dating you exclusively."

She laughed before she relaxed into his kiss. It was so easy to forget, when she was away from him, how comfortable being around him made her feel and how much fun she had. "There's wine too."

"That all sounds great." He gave her one more kiss before standing up. "Take me to it."

She stood up too, reluctantly, and began putting on her clothes. "It's weird, having you here. But maybe it's weird that it's not weirder, if that makes sense."

He smiled at her. "It does, Jess. It does."

Chapter 22

"Down to the three-month mark. As if it hasn't been crazy enough. Coffee?"

Moira was already at the office when Jess arrived. "Good morning to you too," Jess said. She took the coffee from Moira's hand with a nod of appreciation. "Thanks for this, by the way."

"You're welcome." Moira stared at Jess as she made her way to her office. "You're awfully quiet this morning. I would have thought my reminder of how nuts this is going to be would have sparked at least some response."

Jess shook her jacket off. Only in San Francisco did a person need a jacket this late in this year. "That assumes, Moira, that the timeline hasn't been on my mind constantly since the beginning of this, which would be, unfortunately, incorrect. I think it's actually three months and one week, by the way."

"I thought that, too." Moira walked over to lean in the doorframe of Jess's office. "But then I saw that Donathan has requested that we do an opening event before the official launch. 'It doesn't have to be finished by then,' he said. Yeah, right." She rolled her eyes. "As if we could show a three-quarters-of-the way design at the big event. I think this guy's delusional."

Jess's stomach sank. Normally, this kind of request from a client would be no big deal, but given how tight the schedule was, this event would cut into the already lean contingency time Jess had budgeted.

"Crap." Jess sighed. Her day had started off so well. She'd woken up later than usual, blissed out from the night before, and spent the morning with Jack. She'd missed her run, but they'd found other more creative ways to get some exercise in. It was the first time in a long time that she was sad to leave for work. Everything with Jack flowed so easily, and it had felt like a loss when they had said goodbye, even though they'd made plans to see each other the next night.

"What are you thinking about? I wouldn't have thought this riveting discussion about timeline would lead to one of your dreamy-Jess looks." Moira's expression was curious, and not for the first time, Jess wished that Moira wasn't *quite* so perceptive.

"Well, I guess I have some news," Jess said, trepidation in her voice. "I'm dating Jack Stinson."

Moira didn't skip a beat. "Oh good, that'll make getting his approval easier, and we have a *ton* of big design decisions coming up. That reminds me, I've started dating Zac Efron, except the sweet version we all know from *High School Musical* where he was clearly a drama kid and still kind of odd and didn't fully realize how hot he was and get buff for later, bro-ier movies, before the, I don't know, I guess spiritual awakening that he's having now, but adult Zac Efron, not a high schooler, and within an age range that is socially acceptable. That reminds me, can I have Friday off? We have this thing …" She moved to the seat in Jess's office.

Jess glared at her. "Ha ha, very funny. No, I mean it. Jack and I … we're dating."

Moira's jaw dropped. She paused for a second before continuing, slowly. "Wait, you're serious … Wait, are you serious?" When Jess nodded in response, Moira shook her head to recover from the disbelief. "Wow, Jess. I don't really know what to say."

Jess bristled in response to the terseness in Moira's voice. "I'm not sure what you should say. I guess you don't have to say anything, if you don't want to."

"I thought you and I talked about this."

"We did, but the only conclusion was to do what I thought was right," Jess countered.

"Yeah, well," Moira crossed her arms. "I guess we have different opinions about what that is."

The door opened as they both heard Charlie come in. Jess was relieved by his entrance. The conversation between her and Moira was going about as badly as she had anticipated that it might.

Charlie stopped short as he looked at them, congregated in Jess's office. "Um, what is going on with you two?"

Jess looked at Moira guiltily, her eyes pleading with Moira to not have to make her say it out loud again. Moira took the hint and stepped in. "Well, Charlie, Jess here was just telling me how she started dating Jack Stinson."

Charlie dropped the bag he was carrying. "*What?* Oh my word, you are going to be so rich!"

"Thanks, Charlie, very subtle of you." Jess motioned for him to join.

"That's all you have to say about it?" Moira raised her eyebrow at him.

"Good point." Charlie made his way into Jess's office. "Jessica Tyler, Jack Stinson is a smart, sexy piece of ass. So, congratulations, and does he have any gay friends?"

His comment made Jess laugh, surprising given the amount of tension she still felt from Moira. "I'll make sure I ask."

"So how did this *happen?* Tell me everything. Wait, first, let me get some coffee. I can tell this is gonna be a long one."

The silence hung thick between Jess and Moira as Charlie headed to the kitchen. "Look," Jess offered, "I get that this is a surprise. I'm adjusting, too. But, Moira, the chemistry between me and Jack is so obviously *there* that I couldn't keep fighting it. And besides, I don't think anything between me and him will affect Anicca. We talked about that, and he knows that if anything with Anicca ever becomes jeopardized, then we have to call it off with us."

"Oh please, Jess." Moira let out a frustrated sigh. "Everyone *always* says that at the beginning of a relationship, that if it ends badly, they'll still be friends, etc. etc. But how many people do you know who have been able to pull that off? It's rare for a reason,

Jess. Relationships always start well, but they don't often end well, and the end is when shit could hit the fan for Anicca."

Jess hoped what Moira was saying was wrong. She knew she didn't have much experience dating, but in the one relationship she'd had, with Matt in college, they'd ended on terms that could be described as at least cordial. And she hadn't felt for him close to what she was feeling for Jack. It was painful to imagine her and Jack ever not being on good terms.

"Jess, I'm not sure what you want from me with this," Moira continued. "I want you to be happy—I really do—but I'm worried that you don't know what you're getting yourself into."

Charlie rejoined them. "Is it chilly in here? Oh no, that's just the vibe in this room. What is going on with you two?"

Moira responded without breaking eye contact with Jess. "I'll leave this one to you."

Reluctantly, Jess turned to look at Charlie. "Moira has some … concerns … about me and Jack. She's worried that our relationship, or whatever it is, is going to get in the way of this project and jeopardize the future of Anicca."

"Yes, that, and the fact that Jess more or less told me before that she wouldn't date Jack and now, here we are," Moira added.

"Moira, give her a break. Jess doesn't have to be celibate in order for Anicca to be successful. Jess is a professional, and she loves Anicca too much to risk it. And come on! If you had someone as fine as Jack Stinson barking up your tree, you'd eventually cave, too."

Jess was touched by Charlie's comment, the kindness of it as well as the confidence it expressed in her, confidence that she'd sometimes lacked within herself. Of course, she was going to choose Anicca over everything. Hearing him say it out loud made any doubts that she'd had about dating and what it meant for her career appear silly, in the best of ways. She was always going to choose her career, the only thing that had ever made her feel like she belonged. It was ridiculous to think otherwise.

Even Moira was softened by Charlie's words. "First of all, Charlie, you have no idea who may be barking up my tree. And second, it's not that I *want* to be the buzzkill. I'm worried, is all and, I guess, protective of you, Jess. I know you don't have a lot of experience in that realm, and Jack Stinson is … Well, he doesn't come with training wheels."

"I'll say!" Charlie guffawed, nearly spitting out his coffee. "That guy comes fully loaded."

The three of them laughed, then, as Moira playfully jabbed Charlie in the shoulder. "Not what I meant, Charlie! Although thanks for that. Now I'll get to spend the rest of the day intentionally not picturing Jack Stinson, who happens to be essentially our client, naked."

"That one's on you, honey. I'll be picturing Jack Stinson however my mind fancies. Jess doesn't mind. Do you, Jess?"

"I'm honestly not sure whether to be horrified or flattered," Jess said. "I guess I'll choose flattered, if only because that seems easier."

"Probably for the best. Okay, Jess. I'll try to be supportive," Moira said, with some resignation. "But whatever happens between you two had really better not get in the way of our work. We've all given up too much for that."

Jess nodded in response. "That I can agree to. It's not even hard. Like Charlie said, I love Anicca too much to risk it."

"So, are you two boyfriend and girlfriend?" Charlie jumped in, redirecting the conversation.

"No, I don't think so. I wasn't ready for that. But we are dating." Jess took a sip of her coffee before adding, "Exclusively."

Moira pursed her lips. "What, exactly, is the difference between dating exclusively and being boyfriend and girlfriend?"

Charlie shook his head in exasperation. "It's a commitment level! Dating exclusively means 'Hey, I like you enough to see how this goes between just me and you, but I'm not ready to commit to the expectations of boyfriend and girlfriend.'"

"That doesn't make any sense," Moira shook her head. "Those are exactly the same thing!"

"Nope, not at all. If I was someone's boyfriend, and their parents came to town, I might expect to meet them. Or if there was an office function where SOs were invited, I'd expect to be invited. But I wouldn't have those expectations if I were only dating exclusively. That's more like a test drive, with a thirty-day guarantee, before you make the full commitment," Charlie told her.

"Wait a second." Moira set her mug down. "So, are you saying that Jack is just 'test driving' Jess? Jess, I don't like that at all. This guy seems like trouble to me."

Charlie looked at Jess. "Actually, Jess, that *is* kinda what I'm saying. Why did you agree to that?"

Jess quickly looked between the two of them, each staring at her intently. "I didn't know it was a negotiation!" She shrugged her shoulders. "Besides, what if *I'm* the one who is test driving *him?*"

"Why in heavens would you want to test drive a rich, successful, handsome guy?" Charlie looked conspiratorially at Moira as if Jess had lost her mind. "By the looks of him, I bet he's amazing in the bedroom, as well."

Jess blushed and looked away. Charlie gasped and put his hand to his mouth. "Not fair!" he said. "Hot, rich, *and* great in bed? I don't know what you were thinking then, honey. You don't 'test drive' a model like that; you drive it right off the lot!"

Moira cut in, "Jess *should* test drive him! I honestly find it relieving that you didn't commit to being his girlfriend yet. It's good to know that you're not fully jumping into this yet."

Jess wasn't sure how Moira's words felt to her. She knew that Moira intended them to be supportive, but they hurt, nevertheless.

Moira sensed Jess's hesitation. "It's true, right?" she asked cautiously, noticing the hurt expression on Jess's face. "I mean, that's what the concern is about, isn't it? Wanting to test drive the model to make sure that it doesn't careen off the side of the road?"

"Yes, it's true," Jess said, exhaling. "I like him, a lot, but I'm not sure what I'm getting into. To be honest, half of the time I'm thinking of calling it off. I keep wondering if now is the time in my life for this kind of thing."

"Oh, honey," Charlie placed his hand on her shoulder. "it's never the time for that kind of thing. We got you, Jess. It's about time you had fun. Anicca is not going to close just because Ms. Tyler got a little play."

Moira and Jess both turned to him, surprised. "I can't believe my entire dynamic with Jack Stinson is getting summed up as 'getting a little play,'" Jess groaned.

"Listen, honey," Charlie responded nonchalantly, "I'm gay *and* I'm Southern. 'Getting play' is the highest of all possible ends. We *live* for this kind of gossip."

Jess put her heads in her hands. "Ugh, I can't believe I'm doing something worthy of being gossiped about."

Charlie rested his hand on her shoulder. "Seriously, Jess, lean in. We got you covered."

Jess peeked up at him, tentatively. "Thanks, Charlie. I hope you're right."

Moira looked at the two of them, her expression neutral. Jess could tell that she was holding back from saying more, which Jess appreciated. She didn't want her dating Jack to affect anything about Anicca, including her relationship with Moira, which, for now, meant that the less they discussed it, the better it was for the both of them. There was something else too. Some part of Jess, a part that had been there all along, was worried that Moira was more in touch with the truth than Charlie, had maybe had more experience with the hard reality that sometimes, not always but sometimes, a woman has to choose between career and relationship, and that there was some validity to her worries that Jess was making the wrong choice.

"So, I guess you'll need to be extra prepared for your meeting tomorrow," Moira changed the subject deftly. "Are you two free at eleven to meet, maybe give us some time to go through the game plan for this week?" When Charlie and Jess agreed, she continued. "Okay, great. Jess, I … I hope it works out." She smiled, and Jess smiled back. But inside of Jess, some of her elation was tempered. In a way, she was thankful for the comedown. All that excitement had been making it hard for her to work.

Chapter 23

THE NEXT COUPLE WEEKS PASSED BY IN A KIND OF HAZE. JESS'S days were split between progressing with the Jumbl project, responding to other potential clients and tying up loose ends with existing ones, and beginning the hunt for additional staff to help with the increased workload. The last task was still daunting, but Anicca's reputation was steadily building. Word had gotten out that Jess was working with Donathan Lewis on a big project, and even though nothing official had been made public, other Bay Area companies had made soft inquiries as to her availability for their own projects. Jess was equal parts excited and anxious, thrilled to see her dream materialize while at the same time longing for the days when she might sleep again.

And then, of course, there was Jack. As the project picked up, so too did the number of times they interacted each week. Meeting at the site would frequently lead to dinner, and then to the night after dinner, and then to the next morning, which meant late nights and early mornings and not very much sleeping at all.

Not that Jess was complaining, necessarily. It turned out that the chemistry they'd had the first time they had sex was no mistake. Each time they'd been together since, it had only gotten better, with Jess going to places she hadn't known she was capable of going. Jess had had sex before Jack, but it had always been mediocre. Jess had assumed that maybe she just wasn't that sexual, and she was okay with that. With Jack, though, it was completely different. Jack was playful and affectionate in bed, and he was so completely focused on her that she felt bolder and more daring than usual. She loved that he suggested new things that almost always turned out well, and when they didn't, they could both laugh about it. But more than that, his comfort with himself and his sincere desire to make her feel good, not out of stoking his own ego, but out of care for her, got her to open up in entirely new ways. The intensity of his feeling demanded her complete surrender, and to her surprise, she wanted to give that to him. Surrender, with him, wasn't scary at all. In fact, it was liberating.

Her time with Jack had been wonderful in other ways too. Jess had to work late quite a few nights, so Jack would come over to be with her. On some nights, he cooked dinner; on others, they ordered takeout. On the rare chance that Jess had a free evening, they'd spend it exploring the city together: a date night at Mission Bowling Club, an impromptu concert at the Independent, and simply walking around Jess's neighborhood, strolling along Divisadero Street and popping into whatever bar happened to be playing live music that evening. It had felt like a dream. Jack was casually affectionate, a kiss when he got up, holding hands when they walked. Jess felt at ease with him there. She hadn't expected—hadn't thought—that she could feel that way around another person. She sometimes wondered why she'd been so resistant to being with someone. She'd thought dating would make things harder. It was turning out that, with the right person, some aspects of the busy life associated with running her own firm were actually easier.

She'd caught some of her friends up on her growing connection to Jack. Their reaction—"Yeah, Jess, like we didn't all see *that* one coming"—was followed up with a series of questions that, for the first time, Jess was happy to answer. Usually, whenever the topic of dating would come up, Jess turned evasive. This was different, though. She *wanted* to talk about Jack. The more she got to know him, the more she saw him as a kind, funny, and generous person. She was proud to tell the people in her life about him.

What was harder was when people asked what it all meant. As to that, Jess had no idea. It was true that Jack seemed to want something serious. But, then again, it was so new. Because Jess hadn't dated much, she had no idea what the protocol was. They still hadn't had any further conversation "defining the relationship," as Charlie called it, and Jess was still hesitant to bring it up. Everything was so perfect right now, apart from the sleep deprivation. Having a conversation felt too close to having expectations, and Jess still wasn't sure what would happen after this project ended and they weren't automatically in each other's orbits anymore. Jess would move on to other projects, and Jack would turn his focus back to ShineStar. And the two of them? Well, Jess tried not to think too much about that.

After the campus opened, Jess figured, they could talk about what they were and where they would go from there, that is, if there was still any "they" to figure out. There were three weeks left until the opening event at Jumbl. Three weeks was a lot of time for one or both of them to realize that this wasn't working, plenty of time to discover that it was a bond brought about by working together and nothing more. For all Jess's excitement, she made sure that she never forgot that all of this was temporary. Nothing is permanent.

In the meantime, the Jumbl project was all-consuming. There was so much to do between now and the opening that talking with Jack simply didn't feel like a priority. She felt constantly behind, delegating tasks to Moira and Charlie that she usually would have done herself in order to stay sane and, sometimes, to spend more time with Jack. She worried about that, wondering if she was being irresponsible, but Moira and Charlie had so far seemed to handle everything she'd asked them to do, and Jess was finding that the fun she had spending time with Jack made it all too easy to not inquire too much into the details.

Things remained awkward between her and Moira. They hadn't spoken about her and Jack in detail since Jess had revealed they were dating, apart from some superficial catching up that met the bare minimum of checking in that one does for someone in a new relationship. A tension hovered between the two of them, despite Moira's earnest efforts to appear positive for Jess. Jess knew that Moira wanted to protect her from making a mistake, for derailing her career right at its inflection point because of something that might amount to no more than puppy love. The thing that made it harder was that Jess couldn't be sure whether Moira was being overprotective or whether Jess's growing trust in Jack was naive. As it stood, every conversation Jess had with Moira brought with it a reminder: The only thing she could count on was

Anicca. She had to prioritize herself and her work. Everything else could wait.

But that didn't mean she couldn't enjoy herself in the meantime. She was supposed to go to Jack's place that night. He was going to cook dinner, and Jess was picking up dessert. They'd talked about going out to eat, but Jess was so tired that she preferred to stay in. And Jack's apartment was something that she was increasingly curious to see. Jess had been so busy with work that, so far, they'd only spent time at her house, which was more convenient for her. Jack lived in Pacific Heights, which Jess felt a little strange about. It was one of the most expensive neighborhoods in the city, and Jack's family had owned property there for a while. Jess was still getting used to how wealthy his family was. She didn't quite know how to feel about it. She knew he didn't feel awkward about it at all—she *knew* that—but it was easier for him to ignore than it was for her. It was funny how life worked that way, Jess thought, how it was always easier to ignore something that you had but harder to forget something that you didn't.

The building doorman let Jess in. Doorman, doorperson? Jess had no idea what to call him given that she thought people who opened doors for you as a career existed (a) exclusively in New York, (b) in maybe the 1960s at the latest, and (c) not in any place she'd ever go to. After giving her name, she was verified on a list and was told the apartment number. It was a surreal experience, and she wondered whether it was going to be like this every time she went to see Jack. Jess pushed the elevator button and tried to shake it off.

Jess's anxiety was eased when Jack opened the door. He looked sexy, dressed casually in a grey sweater that highlighted his toned biceps. Jess's eyes widened as she, again, reminded herself that he was here for her, that he wanted her.

"I'm so happy you're here," Jack said. He took the dessert she'd brought, Kara's Cupcakes, with one hand and in the other pulled her in close. "I've been dying to see you all day." He kissed her softly yet forcefully, placing his hands around her waist so that she was pressed against him. Her hands moved up around his shoulders as she closed her eyes and let herself succumb to the sweetness of the kiss. She was happy to see him, too. Seeing him now, feeling him now, her body registered how much she'd missed him.

"Me too," she said. "I'm excited to see your place. Do I get the tour?"

"By all means," he gestured her in. "Make yourself at home."

Jess walked around, while Jack went to place the cupcakes down in the kitchen. Jack's apartment was stunning. Tastefully decorated, in a style Jess saw tended towards contemporary but with enough traditional blending to ground it. The white base was complemented by sea-inspired blues and earthy browns, a coastal motif that was reminiscent enough of the beach to remind you that you were in California while subtle enough to remain upscale. The style was different from her own yet obviously professionally done. But the highlight was a window at the far end of the room that took up the entire wall and showed a sweeping view of the bay and the Golden Gate Bridge.

Jess went over to the window, her jaw literally open. "*This* is your view?"

Jack met her at the window and put his hands around her waist. "Mm-hmm." He nuzzled her ear. "But I have to say, it's never looked so good as it does now, with you standing here."

She leaned into his warm chest as he wrapped his arms around her. The smell of him was intoxicating, that cedar scent she'd come to recognize as characteristically him. "You are too much sometimes," she said, smiling despite herself.

He turned her around and gently placed his hand under her chin, lifting it up so that her lips were near his. "Do you want me to stop?" He kissed her cheek and then moved lower, his lips tracing the side of her neck.

Jess's breath caught. "No, no, don't stop." Her heartbeat raced as she felt her desire for him come alive, her body moving closer to him out of sheer need. "Keep going. Don't stop."

"Don't stop, Ms. Tyler?" He lifted her hands over her head and held her wrists together, pressed against the window. He whispered in her ear. "Then tell me what you want me to do."

Jess raised her hips against him. She felt herself become slick, down there, the sound of his voice combined with the smell of him forming a heady blend. "Take my shirt off," she asked, both shied and emboldened by his request.

He readily complied, lifting her shirt over her head and covering her chest with kisses while he expertly removed her bra.

"Look at you, Jess. You take my breath away every time." He shook his head, slowly, as if in disbelief before turning serious. "Put your hands behind your back," he demanded. Jess placed her hands there so that her chest and breasts were now completely exposed, no room for modesty. The exposure took her right to the edge of her comfort zone, requiring her to trust Jack, feeling relieved by knowing she could do so.

Jack took hold of her hands behind her back and bent his mouth so that it hovered over her nipple. "I'm going to make you beg." His tongue gently licked her nipple, tantalizingly soft, toying with her, lick after lick moving between strong and gentle and then strong again. "Mine, all mine," she heard him say, his words bringing her closer, allowing her to surrender, as he placed his mouth forcefully on her breast, sucking and nibbling and biting so that she was fully aroused. Her head fell back against the window, and her eyes rolled up as she soaked in the pleasure.

She felt one of his hands release and start to move lower, towards her skirt. He pulled his lips away from her breast and looked at her fully aroused nipple, blowing on it, the cooling sensation tickling the nerves of the raw skin.

"I'm glad you wore a skirt tonight. That makes things interesting." He tugged at the top of her panties. "May I?"

Jess nodded. "Yes, please."

"That's right, Jess. You know I like when you verbally tell me. Makes it so much easier," he pulled down on her panties removing them with one quick movement, "to know where your limits are." He played with her clit, her skirt ruffled up around her hips, her hands pinned behind her back. A low, soft moan escaped from her lips. "Do you like that?" He kissed her long, deep, massaging her clit and building up her pleasure. "See, the thing is, I want to take you places that you've never gone, and I need you to be able to tell me if we're going too far or too fast."

His kisses continued, one after another, as his hand continued to work her into a frenzy. It was too much to bear, her senses overwhelmed, rationality replaced with the full desire for more, more. She pulled away. "Please, Jack, please, keep going. I need you inside."

Jack's eyebrows raised in delight at her request. "Of course, Ms. Tyler." His eyes sparkled mischievously. "But one thing first." Without warning, he turned her around so that she was now facing the window, looking out over the expanse of the bay and the bridge and the lights of the city. Jack positioned her so that her breasts pressed against the window, the cool of the glass hitting her aroused, assaulted, raw nipples, peaking their sensation.

"Are you ready, Ms. Tyler?" She nodded. "Say it, Jess."

"Yes, I'm ready."

"Good." Jack slid his finger inside her and began moving, quickly, in and out, building her up until she was ready for him to join another finger. She panted, her breath coming in spurts, at her edge. Jack kissed her back forcefully, in what Jess realized was a move to keep her breasts pinned against the glass while his fingers continued their merciless onslaught.

Jess moved her hand down to her clit and began massaging her swollen center. "Yes, Jess, I want you to make yourself feel good. That is so fucking hot." Jack showed his delight by increasing his pace, moving now so that he was pounding, quickly, unrelenting, moan after moan escaping from Jess's lips as the sheer eroticism of it overcame her and she realized she was about to orgasm while pressed against a window overlooking San Francisco. She knew it was unlikely that anyone could see them from this height, almost impossible, but the possibility that someone *could* awakened some latent exhibitionist instinct in Jess and sent her over the edge so that she came, releasing in Jack's hand as he moved faster and faster for the last few strokes until she came undone.

Jack slowly removed his hand and kissed her chest and neck while Jess's breath evened out. "Did you enjoy that?" He kissed her ear lobe and whispered in her ear, "It seemed like you did."

Jess turned around to face him again. She nodded and placed her arms around his neck. "Mm-hmm," she kissed him. "And now I want some more."

"That's exactly what I want to hear." Jack moved his tongue against her lips. "What do you want?"

She kissed him back for a moment and then, suddenly, pushed his chest with both hands so that he took a step backward. "What do I want? I want you, on your back. Me, on top. I want to have all the power." Jess was surprised by her boldness. The combination of her orgasm, exhibitionism, and her feeling so comfortable with Jack arose something deep from within her that felt powerful, domineering, that wanted to know that Jack Stinson was under her control, to see him lying on his back, deep inside her, with her calling the shots.

Jack's eyes glinted, sultry, full of desire. He nodded and moved to lie down. "No," Jess stopped him. "I want you to say it. I want you to say you want that, too."

The corners of Jack's lips turned up. "Yes, Ms. Tyler, I would like that very much."

"Good. Now take your clothes off and lie the fuck down."

Jack took his shirt off, revealing the taut abdomen that led, tantalizingly, down to his waistband. Jess watched appreciatively as Jack slowly undid his belt and then his jeans. "I don't know that I've ever been so openly watched while I took my clothes off," he said. "I feel like I'm doing a striptease."

Jess pursed her lips, in no mood for joking. "Maybe that's because you fucking are," she said. "And guess what," she stepped closer to kiss him before he finished removing his pants, "you better make it a fucking good one."

Jess saw Jack's breath hitch as he smiled, slowly. He stepped away and slowly, seductively, pulled his pants down over his hips, pausing for a second to show her his perfectly sculpted ass in true striptease style, before he removed them.

"That's better," Jess said. "Now lie your ass down because you are going to get so fucked."

Jack lay down. Jess grabbed a condom from his jeans pocket and placed it on his erection before climbing on top of him, straddling right over the top of him. She placed her hands on his chest and looked at him, intently, right in the eyes. "Now I'm going to make *you* beg."

With that, she lowered herself down onto him. She started riding him, slowly, deeply, pulsing on and off while she watched him close his eyes, locked deep in pleasure. She moved faster, harder, the sight of his breath quickening urging her to continue. It was exciting, arousing, knowing she had the control, seeing the effect she had on him. She rode him until he was right at the edge, and then she stopped, suddenly.

"Why did you stop?" he asked abruptly.

"Because," she said. "I already told you. I want you to beg."

"Fuck, Jess, please, I'm so fucking close."

"Aw," Jess placed her hand caringly on his cheek, "you can do better than that."

"Please?" Jack asked imploringly.

Jess leaned in to whisper in his ear. "Jack fucking Stinson, that is the most pathetic begging I've heard in my life. If you want to cum," she intentionally rode his cock again to work him back up a little, "then I need you to fucking beg like you fucking mean it."

"Please, Jess. Fuck, please. Whatever I can do, please, I'm begging you."

Jess sat up and placed his hands on her breasts. "That's fucking better," she said. And then she rode him, hard and fast, not stopping, moving quickly, determinedly, now on a mission. She saw him get closer, his hands massaging her breasts, and she took her hand to her clit and started touching as she rode him. She kept going, in and out, moving her hips all around him until he came, exploding inside of her, calling out.

"Stay inside; I'm close!" she called out and kept riding, her hand still touching her clit, until she came again, spasming around his cock.

She let herself collapse onto his chest. He wrapped his arms around her and kissed the top of her head.

"Wow, Ms. Tyler." He kissed her again. "I had no idea you had that in you. That was … incredible."

Jess laughed, relieved by the intensity of her orgasm and amazed by what she had just done. "Neither did I, Jack. Neither did I."

They lay like that for a while. Jess felt relaxed on a level she didn't know she could be. Something was changing inside of her, she knew that, but a curious thing was happening. Usually change felt scary, stepping into the uncertainty of what was to come. With Jack, though, it was different. She felt comforted by him. Change was different, this time. Instead of being scared, she felt free.

Chapter 24

"NICE USE OF COLOR, JESS," REBECCA SAID, POINTING TO ONE OF the walls of the main work area at the Jumbl site. "It's thoughtful of you to have extended the aesthetic from the lounge and the café through this area. Often, and regrettably, campuses like this prioritize the design in common areas and neglect to bring it to areas where people work and spend most of their time."

Jess beamed at the compliment. She had invited Rebecca over to give her thoughts on the space before it was so close to final that nothing could be changed. It was a delicate offer. Jess was feeling out what her relationship with Rebecca would be now that they weren't employer/employee but also weren't quite friends. Although Jess would have appreciated if Rebecca had offered critical feedback on her design, knowing that it would have come from a good place, it would have been hard to hear regardless. Jumbl remained the largest project Jess had taken on, and even though things seemed to be going well enough, the whole thing felt precarious, as if something could go wrong at any time. Jess found herself counting down the days until it was over.

"Thank you, Rebecca." Jess joined her at the wall. "I tried to make the feel seamless, like the ripples on the lake, having no clear start and no clear end."

"Yes, and impermanent too. It's very Jess." Rebecca smiled knowingly.

"Too true," Jess laughed. "What can I say? At least my preference for impermanence doesn't change, which is ironic, I guess."

"I guess so. But then again, some things I'm glad to have stay the same." Rebecca gently placed her hand on Jess's shoulder. "Does it come off as condescending if I say I'm proud of you?"

Jess shook her head. "Not at all."

"Well, then, I'm proud of you." Rebecca gave Jess a hug. "Although I'm losing more and more hope of ever convincing you to come back to Unoa."

"Yep, I wouldn't plan on it. Although I will say, this project gave me a newfound appreciation for all that you have to deal with. Having everything come together has been stressful, to say the least."

"Tell me about it." Rebecca looked knowingly at Jess. "You don't seem too worse for the wear, though. If anything, you look kind of radiant."

"Ha, I have no idea why that would be." Jess gestured towards the next room. "Come, let me show you the outdoor pavilion."

"Ooh, exciting." Rebecca followed Jess to the door. "I'm curious … Does the radiance have anything to do with, oh I don't know, Jack Stinson?"

Jess felt her energy shift, pulling closer to herself, protective. "Why would he have anything to do with that?" Jess hoped her tone didn't betray how flustered she was by the question.

"Well, a couple people saw you leave the aquarium together, and I guess here and there throughout town. There's been a bit of a buzz about it." Rebecca paused, noticing the stiffness in Jess's shoulders. "I didn't mean to upset you, Jess. If anything, if there is anything going on, I'd be happy for you."

The sincerity that Jess felt from Rebecca relaxed some of her tension. Nevertheless, some discomfort remained. "I'm not upset. I'm … surprised? I didn't know people were talking, and I don't like that that's happening."

"Fair enough," Rebecca offered. Her expression was hesitant, as if debating whether to say anything more. "Jess, please tell me if I should mind my own business, but I thought you would have assumed that would happen. In those circles that care, Jack's well-known, and people talk. Not bad things, necessarily, but things."

Jess was silent. She moved quickly through the rest of the building, anxious to be outside. The walls felt claustrophobic. The building was full of her designs, and having this conversation inside felt sacrilegious, manifestations of who she was bombarded by the unwelcome knowledge that people who didn't know her and had never met her, were discussing her personal life.

"I'm not sure how to respond," Jess said, after a while. They had reached the door to the outside, and Jess turned to look at Rebecca before pushing the door open. "This is the pavilion area, overlooking the lake." Jess gestured half-heartedly at the scene.

"Jess," Rebecca approached cautiously, "I'm sorry I said anything. I really didn't mean to upset you, or hurt you, or whatever is happening."

"You didn't, or at least I know you didn't mean to."

"Not at all. Look, Jess, people talk. It is what it is. If it weren't about Jack, it would be about something else. Soon enough, with Anicca on the track that it is, you're going to be in in the public eye, and part of what comes with that is the sacrifice of anonymity. I honestly thought my mentioning Jack would be a nice transition for you to tell me about this new and exciting part of your life. Isn't it at all that?"

"Yes, it is." Jess's jaw, which had become tense, loosened. "It's going well, as well as something new can be going, I suppose." Her voice was dreamy, distant. She found herself disoriented and sat down at a nearby table for some support. "Rebecca, I'm not sure I want *this* to be the thing I'm known for. I'm not sure I want to be known at all, but if it's going to be for anything, I want it to be for my design. I don't want that to be overshadowed."

"Then don't let it be." Rebecca sat next to her at the table. "Jess," she gestured to their surroundings, "this, what you've created, is the star. The secret to not being overshadowed is to make the rest of what you do undeniable. I think you've done that here. When people see this space, the only thing anyone will care about is Anicca."

"I hope you're right." Jess sighed. A heaviness that she had been keeping at bay seeped into her. Months of intensity, years of hard work, a lifetime of feeling out of place—it all came pouring in thick into her chest. Jess looked up to the sky, clear blue with whispers of white clouds, and let herself surrender to the vastness of its presence, finding therein what felt like the closest she could come to calm.

"I know I'm right," Rebecca told her. "Listen, I know when you and I spoke, I mentioned this next period of time being crazy, and that's certainly going to be the case. I gave my all to Unoa for years, sacrificing basically my entire social life. But your path will be however it will be. Jack, he treats you well, yes?"

"Yes."

"He understands you?"

"He seems to," Jess agreed.

"Then why not go for it? There's worse things to be known for than being a fantastic designer who has a hot boyfriend."

A faint smile appeared on Jess's lips in response to Rebecca's welcome attempt at humor. "I guess you're right. Rebecca, you really think people will like this space?"

"Jess," Rebecca's eyes conveyed deep warmth, "people will love it."

Jess nodded. They spent a few more minutes talking through what remained of the design implementation, with Rebecca providing a few helpful tips for timing of installation and dealing with the sometimes-eccentric personalities of the design world. They didn't speak about Jack again, and after said goodbye, Jess was too distracted by the complexities of the project to devote too much time to further reflection on it.

But when she got home, she replayed their conversation. She hadn't given really any thought to the impact that dating Jack could have on her career, apart from how it could serve as a distraction to her work. Jess recalled Moira saying early on how people might speculate that Jess had only received the Jumbl commission because of her relationship with Jack, but, thankfully, Rebecca had not indicated that that was happening. Regardless, the importance of her succeeding with the Jumbl project felt highlighted in a way it hadn't previously, which Jess could hardly believe was possible. The only thing Jess could hope for was that these last few seemingly unending weeks would go by without complication and that her design would speak for itself. It was a familiar feeling, that whether she would be accepted depended on how much people liked what she created, and Jess was growing weary of it. Regardless, here she was again, and the only comfort Jess had was knowing that, tired as she was of having to prove herself in order to fit in, she at least knew how to do so.

With a heavy sigh, she opened her laptop and went back to her work.

Chapter 25

"Good morning, sleepyhead."

Jess covered her ears with the sheets. "Too early. Not fair."

Jack chuckled as he gently pulled the sheet down. "Come on, sunshine. We have a big day ahead of us."

"Fine," Jess groaned. She forced herself to sit up and saw Jack sitting next to her, coffee in hand.

The sight of him, happy and generous in his kindness, made Jess's heart melt. She was getting used to the sensations that she felt being with him, but it was still, at times like this, surprising to find how powerfully he affected her.

It had been several days since she'd seen Rebecca, and she hadn't spoken with Jack about their conversation. She had no idea what she would have said. She was sure Jack would have been understanding—he usually was—but about what, that she wasn't comfortable with people talking about them being together? Jess wasn't sure how to convey that without it being hurtful to Jack, and so she'd kept it to herself. Things were going so well between them, and Jess wanted their time between now and the end of the Jumbl project to remain in this sweet fantasy place before conversations about what they were or what anything meant had to happen.

Jess's heart felt light as she thought about their day ahead. It was a beautiful Saturday, and they were planning to spend the day in Petaluma, a small town in Sonoma County, to do a little antique shopping under the guise of finding some final pieces for the Jumbl project. Jack suggested they add some wine tasting to the agenda and spend the night there afterward. Jess had agreed. Although she worried that any time not working on the project would come back to haunt her, the day that Jack had planned for them sounded too exciting to pass up.

Wine tasting on a Saturday—it was something Jess had barely been able to do despite her many years of living in the city. The idea made her feel like she was only twenty-nine years old, not decades older as she often felt. Jack was so solid and dependable that she could, almost unbelievably, unwind around him. The stress of starting Anicca had weighed on her more than she ever realized, and with Jack by her side, Jess noticed some of her younger, dreamier self emerge, the self that got lost in the potential of things, that could spend an hour daydreaming upon some flowers, that felt free.

Jess took the mug of coffee from Jack and gave him a kiss before taking a sip. She motioned for him to come lie next to her, and he readily complied. They shifted so that they were looking out his bedroom window, which had a view of the western part of the city, down to the ocean. It felt perfect, lying there, completely at ease, having spent hours the night before making love.

Jess's eyes became dreamy as memories from last night flooded her mind. She was going places with Jack she'd never been, physically and emotionally. And it was all happening so quickly that she could only be witness to it.

Jess sighed contentedly. "Careful, Jess." Jack took her mug and placed it on the nightstand. "Don't fall asleep now and spill your coffee all over the bed."

"Not sleepy." Jess turned to rest her face in his chest, breathing in his cedar scent and welcoming in the relaxation throughout her body that naturally followed. "Just reliving some of last night. I didn't know my body could do that."

"I'll have to thank Bridget and Moira for making you go to those yoga classes." He gave her a kiss. "I had an amazing time last night. I'll have fun thinking about how I'll make it up to you. In fact," he kissed her again, "we could get started on that sooner rather than later."

"What happened to your 'get up and go'?" Jess nuzzled against him.

He moved his mouth in soft kisses down her neck. "Well, there are always exceptions ..."

"Oh, good to know," Jess laughed. "And here I thought we were on a tight schedule."

"People will understand," he said in between kisses.

Jess tilted her head to expose more of her neck, surrendering to the softness of his touch. Everything felt so right when she was with him. It was so easy to forget that anything else existed. She considered whether they might have time for a long morning, but, then, she looked over at Jack's shoulder and saw what time it was.

"10 a.m.! I can't believe I slept in this late," Jess said, squirming away from him. "We have to get up to Petaluma and at least attempt to be productive."

Jack made a pouty face before gently releasing her. "I can't wait for this project to be over, so we can spend all day right here and not worry about the rest."

"The project will be over soon enough," Jess replied. His reference to days spent together following the project made Jess feel strange. Continuing their dynamic was something she wanted, some of the time, but counting on their being together was scary. She was still not sure how different they would feel once they no longer had to be in each other's orbit. "Do you think I have time for a quick run before we go?" she added, changing the subject.

Jack nodded his head in assent. "Sure, it's only about an hour away. Mind if I come with?"

Jess hadn't considered the possibility of running with him. It was usually something she did solo. But the idea, she found, was kind of nice. "Okay, let's do it. Forty-five minutes?"

"Sounds good." He gave her another kiss. "But first, let's enjoy our coffee. I like having you here, with this view. I don't want to change it just yet."

Jess smiled as she settled in. For now, she felt the same way.

• • •

On the way to Petaluma, Jess heard the phone vibrate and hurriedly shut it off after realizing who it was: Bridget. She had been avoiding her calls for the past week. She knew she was being rude, but she also knew that a conversation with Bridget would inevitably turn to Jack, and she had no idea what to say.

"Who was that?" Jack asked. He was casual in his tone but seemed concerned. Jess didn't blame him. She'd rushed to turn off her phone pretty conspicuously.

Jess shrugged her shoulders in an effort to appear casual. "Oh, just my sister Bridget. No big deal. I'll call her later."

"You can call her now if you'd like. I don't mind." He pointed to the car's Bluetooth button. "You can even connect into the car if you want, but no pressure."

Jess looked uncomfortable. "Thanks, but it's okay. We're due for a long chat. I'll call her after we get back tomorrow."

"Jessica Tyler," Jack took her hand, "are you afraid to be caught in the car with me? Are you keeping me a secret?"

Dammit, Jess thought to herself. Was she that transparent? Probably. She wasn't used to having to hide things because usually there was nothing to hide. "I wouldn't say a secret, necessarily," she said. "But maybe an undefined, nebulous thing that doesn't easily fit into questions from others?"

Jack squinted at her.

"Keep your eyes on the road!" Jess retorted, playfully tapping his shoulder.

Jack complied but was silent for a moment. "You know, Jess, it's only an 'undefined, nebulous thing,' as you call it, because you wanted it that way."

Jess exhaled. They were about to have *that* conversation. "I know," she said. "So, did you want to talk about that?"

"Here's what I think, Jess. This thing between you and me is new, really new, but I like it, a lot. Every time I see you, I want to keep spending time with you, and the only reason I don't is because I know you're busy and because I understand that most everyone would warn me to take things slowly. So, I'm trying. But that doesn't change how I really feel." He paused to take a breath before continuing. "We're about to spend the night out of town. What do you think? Are we due for an upgrade?"

Jess felt her heartbeat quicken. She put her hands on her belly to relax herself and looked away, unable to maintain eye contact. She'd been planning to delay any kind of conversation like this until after the project finished, yet somehow, here it was. She didn't feel prepared.

"The Jumbl opening event is in two weeks, and the official opening is not too long thereafter." she forced herself to say. "What happens then?"

"I don't understand. Do you mean are we dating just because of the Jumbl project?" Jess nodded, and Jack continued. "Well, I didn't think so. But is that what you thought?"

"Maybe. Or, I don't know, maybe I thought that since we didn't have to be around each other, we would kind of naturally drift. Or ... I don't know what I thought. I guess I thought you would lose interest." Jess hated how exposed she felt. This feeling was one of the reasons she'd avoided dating in the first place.

"Jess, do you have any idea how I feel about you?" Jack sounded a combination of sad and exasperated. "Why you have these thoughts, I have no idea. But I know that they have much more to do with how you feel about yourself than with me. Whatever it is that is making you think I'm going to disappear, I wish I understood it more. If it's something I'm doing, then I want to know. But I think I'm trying to be honest and haven't given you any reason to doubt."

Jess put her hand on his shoulder. "No, Jack, you're being great. You've been great." She closed her eyes briefly to collect herself. "You're right. These are my fears and insecurities. I didn't think that I would be in this position, of my career being on the verge of a breakthrough and then *that* of all times being when I start a new relationship. Did you know that starting a new relationship is considered a life stressor? Along with moving, changing jobs, etc. I guess it's a better stressor than most, but still, I don't want to lose everything I've built."

Jack's eyes softened. "I get that. I don't want that either, you know. I would hope that you wouldn't feel like that was a choice you were being asked to make."

"Jack, you're not asking me to make it, but I might have to make it all the same. That's just how it is for a woman. Maybe not now, but what if, in the future, you want kids or your career takes you somewhere or all of these other unnamed things happen? It's usually the woman who bears the burden. And I don't want that to be my narrative. It's—" she caught herself. She was about to mention her conversation with Rebecca but stopped. Too much, too fast. "It's a story that's all too common," she said instead.

They were both silent again. It was a minute before Jack spoke. "Jess, I am listening, I really am. But maybe, before we have to decide anything like that, maybe we take a step back and realize that right now, all we're doing is getting to know each other. I don't know the answer to the questions you have. I certainly wouldn't want you to live a life full of regret. But at the same time, we haven't been dating for that long, and who knows? Maybe by the time it's really time to ask those questions, we'll have more options than we think? All I'm saying is that, right now, I'd like to be your boyfriend."

They both paused briefly before laughing, breaking some of the tension. "Yeah, in my mind that came out more smoothly," Jack said.

"God, why is the word 'boyfriend' kind of cringey?" Jess shuddered. "I mean, it's an established term."

"Right. 'Girlfriend' is not much better. But, Jess, seriously, unfortunate nomenclature notwithstanding, what do you think?"

Jess thought. Here was a man who was great, a total catch, smart, sexy, kind, and not afraid to be completely into her. She was having trouble thinking of a good reason to say no.

"Okay, Jack. Okay." She squeezed his hand, and he squeezed back. "Boyfriend"—Jess let the word sit with her. She was spending the weekend away with her boyfriend. She liked the sound of that.

• • •

Petaluma was gorgeous: relaxing, sunny, old-town charming. Jess had only been to Sonoma County twice, once to the Russian River in Guerneville and one other time to wine tasting in Healdsburg, as part of a networking event through Unoa. Petaluma was smaller than those other towns, with a more industrial vibe, but it boasted an adorable downtown area where she and Jack spent most of the day.

They found a handful of Bay Area-themed antiques that would add character to the Jumbl project before visiting a couple wineries for tastings. Afterwards, they had dinner at the Wild Goat Bistro, right by the water. Dinner conversation was lively and full of laughter. Jess couldn't believe how good she felt. She noticed something: she was getting used to the title "girlfriend," and "boyfriend," even though it still felt odd, was terminology that was also growing on her. It made her less anxious than when they had been only exclusive. She could relax a bit more, knowing that they had made certain obligations to each other, knowing that Jack wanted to be with her in a more serious way.

They were staying at the Hotel Petaluma that evening. They had a suite overlooking the nearby park and the downtown area. Jack had insisted on paying, which had made Jess somewhat uncomfortable, but he'd persuaded her by pointing out that she could easily have billed an expense like this to Jumbl anyway, and it made him feel less like he owed Donathan to simply pay for it directly. Jess reluctantly agreed. Even though she was adjusting to their income disparity, she still didn't like that it existed, particularly since she now knew that people were talking about them being together.

Regardless, the heady combination of wine, laughter, and sunshine left her buoyant by the time they got to their suite. They'd decided to skip dessert at the restaurant in favor of ordering room service to have with their view, so they cozied themselves up by the window and prepared to enjoy the selection of cheesecake, chocolate cake, and strawberry parfait.

"Jack," Jess said as she made herself comfortable under a blanket, "I'm having a really nice day."

Jack smiled as he leaned over to kiss her. "Me too, Jess. You know, I thought about moving here for a while. It feels so peaceful here up in the country, and running my own business means I could set my own standards on how much to be in the office."

"Mr. San Francisco move away?" Jess tried a piece of the cheesecake, and it was so good she had to close her eyes. "Wow, that's good. But seriously, *you* leave SF? I bet your family would, um, not have been happy about that."

Jack tried a bite of the cheesecake and shook his head. "Mmm, that *is* good. You weren't kidding." He placed his fork down. "You're right about my family, though. That was exactly the issue with Petaluma, or at least one of them. It would have upset them, absolutely. But at the time, that would have been something I was okay with. We ... haven't always had an easy relationship. My parents have certain understandings of how the world works and what it means to be successful in the world. It's a lot of pressure your whole life to have people expect great things from you."

He hesitated, unsure whether to continue, but Jess gave him a reassuring smile and encouraged him to go on. "I remember telling you about how Donathan and I became friends because we both knew how it was to be outsiders, albeit for different reasons. Well, sometimes I felt like he was my only real family. I didn't feel like I fit in even at home."

Jess considered what he was saying. "It impacts you, I think, not knowing where or how to be. That's all a kid wants, right, to belong? To not have that ... it certainly leaves an impression. Did you feel like they disapproved of you?"

"Not disapproved, necessarily." His expression was thoughtful. "Although probably they did on some level, now that I think about it. It was more like our values were different. They're not bad people, not at all. It's not like they dismiss others. They just don't think about them that much, which, when you're living in certain parts of San Francisco, is very easy to do. But I was always curious as to why some people seem to have everything and some nothing, and I think they didn't understand that fascination. They certainly don't really understand why I'm doing what I'm doing now."

"You mean with the solar company?"

"Yes, or specifically with my project to make solar technology more accessible. It's not glamorous in a way that they would get. But then again, it's not supposed to be." He picked at a chocolate shaving and ate it in satisfaction. "It's supposed to be about doing what you can with what you have to help. Honestly, I could be doing more too."

Jess put her fork down and placed her hand on his chest. "Is this what you tell all the girls? Because I have to say, it's kind of working on me," she said, in an attempt to lighten the mood and bring some comfort to Jack.

Jack smiled but without emotion. He touched her hand on his chest. "I never tell anyone this, Jess."

Jess was once more struck by the sincerity of his words. "I'm sorry, Jack. I … I didn't mean to be dismissive. Well, I guess I did kind of, but only to make you feel better, not to hurt you."

"It's okay, Jess." He gave her a kiss. "I know it's not in you to try to hurt me. And I know I can be intense."

"Yes, but," she leaned in closer and gave him another deeper kiss, "I like that about you."

He pulled her in, placing his lips on her forehead and nose and cheeks in gentle, sweet touches. "Do you now?" he said in between kisses. "What else do you like?"

His tone was sensual, sparking something primal within Jess. She felt her body start to come alive in that way that it did—it always did—with him. "I like your kisses."

His mouth moved down her neck, making her breath flutter. He held her, solidly, with his hands while he let his tongue flick against the hollow of her neck. "Very good. What else?"

Her breath caught with the movement of his tongue. It was so sexy. She didn't know she could be this turned on from someone kissing her throat. But the way he did it was so possessive and confident; it made her want to surrender.

"I like it when you touch me," she said. He kept his lips at her throat but moved his hands down, softly, strongly, taking their time in a methodical, determined way. He traced them along her stomach, down to her hips. Jess felt her skin tingle. It was like her skin was only now becoming known to her, only now realizing it could feel this charged, and Jack was the one that understood how to take her there.

Jack pushed the table out of the way and, in one swift motion, moved Jess so that she was sitting with her legs wrapped around his torso, both of them upright. "Show me where." Jack took her hands and placed them on her body. "I've been thinking about last night, quite a bit, as it turns out, about how hot you were, about how I'm going to make it up to you. So, Ms. Tyler, I'll say it again. Show me where you like to be touched."

Jess's eyes grew fierce with longing. It felt almost danger-ous, being asked to reveal herself like this. She felt more exposed than ever before, even that time when she'd taken control. But his confident insistence coupled with her deep trust in him allowed her to push past the fear, to explore what her body wanted to do, was already doing, in ways her mind couldn't yet consciously comprehend.

She massaged her hands against her stomach, moving slowly, languorously, downwards, approaching her hips but then reced-ing. She knew they were her hands, but there in that moment, with his gaze fixed intently on hers, it was like he was command-ing her to move them. Her will was not entirely her own. She had surrendered it to him and was grateful for the surrender. As if by some silent agreement, she moved her hands upward, now to her breasts, and touched them. Her gaze locked intently on his as she pulled her shirt overhead and removed her bra so that she was naked from the top up, touching herself, fixing her eyes on his as she saw them become big with need.

She felt Jack grow stiff and large beneath her, as she continued to show him how she liked to be touched, moving her hands along her breasts, more confident with every touch. Her hips started to move in some primal rhythm along him, knowing what was underneath and prolonging the pleasure of the before, both of their bodies saturated with need.

"Jess, oh my God, what you do to me." Jack moved his hands onto her hips and helped her feel the rhythm. She pulled one of his hands up to her breast, and he kneaded it, slowly and forcefully, pulling and teasing her nipple until it stood erect. She closed her eyes and felt her head relax. This, *this* was what she wanted. And it felt so liberating to let it happen to her, to know that he knew what he was doing and that all she had to do was say yes.

"Jack, I want you." The words came out before she even realized she said them. With his other hand, he pulled her close to him, kissing her fiercely while continuing to play with her breast. Jess felt herself become almost dizzy with how much she wanted him. She needed him, now. She moved to pull up his shirt, and he obliged, revealing his taut torso. Still on top, she began kissing him, moving her mouth lower to place kisses on his chest, his arms, his belly, taking in his heat and his scent with every kiss.

He lifted her head up to meet his again for another long kiss as he sat up, still kissing her, and positioned her so that she was straddling against him. "Jessica Tyler, tonight, it's my turn to be in control. And now, you are going to take your clothes off, and then I'm going to touch you and tease you, until you beg me to stop."

Jess felt herself get wet at his words. She realized she was always in control, always, with her regimented run and her morning coffee. Even their times before, although she had pushed herself, had been on her terms. She felt powerful in control. But somehow, right then, she wanted nothing more than to let someone else—to let him—take over, to let herself receive, to give him the pleasure of giving.

She slowly got up and took her pants off until she was standing in just her underwear. "Keep going. I didn't say to stop," Jack prodded. With her eyes locked on his, she pulled down her underwear, feeling her heartbeat race as they got lower, until she was standing completely naked before him. "My God, Jess. You are a piece of art."

His words disarmed her self-consciousness. She felt confident, sexy, and she relaxed as he moved over, pillowcase in hand, and tied her wrists behind her back. He took her hand in his and led her over to the armchair and positioned her, knees tucked, facing the back of the chair with her arms tied behind her back. "Stay there," he said as he grabbed the other pillowcase and used it to blindfold her. She was completely naked, completely vulnerable, completely turned on.

He started slowly, rubbing her back and neck. She moaned with pleasure as she felt some of the stress these many weeks had built up release. He stayed there for a while, so long that any remaining nerves she had from being so exposed were soothed. She felt only comfortable, as if she wasn't blindfolded in a hotel armchair but was simply relaxing, receiving, present in a place without time or space. She leaned her head forward to luxuriate in his touch and then felt him move lower, massaging now her breasts, kneading, relaxing, soothing, and scintillating at the same time. She had no cares or concerns right now, only to be here with him, no expectation other than to let herself feel. Her whole body relaxed from deep within as she let it happen.

He kissed her back and then moved his hands downward until they were over her hips and then even lower, touching her right at the parting of her lips, down there, slowly moving one finger in and out, building her up. She gasped as she felt him move deeper, felt his knuckles move over her G-spot, her breath turning into panting as his movement quickened. She wanted more. She needed him to touch her clit, knew that she needed to be stimulated there to go over the edge. He knew she needed that but was denying her the ability to touch herself, building her up more and more.

She felt like she couldn't take any more. "Jack, please, please!" she cried out.

"I know, Jess, I know. But you, my dear, are going to have to be patient." He lifted her hips up and spread her legs wide open. "I recall the other night someone telling me I had to beg." He moved his fingers inside, making her moan. "I thought I might return the favor."

His words exhilarated her. She had no idea what he had in mind but found herself incredibly turned on regardless. She was sopping wet, and she knew it, but he had her positioned so that she was unable to touch herself. Her only choice was to surrender to his touch. He had her right on the edge of what she could tolerate and wasn't pulling back.

"Jack, please!" she cried again.

"Please what?" he asked in mock innocence.

"Please, Jack. I want you inside me. I want you to make me cum!" Her need for him was stronger than her need for restraint. She didn't care what he thought, how she appeared. She wanted him more, now, forever.

He nipped her ear. "Alright Ms. Tyler." He untied her hands and braced them against the armchair. "But only if you stay exactly like this."

She nodded in agreement, desperate for him to keep going. He lifted her hips and started licking her, down there, from behind. She cried out. She had never been touched like this, from this angle. It was exhilarating. She felt him lick and nibble, and she felt that feeling, almost like a tickle but with that deep ache, start to form within her as he played with her clit and then licked upward, right around where she opened, and then back to her clit.

"Do you want me to keep going?" he asked.

"Yes, oh my God, yes!" She moved her hips towards him in further response.

"Is that what you call begging? I think you can do better than that."

She knew he was toying with her, paying her back for the other night, but she didn't care. "Please, Jack, please, don't make me wait!"

"That will work, Ms. Tyler." She heard him unbuckle his belt and tear open a condom. "Get ready for me, Jess." He slid into her in one long, slow movement. She felt his thickness open her further, almost dizzying, and she leaned further into the chair. She relaxed her body to accommodate him inside. "That's right, Ms. Tyler, relax for me." He began moving, going deeper, rhythmically, more of him coming in as more of her adjusted to him. He was methodical and steady.

She wanted him to move faster and then realized he intentionally wasn't, again teasing her, preventing her from reaching climax. She moved her left hand from the back of the chair to his hips and pulled him in tighter, urging him to go faster. He quickly removed her hand and placed it back on the armchair and then leaned over her back and whispered forcefully in her ear, "I *told* you to stay just like this." He moved his hand to her breast and began moving more quickly, sliding in and out of her as he whispered again into her ear, "But now you're going to get it."

She cried out again as he moved faster and faster. His hand lifted from her breast and moved to her clit, massaging her as he slid in and out of her. Her body moved back against his in a steady rhythm, the two of them naturally finding their own pace as the sensation built and built and built. He suddenly took his hand away from her clit, and Jess moaned out, "Jack, please!" But instead of placing his hand back there, he moved her hand down to her clit.

"Touch yourself, Jess. I want you to touch yourself while I fuck you." She started touching herself and felt herself get heavy with pleasure, surrendering to the flow of his rhythm, unsure who was in control but beyond a place where she cared.

They kept moving like that, in sync, him pushing her to her max. "I'm going to cum!" Jess screamed as he quickened his pace to take her over the edge. He kept moving, prolonging her orgasm, crying out as her orgasm pushed him to find his own release.

He stayed inside of her for a moment, breathless, before kissing her back as he slowly stood up and removed the condom. He untied the pillowcase that was serving as a blindfold and kissed her deeply. "You are amazing, Jess. Every time. Never has it ever been like this for me."

She responded in kind, kissing him passionately and turning over. She maneuvered so that he was sitting on the armchair and she was straddling his lap, kissing him, with her arms around him. "Me neither, Jack. I didn't know it could be like that. Did you?"

"I imagined," he said, pausing between kisses to move a strand of hair away from her face. "But only ever with you."

They spent the rest of the night like that, kissing and cuddling, in between bites of the dessert that they had left mostly untouched. When it was finally time for bed, Jess lay there in his arms, her head on his chest, and felt complete. She was falling for him, fast. Some part of her still begged for her to slow down, worried about what the consequences could be, but she didn't know how much control she had any more. This was happening, it seemed, whether she liked it or not.

She yawned and reached her lips up to kiss him on his cheek. She could only hope that whatever was happening would somehow work out in the end.

Chapter 26

JESS SPENT THE NEXT MORNING WITH JACK ENJOYING BRUNCH AT the hotel. They both had to be back in San Francisco relatively early but wanted to make the most of their time in the peaceful country before returning home. They walked around the downtown area with some to-go coffees from Avid Coffee, the locally famous cafe, looking at stores selling country kitsch that they both discovered they had a soft spot for. Jess appreciated how easily their conversation flowed. Then again, their whole relationship had flowed easily. Jess barely felt like she was trying at all. The ease of their connection was what had let the relationship progress to the point that it had.

Jack insisted that they stop at Petaluma Creamery before they headed home. "No way am I going to take you to the land of dairy and have you come home empty-handed," he'd said, as he pulled the car into the driveway. Jess had joked that if Jack wanted a charcuterie again, there were easier ways to go about it, to which he'd countered that he was open to those ways as well. They'd left with a selection of cheeses that Jess would bring to the office the next day. Jess hoped some aged cheddars and mozzarellas would help lift whatever remaining tension continued to exist within her relationship to Moira. Moira's hesitation, combined with her warning about people talking that was turning out to be all too prescient, continued to haunt her, and Jess did not love the idea of revisiting the topic of her and Jack in any serious way with Moira until the project was over. In the meantime, it was much easier to put a Band-Aid on everything through the gift of gourmet cheese.

Jack dropped her off at her apartment shortly after lunch time. Jess was happy to be home, back in her comfort zone in more ways than one. As she opened her computer, though, to check the week's schedule and coordinate necessary vendors, she saw one from Brian, from the Aquarium of the Bay. She hovered over it briefly before opening it. Here it was, another possibly life-changing opportunity. Jess took a deep breath and clicked her mouse.

> Hi Jess,
>
> Brian here from Aquarium of the Bay. Wanted to let you know that YOU GOT THE COMMISSION! We'll send you the official letter and the contract information separately, but I was so excited that it was you that I couldn't wait. We completely loved your design and how your vision for the aquarium merges the best of what's old with what this place could become.
>
> Excited to work with you on this project! It needs to start ASAP, so we'll send over the necessary documentation with the hope that you can start as soon as this week. Please send us your availability for an initial on-site.
> Congratulations again!
>
> Brian Chang
> Director of Operations
> Aquarium of the Bay

Jess sat back in her chair. It took a minute for the news to set in. She had been chosen to redesign the Aquarium of the Bay! It was a huge deal. Between that and the Jumbl project, Anicca was on track to be among the elite design firms of San Francisco, right up there with Unoa. It was almost unbelievable that it could be on this trajectory after two short years of opening. All that doubt she'd had about how she was going to build her clientele, and now she had the opposite problem. It was daunting to think of how she was going to finish the Jumbl project in two weeks, which already required every second she could spare, while also now taking on the Aquarium of the Bay project.

Thinking about all she had on her plate, Jess felt a combination of excitement and panic and needed to take a step back. She got up from her computer and went to her fridge to grab some cheese. When even cheese didn't help, she knew she needed to talk it through with someone. The natural person, the person she *should* want to talk it through with, was Jack. But as much as she was growing to trust him, this was still too vulnerable to let him in on. Besides, he was so involved with the Jumbl project that it wouldn't have felt right to express that she now had concerns about taking on this other project. She couldn't wait until these two weeks were over and she no longer would have to navigate this personal/professional line.

Instead, she called Bridget.

"Hey, Jess, nice to hear from you! You're back from Petaluma already?"

"Yes … Oh Bridget, I don't know what to do." Jess got up and walked towards her window, maneuvering her cheese and cracker spread with one hand.

"Did you two get in a fight? Is that why you're back early?" Bridget's voice grew tense on the line.

"No, it's not that. It's … Oh Bridge, everything is going so well on paper, and all I can think about is how overwhelmed I feel." Jess positioned herself by the window so she could look out at the sky. It felt better, to look at that vast space. She let her eyes wander over the colors of the landscape outside, resting her head against the glass.

Bridget's voice softened, "Aw, Jess. Do you want me to come over?"

Jess nodded, tears starting to form. "Yes, please," she said quietly.

"I'll be right there."

Jess hung up and looked back at the sky. She felt relieved now that Bridget was coming over. It was all going to be okay, somehow. She watched as the clouds moved slowly but steadily against the bright blue backdrop, the interplay of a tree's rustling leaves as they moved against that same backdrop, interacting with the sky and the clouds. This was where she belonged, right here, just her and the world, observing it, returning to that private connection they had always shared. She had gotten away from that with so much of her time and attention now being focused on Jack. She missed this. Staring at the slow dance of the blue and green and white, she felt better. Nothing could be so bad, nothing at all, in a world this magical.

• • •

In forty-five minutes, Bridget was there, bringing with her wine and Thai takeout. She gave Jess a big hug as soon as she came in.

"Sorry it took me so long. I figured we needed some comfort food and stopped at Lers Ros." Bridget observed the scene around her as she set down the takeout. "Oh no, this must be bad. You're doing your silent observing thing, huh? You got the whole pillow-by-the-window set up and everything."

Jess shrugged her shoulders and got out a couple plates. She hadn't thought she was hungry, but takeout from one of SF's best Thai restaurants sounded like exactly what she needed.

"I don't know how to explain it, Bridge. The thing is, everything on paper is going great. More than great, actually. The Jumbl project is almost complete. My dating life … well, first of all, it even exists. But second of all, it's going great. Jack and I had a wonderful time in Petaluma. He … he wants to be my boyfriend." Jess could barely get the words out. It was different having to say it out loud to someone else.

Bridget was astute enough to know not to push this point just yet. "Okay, so what's the problem?"

Jess handed Bridget a plate. "Well, today I found out that I won the Aquarium of the Bay contract." Bridget gasped and was about to say something, but Jess stopped her. "No, I know that it's a great thing, and I'm happy for me, too. But honestly, even though I know I should be excited, all I can think about is how much there is to do. They want me to meet with them later this week! But I need every spare second I can to finish this Jumbl project. The deadline is just so tight. I only have two more weeks until the soft opening, and the deadline seems to be the only thing that Donathan actually cares about!"

"So, tell them that you're finishing up this project and ask if you can push the meeting." Bridget scooped out some pad see ew. "I mean, they have to understand that you weren't just sitting around and waiting for their call, right?"

Jess considered that. "I guess I could, but I don't know. I'm still growing into this role, and I'm worried that a more seasoned designer would know how to handle this. I can't imagine Rebecca telling a new client that they'd just have to wait for her to get around to them. She'd send someone over. Except I don't have anyone who could do that. I mean, maybe I could send Moira, but …"

Bridget placed her hand on Jess's. "Hey, it's okay, Jess. It was just a suggestion. It wasn't intended to stress you out even more." Bridget grabbed a couple skewers of chicken satay and handed Jess the box. "So, you're at the top of your game, both personally and professionally, and realizing it's way too much for one person to handle all at once."

Jess took the box of satay. "Basically. Crap, when you put it that way, I think I maybe just sound whiny."

Bridget smiled. "Well, a little. But I'm not going to minimize it like that. Success can be really stressful and uniquely challenging for the reason you just expressed, that you don't *feel* like you can complain about it. And then it just gets all bottled up inside and then one day you have a nervous breakdown." Bridget paused. "Sorry, I don't think that's your trajectory. Just thinking of a couple lawyers I know."

"Yeah, thanks for that." Jess put a few skewers on her plate and made her way to the dining table. "What am I going to do?"

Bridget sat down next to her. "What do you want to do?"

Jess took a bite of pad see ew as she thought about it. "Besides have another bite of this? I don't know. I have to say, whining about things helps a little bit."

Bridget laughed as she ate some Satay. "Mmm, that's good. Well, Jess, I know you *can* do it. *That* I'm not worried about at all. Whether you *want to,* though, that's a different question. Maybe you don't really want to go it alone. Maybe you thrive best in partnership."

Jess scowled at her. "Jeez, Bridge, okay we all know you're pro Jack and pro me dating. You already gave me the Mom's-story-is-not-all-that-meets-the-eye lecture, okay?"

"Okay, okay, seems like I struck a nerve …" Bridget's shoulders looked tense.

"Sorry," Jess replied. "I shouldn't have snapped at you just now. I'm not handling this stress well."

Bridget nodded slowly. "It's okay, Jess. I've been there. But—and this is not to put pressure on you at all—but it might be worth considering whether the route that you have planned out for you, where you're putting so much pressure on yourself, like this project defines you, is really what fits you now, with your life and business at the place that they're at. It's a good thing to revisit, periodically, whether the way that we're living our lives reflects where we're at as people. Because we grow, and we change, and it helps when life matches that.

"Speaking of which," Bridget continued, "and I hesitate to do bring this up when you're stressed and have a sharp skewer in your hand, but did you get a chance to talk to Mom?"

"Right, that," Jess ate the last piece of chicken off her skewer. "Wow, that *is* good. Okay, okay. Yes, I did, when I went home. And you're right; it's more complicated than I thought. And you're right; it gave me a lot to think about. But the fact is that her career would be in a different place if she'd made different choices. Unlike her, I'm not disillusioned with my career, far from it, and the thought of having to give it all up? I'm not ready for that in any way, shape, or form." She shook her head. "Yeah, I don't know what to do."

"Well, Jess—" Bridget grabbed the last piece of satay over Jess's protests. "Hey, I'm your big sister, *and* I brought this here!" At Jess's sad face she ripped off half and gave it to her. "You are the absolute worst. *As I was saying,* I think you have a really neat story going on for yourself over there about dating and what it means to have it all and how you define success. But I think the truth is that you're making it all about Jack when it isn't all about Jack. Okay, okay, I know you're talking about being busy generally. But the Jumbl project will come together. You'll put off the Aquarium of the Bay for two weeks. Yes, you *can* squeeze in one meeting, despite how busy you think you are. And as for Jack? He seems like a good guy who would totally get it if you were busy for a couple weeks. So, what I'm really wondering is, what are you actually afraid of, and why is it so important to you to keep denying how you feel about Jack?"

Jess was taken aback by Bridget's words. She'd always been direct, for better or worse. This time, Jess was worried that Bridget was uncomfortably close to the truth. "I don't know, Bridge. I honestly don't."

"Well, you better figure it out. Because you're becoming a big deal, little sis, and I hope that whatever story you have going on in your mind telling you you don't deserve it doesn't hold you back." Bridget pushed her plate away and took her hands to her belly. "I am so full. I honestly could keep eating, but it would be a terrible idea. Can we go for a walk or something?"

Jess shook her head. Only Bridget could drop some serious insight at the same time that she ate herself to the point of discomfort. "Sure, I'll grab a jacket."

Chapter 27

THE FOLLOWING DAY AT WORK WAS CHAOTIC. JESS HAD TAKEN Bridget's words to heart and realized that, even though she *felt* too busy, she *could* squeeze in a meeting with the Aquarium of the Bay people Friday, which would buy her time until Jumbl finished in the now less than two weeks remaining. She'd have to let Brian know that she wouldn't really be able to dive in for a couple weeks and hope that he'd be understanding. Having too much business was a new problem for her to have to tackle, and she hated letting people down.

Even assuming Brian's understanding, this last stretch of the Jumbl redesign would be stressful. This close to the end of a project, she tried to be on-site as much as possible, usually every day, to work on installation, any necessary construction, and the finalization of the design. Some of the contracts had had to be amended to accommodate changes in timeline or availability of product, though, and so Jess had to allocate at least a couple days to office work. It wasn't ideal.

Between her, Moira, and Charlie, at least one of them would be monitoring the progress on-site at all times, but it worried her when she couldn't be there herself. She trusted them but wished they had more seniority. She reasoned, though, that they were both gifted beyond their years and that opportunities like this were what had contributed to her own growth. And, as nervous as she was, she knew she had to learn to rely on her team for her firm to grow.

"Okay, I've got the contracts printed and reviewed. All they need is your sign-off, and then you should be ready to head to Jumbl." Charlie walked into Jess's office and handed her the papers. Charlie's confident demeanor settled Jess. It was interesting to see him in this role, which was usually Moira's. Moira, however, had been assigned to be on-site, so Charlie was tasked with helping Jess finalize things at the office.

"Thanks, Charlie. You're the best." Jess grabbed the papers and reviewed them. The numbers were astronomical. The grander her vision had become, the more costly it had become and, oddly, the more Jack had said Donathan would want it. That was the thing with these big tech companies, Jess was realizing. Expensive add-ons were seen as an investment in the brand. Innovative campuses meant attracting the best employees, and attracting the best employees meant more profit for the brand. Jess was still getting used to that mentality but appreciated that it gave her the opportunity to actualize some of her more extravagant visions.

"So, should I send them to Jack, or is that something you'd rather handle?" Charlie gave Jess a meaningful look.

Jess looked back with a scowl. "Ha ha. I think you are perfectly capable of emailing these to Jack." She handed the contract back to Charlie. "To my boyfriend," she added spontaneously.

Charlie gasped. "Are you serious? Well, not like I didn't see *that* coming. But wow, Jess, so you two are official?"

"Mm-hmm," Jess nodded. She had decided on a whim to tell him, not sure what her motivations were. Maybe it was easier to do when it was just the two of them, with Moira not there. Now that she had, though, she was excited. "Things are going really, really well. We went away this weekend, and it came up, and so I went for it.'"

"I love it!" Charlie clapped his hands together. "It has always been so crazy to me that someone who is so through and through an artist like you are is so guarded when it comes to your romantic life. Live a little, girl! You're young and hot. And no social media campus is worth prioritizing over some fine ass Jack Stinson!"

Jess laughed. "Thanks, Charlie, I'm glad you approve. I guess I should tell Moira," she added with a sigh.

Charlie tilted his head understandingly. "Yeah, I guess so. I know she didn't have the best reaction last time. But she's just protective about you. Seriously, for someone who does so much yoga as she does, she needs to chill out. I mean, shoot, I know I do, too, but that girl is tightly wound."

"I think you might be right. Guess I'll cross that bridge when I get to it." Jess stood up and gathered her things to head to the Jumbl site. "Anyway, I think we could all use a break after this is over. Lord knows I could. I almost want to tell the aquarium no, but I know that's just my desire for a week in Hawaii talking."

"Exactly. We'll get through it. And besides, you could always work from Hawaii for a couple weeks, you know. Part of the perk of being your own boss." After a moment's hesitation, Charlie reached out and gave Jess a hug. "Proud of you, Jess. The Jumbl campus is going to be amazing, truly blow people away. And Jack is lucky to have you. Take him to Hawaii with you! Damn, I bet he looks great without his shirt on."

Jess looked away, guiltily.

"I knew it!" Charlie added. "Okay get out of here before I realize I'm jealous of you."

Jess opened the door to leave. "Thanks, Charlie, for everything."

"You're welcome. Now go check on your project!" He shooed her away.

Jess made her way to the Jumbl campus. Her conversation with Charlie had made her feel lighter. She had good people in her life and a team she could trust. She felt like maybe these last couple weeks before the project finished just might be okay after all.

• • •

That reassured feeling lasted for approximately the thirty-five minutes it took her to get from her office to the campus. Once she got there, she saw Moira in a panic.

"Jess, thank God you're here." Moira ran over, clipboard in hand.

Jess was taken aback. "What's going on?" It was unusual to see Moira like this. Jess immediately became anxious.

"There's a problem with the indoor lake area. Some of the specifications were miscommunicated. To be honest, I'm not sure if it's our fault or theirs. But what was supposed to be installed tomorrow is now going to have to be installed Friday morning so that there's time to adjust the specifications. But that means that the rest of this schedule is going to be thrown off this week as well."

Jess shook her head. This was not good. "Okay, okay. So, it sounds like it's doable but just barely. Is that right?"

"Basically," Moira agreed. "But the thing is, now I think we have to double check everything else we submitted. I'm hoping that nothing else is wrong, too. It might be that this was just a mistake on the vendor's end, which I guess leads to contract renegotiation or something but at least it's on them. I also think it makes sense for us to revisit the installation schedule and see if we can move things around to not be so screwed come Friday."

"Agreed," Jess said. "Crap!" she exclaimed. "I just remembered I have that Aquarium of the Bay meeting Friday too, so I have to be gone at least half of the day."

Moira went pale. "Is there any way you can move it? That is … that is not ideal."

Jess shook her head. "I don't think I can. It was challenging to schedule, and I don't think it's a great look to have finished scheduling something just this morning and then to have to reschedule a couple hours later because there's some chaos going on with my current project."

"Right, right ... Well, I don't know, I guess we'll have to try to see if people can come Friday evening or something. I don't know what else to do."

Jess hesitated. She was supposed to go to Jack's Friday evening. But what was she thinking? How could she even imagine bailing out on Friday when all this was happening? She'd have to cancel, and he'd have to understand.

A nagging voice inside of her reprimanded that it was thoughts like this that had created this kind of problem in the first place. The old Jess, the pre-Jack Jess, would never have let something like this happen. She thought of how many nights recently she had put her laptop away earlier than she would have normally, or asked Moira and Charlie to take over a job that she usually would have handled, so that she could spend time with Jack. Even this last weekend in Petaluma had been an unjustifiable decadence, her already flimsy excuse of antique shopping looking more and more pathetic with each second the consequences she was now facing were sinking in.

"Okay, we'll do what we have to do, I guess." Jess put her hands on her hips and tried to monitor her breath so that the now-crippling weight on her chest didn't lead her to melt down in front of Moira. Moira had been warning her the entire time about the impact that dating Jack could have. Jess couldn't let on that the situation was breaking her down. "Okay, plan for today. I'm going to take a look around here and see that everything else is on track.

Then you and I will go through the schedule to see what can be modified. Then we'll look at our other specifications to make sure there's nothing else wrong. Sound good?"

"Okay, works for me," Moira said. "I'm going to, I don't know, go for a walk or something. I need to do some deep breathing. At least we're already at the lake."

• • •

By the time Jess got home that evening, she was exhausted. She and Moira had reworked the entire schedule, which had involved coordinating with multiple vendors and seeing if they could make changes to their schedules as well. Most had been able to accommodate, but some had not. It looked like they would end up working Saturday, which meant that certain vendors would charge extra, which meant that she'd have to run the additional costs by Donathan and explain what had happened. It was a nightmare.

And thoughts of how she was at fault began to run through her head at an extraordinary pace. She wasn't her usual self, because of Jack, because she'd let herself become distracted, because she'd decided that the only thing in her life that had ever meant anything to her was worth losing. She tried to calm herself by looking at the sky, but she'd gotten home so late that it was already dark, and that, combined with the extremity of the guilt Jess felt, meant that she couldn't find the comfort she usually did when she let her eyes scan the expanse.

As she sat by her bay window, she heard her phone buzz. Jack was calling her. She hit the silent button. He was the last person she wanted to talk to right now. What would she say? "Hey, this day has been exhausting because the project I'm working on, which is also, by the way, the project you're supervising, is kind of falling apart less than two weeks from the deadline, and at this point I'm wondering why I thought it was ever realistic that I could take on something this size?" Jess heard another buzz indicating that she had a voicemail. She turned the phone on Do Not Disturb and tossed it to the couch.

Maybe this situation was all because of Jack. It wasn't his fault, *per se*; that wouldn't be fair. At the same time, Jess couldn't help but think that if she hadn't been navigating bringing this person into her life, this wonderful and glorious and sexy but altogether distracting person into her life, then this wouldn't have happened. She and Moira had rechecked the faulty specifications and found that they sent them out correctly, so she assumed there had been some mistake on the vendor's end. But still, Jess usually triple checked everything to make sure things like a vendor's error didn't slip through the cracks, and she hadn't this time. She hadn't been as careful as she usually was, rationalizing the time she spent with Jack by telling herself that she was probably overcautious and needed to loosen up. Now, as a result, everything was coming apart at the seams. It was a terrible feeling.

Jess went over and grabbed the phone. It had been a little rash to toss it, even though it had felt good at the time. She listened to Jack's message. "Hey, Jess, calling to see how your day went. I know you were on-site today to make sure everything was on track. I'm sure it all went well, knowing you, but I wanted to hear how it was anyway. Been thinking about how great our weekend was. Call me when you can."

The weekend—she couldn't believe it was just yesterday that they had said goodbye to each other. It felt like a week ago.

Jess put the phone down. She didn't know what to do about Jack. He wasn't a bad guy, not at all. But the timing might just not be right on this one. Today was a disaster, but it was fixable. But what if something else went wrong, and next time it was worse? Jess didn't know if she was ready to take that chance. She had no idea what to do about Jack. All she knew was that she was tired, had made about a million decisions that day, and couldn't make any more.

She drafted a text back. *Hey, thanks for calling. Had an exhausting day and going to bed. Will catch you up later. Had a good weekend, too.* She felt a little abrupt in her text but didn't have the capacity to think about it more. She quickly pressed send and then got up to go to bed. She'd think about what she needed to do tomorrow.

Chapter 28

JESS WAS LISTLESS THROUGHOUT THE WEEK. SHE MADE THE NECessary changes to the schedule—thank God for Moira and Charlie—coordinating with different vendors and thanking everyone for their flexibility. There had been a few more hiccups throughout the week but nothing explosive. Those hiccups, though, had caused further delay and further readjustment. It was challenging. It took everything she had to not break down. This was her dream project, her big break, and here she was scrambling at the last minute to pull it all together. She felt like an amateur masquerading as a professional, sloppy. Jess moved on autopilot from one project to the next all week. By the time Friday morning came around, she barely felt like herself.

She'd talked with Jack here and there throughout the week but not much. She had explained that she would be busy and not very available this week. He'd been understanding, even if he was disappointed. Jess thought about trying to find time with him, but when she thought about how she'd fit seeing him into her schedule, she became even more overwhelmed. It was like she was watching herself in a movie, seeing her worst fear, that she'd get in a relationship and then lose everything she'd worked for, come perilously close to coming true. Taking care of herself this week was all she could manage. She couldn't be responsible for Jack too. She knew that her going MIA, the one thing she'd promised that she wouldn't do, would have consequences, but she couldn't worry about them right now. They'd have to talk after all this was over and then, she guessed, to see where they landed and go from there. There was no other choice.

Jess got to the office Friday morning to prepare for her meeting at the Aquarium of the Bay. She tried to focus, but her mind was racing. She ran through the designs she'd put in the pitch but felt detached from them. She couldn't remember why she had thought they were good. She couldn't believe that the people at the aquarium had picked her proposal. It seemed so ordinary and empty now. She pushed herself away from her desk. This was going nowhere. She felt completely disconnected from the design, left with little confidence after a brutal week.

Just then, Jack texted, *Hey stranger, sorry this week has been crazy. Dinner tonight to relax?*

Jess felt nothing at the text, like she was experiencing herself receiving it but from a distance, not engaged with her own body or her own life. Dinner … It vaguely dawned on her that Jack wanted to get dinner. It was a simple request, and yet she had no idea what to say. Odds were that she wouldn't she even have time to get dinner, given that she had to monitor additional installation tonight at the site. Her stomach sank imagining what new disasters could emerge today on-site while she was at the meeting at the aquarium. Even if they did get dinner, Jess couldn't imagine why anyone would want to be around her right now. She felt barely human, disconnected from herself, heartbroken and overwhelmed and numb. This version of herself wasn't who Jack wanted to be with. The Jess he'd gotten to know was inspired and courageous, able to see the world in a certain way and to communicate the essence of what she saw into her work. This person, whoever she was now, was no good for anyone.

Hey there, she watched herself write back. *Raincheck? Thinking today is going to be another killer.*

:-(okay. Hope it goes better than you think it will. Miss you.

Jess put the phone down. With a sigh, she returned to her presentation. She was going to have to pull through, again, to make it work no matter what. She was used to this, being alone, having only herself to rely on. She was the only one who could do it, so she would. She dug deep and tried to find some of that inspiration that had won her the aquarium project in the first place. She muscled her way into finding something close. Looking at her designs now was like running into an ex. She recognized them, knew they had mattered to her at one point, but felt disconnected from them, like the person she'd been when she created them was no more. She hoped that she was able to seem excited about them during the meeting.

She called Moira and Charlie in for a morning meeting to run through the plan for Jumbl for the day. To her relief, they were both organized and ready. Moira had a set plan for handling everything that day, and Charlie had been in contact with those vendors who needed to be on-site today to make sure that they would be ready and available.

"Okay, looks like we're all set, at least as much as we can be," Jess said. "I really can't thank you both enough for all of this. I …" she rested her head on her hand, "I really don't know what I would do without you."

Moira placed her hand gently on Jess's shoulder. "Hey, Jess, it's going to be okay. You know that, right?" Jess nodded slowly but without enthusiasm. "This whole week is a nightmare; that's sure as hell true," Moira continued. "But in the grand scheme of things, it's just a week, *maybe* two, and then it's over and you'll forever be associated with this fantastic design. Because it is fantastic; it really is. And I hope you know that."

Jess looked up, the beginnings of tears in her eyes. "Thanks, Moira. I really needed to hear that. I … Some part of me knows that you're right. But I'm so tired and it's so much, and I can't believe I need to be on and selling myself to new clients today. I feel completely spent."

"Of course, you do, honey." Charlie leaned over and gave her a hug. "Of course, you do. You're pushing yourself to new limits. It's impossible for that not to feel scary. But Moira is absolutely right. This week is going to suck, and then it's over. And that tired-ass, janky aquarium is going to be so, so lucky that you pumped some life back into it!"

Jess laughed and wiped a small tear from her eye. "Thanks, Charlie. And you too, Moira." She took a deep breath and sat up straight. "Okay, time for this meeting. Time to show that 'tired-ass, janky aquarium' who's boss."

She packed up to leave amid Moira and Charlie's encouragement. It had helped immensely to have her pep talk with them, to have some laughter remind her of what it was like to feel something, anything. She just needed to get through today and then one more week, and then she could collapse.

Her mind briefly scanned to Jack. He was a problem that she would deal with later. Yes, later—that was as good a time as any.

Chapter 29

THE MEETING AT THE AQUARIUM OF THE BAY WAS WRAPPING UP.

"Jess, this design looks great!" Brian stood up to shake her hand. "You've really impressed us both."

Danielle Johnson, Head of Marketing, joined in Brian's praises. "Couldn't agree more, Jess. I think your vision is exactly what we need to revamp our image and take this place into the future. Can't wait for you to start."

Jess turned to shake Danielle's hand. "Great to get to know you both even more. I am very excited to be part of the aquarium's revitalization. Like I said, this place was special to me when I was a child, and I can't wait to see how the new design helps inspire a whole new generation."

"Happy to hear you say that," Brian said as Jess shut down her laptop. "We were already leaning towards your design after your pitch, but then when Jack let me know that you had a personal connection to the aquarium, it became even more clear that you were the one to do the redesign."

Jess looked up from her computer. "Jack talked to you?"

"Mm-hmm. Maybe a month or so ago? He told me about how you two are working on the Jumbl redesign together and how fantastic the space is going to look. 'Revolutionary, even for tech,' I think is what he said. I knew we had to bring that same energy to the aquarium."

Jess felt the blood drain out of her face and buried herself in the process of packing up to avoid letting them see her expression. "That's great," was all she could find the strength to say. It was all too much. The mishaps with the Jumbl project, all of which she felt responsible for, the news that she was suddenly the subject of SF gossip, and now this, that Jack had been involved in her obtaining the commission from the aquarium?

"Is something wrong, Jess?" Danielle tilted her head curiously. "You look a little pale."

"I'm fine," Jess said as pleasantly as she could. She picked up her portfolio and mustered up the energy to face them. "Ate something that didn't sit right with me, I think, but I feel okay. I'm so grateful to you both for putting your trust in Anicca. We'll make this place something unforgettable."

"I have no doubt," Brian replied. "We'll send you over the formal proposal and plan to touch base after you and your team have had a chance to review it. I'm sure there will need to be modifications, but with any luck, we'll be able to start soon. I'm sure your plate is filling up."

"You have no idea," Jess said, more sincerely than was possibly appropriate given that she was trying to convey an air of capability to her new clients. But the shock of Jack's involvement was throwing her off kilter. "But nothing more important than this," she added with what she hoped was reassuring confidence.

They parted ways after a few more optimistic exchanges, and Jess immediately took an Uber over to the Jumbl site. Her mind raced the entire ride, wondering what Jack had said, wondering why he hadn't told her anything about his meeting with Brian. Above all was the horrible thought that maybe she had only gotten the commission *because* of Jack. Moira had been worried that people would assume Anicca got the Jumbl job because of Jess's relationship, and while that fortunately didn't seem to be the case, they could say something similar about the aquarium.

What made it even worse was Jess's sneaking suspicion that any gossip of that sort would be right. She was glad the meeting was over. It had gone well, she could tell, but inside, she'd felt like a mess. She knew what she was capable of and knew that the designs that she had delivered weren't it, even if they had been good enough. By some miracle, she'd managed to impress Brian and Danielle, but she knew she could do more. She recalled that morning preparing for the meeting, reviewing her designs and wondering why they had chosen her. Now it all seemed to make sense. They'd chosen her not because of what she could do but who she was doing.

Jess headed straight to the site, not even bothering to stop at the office beforehand. When she arrived, Charlie had a fake smile plastered to his face. It was troubling.

"Charlie, what is going on? That smile is terrifying." Jess approached him cautiously, almost superstitiously, as though approaching him too quickly would make bad news come true.

Charlie's smile faded. "Okay, it's really not a big deal, Jess. It's really not. One of the vendors that we rescheduled didn't fully get the memo on the reschedule, and so instead of coming this morning, they're due here at about 4:00 p.m. So, we should plan on a late night."

Jess's shoulders slumped. "Okay, well first, please don't freak me out like that unless it's something really huge, okay? Second, well, we knew we'd have to be there at least a part of tonight, and now, I guess even longer. At least it's not worse news."

"That's how Moira and I were hoping you'd take it!" Charlie clapped his hands in relief. "It'll be fine. We'll get some delicious takeout and put some music on or something. Did your meeting go well?"

"Yes, it did." Jess put her portfolio down. She hoped Charlie wouldn't ask for more details. Jess wasn't sure she could recap the meeting and avoid mentioning the likelihood of Jack's involvement, which felt too raw to share. "But maybe I can catch you up later? Seems like there's a ton going on."

"Sure. Glad it went well. Not surprised, but glad."

After getting a quick update on what was happening on-site and mapping out the day's agenda with Charlie, Jess sent a quick text to Jack. *Another long night ahead. Definitely a no on dinner. Another time.*

Jess set the phone down. The truth was, it was convenient to have an excuse not to see him that night. She was confused after this week, overwhelmed, and angry. She didn't know what Jack had told Brian or why he had even needed to say anything at all.

Maybe he knew that she wouldn't get the commission without his help. The thought was sickening.

No, seeing Jack would have to wait. She needed more time to think about things. Jack was great, she knew that, a total catch. But this news felt like an invasion. Jack had overstepped his boundaries, and even though Jess imagined he'd have some excuse or maybe was "just trying to help," it upset her all the same, not to mention the pervasive feeling that, if she hadn't been so distracted by her new relationship, her designs would have been better in the first place, and he wouldn't have felt compelled to step in.

It was a bitter end to an already terrible week. The error of this week, although small in the grand scheme of things, triggered a deep fear within her. The whole reason that this week had gone off track was because she had been prioritizing her time with Jack over her career. She didn't know how to handle it, hadn't had time to process what she was feeling. A combination of anxiety and dissociation had fueled her through the week, and while she appreciated whatever it was in her that compelled her to push through, those same things made her completely unavailable for connection to Jack.

She'd responded by numbing out to him, avoiding him to the extent she could, and being distant when they were in contact. She knew she was pushing him away, but she didn't know how badly she should feel about it. She'd promised not to disappear on him again, but she couldn't help it. She had no idea what to say to him, and doing the work of being transparent with him only mattered if they were going to be together, which after this week seemed less and less appealing. Moreover, he would need to understand that her being less responsive during one of the craziest weeks of her life wasn't the same as disappearing. She did plan to talk to him, at some point. It was important that he understand that and be willing to give her the space she needed to finish this project without taking everything personally.

Jess walked into the cafeteria area and looked favorably upon the progress that had been made there: shades of green were thoughtfully mixed on the walls around her, moss mingling with pine and the occasional flicker of gold to evoke the radiance of the lake. She'd had to call in a favor from a local artist she hadn't worked with since Unoa to get the look she wanted, but now that Jess could see it, it was better than she'd even imagined it. Serene energy surrounded her. The water of the lake circulated around the room through an elaborate series of half-pipes constructed from native wood, perfectly complementing the green background and the hints of blues that Jess had interspersed into the furniture and décor. It was reminiscent of the lake without being gauche. Jess remembered why this room had spoken to her so immediately. The energy of the lake moved through the space, changing yet unchanging, in that ancient rhythm that the water understood. It grounded her in a way she hadn't known she had needed. This, *this,* was her passion: design, art, her connection to the earth, to the subtle language of life energy that she felt deeply resonant with. She'd fallen away from her path with her new relationship, and she missed it. This was what called her back, time and time again. This was what fed her soul and nourished her being.

She closed her eyes and let herself expand into it.

• • •

Jess finished packing up around eight thirty that night. It was late but earlier than she'd expected to go home. She was going to have to come in over the weekend and figured she'd spare what she could of this night for some rest. She ordered an Uber to take her to her apartment, but as she waited for it to arrive, she changed her mind. She wanted to see Jack. She needed to tell him that this was not working.

She updated the address in her Uber order and sent a text to Jack letting him know she was coming by. She felt horrible. He would probably be excited to get that text. But Jess wasn't coming to get dinner or relax on the couch or have sex. She was coming because she needed to tell him … what? The hours since her meeting at the aquarium had given her space from the news of Jack's involvement, but she still felt betrayed, about what, though, she wasn't sure. Maybe that he hadn't told her about what he had said to Brian. Or maybe, worse still, that he hadn't believed in her.

But the hours since the meeting had also solidified her resolve. She had to tell Jack that this wasn't working out. It wasn't the time in her life to be with someone. She'd made a promise to Moira, to everyone, to herself, to choose Anicca if she ever had to make the choice. If this whole week hadn't been a demonstration that she needed to choose, she wasn't sure what would be. Jumbl and the aquarium were only the beginnings of a chaotic few years ahead of her. Whatever they had had been nice while it lasted, but it wasn't sustainable long term. It was better, Jess tried to convince herself, to end things now before things got ugly.

She arrived at Jack's apartment after letting the doorperson—she still hadn't adjusted to that—know where she was headed.

Jack opened the door wearing a casual white t-shirt and pajama bottoms. He looked excruciatingly handsome, and it broke Jess's heart that she was going to have to say goodbye to him. He went in to give her a hug as she came in, but she resisted, slowly shaking her head and not making eye contact.

"Jack, we need to talk," she said as she moved to the sofa.

Jack joined her. "Okay … Should I be worried?"

Jess tried to smile. She wanted to reassure him, badly, that it was all going to be okay, but she couldn't. She wasn't here because it was all going to be okay. She was here because it wasn't okay, hadn't been okay, and needed to change.

"I know I've been distant—" she started.

"It's okay," Jack interrupted. "Don't get me wrong. I've missed seeing you this week. But I get that you're going through hell with the Jumbl project."

Jess looked up at him and saw the understanding in his face. It was devastating. She almost wanted him to be a jerk, to be resentful of her having to work this week. That he was so kind and patient almost made what she had to do worse.

"Thanks, Jack. That's very kind of you. I feel like I don't deserve it." Jess wiped the beginnings of a tear from her eye before she went on. "I had my meeting at the aquarium today."

"I know! I've been waiting to hear how it went."

"Did you say something to Brian about me?" Jess didn't fight to hide the betrayal in her expression. She was falling apart from within and without and past the point of caring enough to soften what she was feeling.

Jack's expression was puzzled. "Nothing worth mentioning. I mean, I speak to him periodically because my family is a donor, but those conversations are usually about how much the Stinsons are planning to give that year. I think in this last conversation he asked about Jumbl. I guess he found out I was involved somehow, and I think I probably said something like you were doing a good job, but honestly, Jess, it must have been at least a month ago, and it was so minor that I probably forgot about it."

Jess focused on him to see if he was telling the truth. His energy felt open, sincere. There was a part that felt guarded but not in a way that conveyed dishonesty. It felt more like Jack was hurt. He sensed that he and Jess were not okay, and that hurt him. Jess felt some of her anger subside, but some remained.

"You should have told me. People are already talking about you and me dating. And now, if word gets out that you were in any way involved with Anicca getting the aquarium commission, people are going to assume that I didn't deserve it."

Jack took a deep breath. "Okay, right. I get that. Look, I'm sorry I didn't say anything. It seemed like nothing at the time. And as for people talking about us dating ... People have been gossiping about me my whole life. I mostly try to tune it out, but yeah, I can understand how that would take some getting used to for you, part of the wonderful package of dating Jack Stinson. Let me know what I can do. Do you want me to say something to Brian?"

"No!" Jess exclaimed. "That would only make it worse." She ducked her head into her hands. "There's nothing you can do, Jack. It just is. It's not just people talking about us, not just people assuming things about me and Anicca. It's more than that." She looked up at him. "This week, everything went haywire with Jumbl. I didn't tell you, and I guess I probably should have, but I was stressed, and embarrassed. And you're my boyfriend," she paused, the words sticky in her mouth, "but you're also the client. And I wanted things to be under control, and it took everything I could do this week to get them that way.

"Everything is back on track, thankfully. But Jack, it was *this close* to going the other way. And then we wouldn't have been ready in time, and then everyone would have shown up to that opening and seen what a colossal failure I am. What Anicca is," she corrected herself.

There, the words were out. Jess felt herself dissociate, operating in a fugue state where nothing mattered. The same autopilot that had gotten her through the week was coming into play now, and Jess let it happen. Some small part of her suspected what she was doing would have been too painful had she been more present. This numbing was protective, soothing, consequence-free— exactly what she needed.

Jack shook his head. "That's exactly the problem, isn't it? You see yourself as only as good as what you've achieved. You *are* Anicca, Jess. This whole thing about you needing to prove something just to fit in … It's destroying you. Trust me, I get it. You think I didn't feel the same way about ShineStar at some point, like I needed to prove that I was successful on my own merits to be seen as a person and not just some trust-fund kid? I'll let you in on a secret. That feeling never goes away, no matter how much you achieve. The only reason it ever shifts is because you decide it needs to, because the part of you that wants to feel free of that burden becomes stronger than the part that's afraid of letting it go."

He was impatient. Jess wasn't used to seeing him this way. Through the haze of her dissociation, she registered only that, if he was getting upset, something bad must be happening.

"You and I have something real, or at least I thought so," he continued. "But I guess if one offhand comment to Brian and one off week at work is enough to call everything off, then maybe I was wrong. Because that's what this is, right? You came here to break up?"

Jess nodded and looked away. A small part of Jess that was still able to feel was hurting. She pushed it away, inconvenient at a time like this. She was there to complete a task. She let herself dissociate further, now moving away from her body to hear the words come out of her mouth, barely audible. "Yes."

Jack was silent. "Okay," he said after a moment. "Okay."

Jess looked at him then and saw the devastation in his eyes. That part of her that could still feel was starting to feel more, coming dangerously close to understanding the impact of what was happening. "Okay?" she asked. "That's ... that's all you have to say?"

"What do you want me to say?" Jack questioned. "That I think you're making a mistake? That you're making the wrong choice? I don't know, Jess. I guess I assume that you're saying what you're saying because you've really thought about it. And I have no interest in trying to convince someone who doesn't want to be with me that they should be with me. I feel like this whole relationship has been me trying to convince you to give us a chance. But why? Maybe you were right. Maybe I was lying to myself. All I know is, I'm tired."

His tone had an edge to it. He was hurt, Jess could tell that. She had expected that, she supposed, but the actual witnessing of it was something different.

Jess pursed her lips and sat up. "Thanks for understanding." It was an awkward thing to say, but Jess couldn't think of anything better. "I guess this is it, then. What do you want to do about this week at work?"

Jack shrugged his shoulders. "You tell me, Jess. You're the one leading the project and the one making this decision. I'll do whatever you think is best."

It hurt to feel Jack's abruptness. He was always so sweet to her, that to feel him be short was jarring. She was beginning to understand how deeply she'd hurt him, beginning to feel some of that hurt herself around the protective edges of her dissociation. She had no use for that feeling, though, not now. Figuring out what this all meant was something that would have to wait until later. For now, she needed to be logical, put one foot in front of the other, finish what she came to do, and leave.

"I think we'll be okay having minimal contact this week. Honestly, Moira can probably catch you up on whatever you need; it's not much. And as far as the opening goes next Friday, I assume Donathan will want you there, and we'll be professional."

"Okay, sound good." Jack was distant now. Jess couldn't tell what was worse, feeling his hurt or accepting his distance.

She got up to leave, and he walked her to the door. At the door, she paused. "Jack, I'm sorry. I wish, I really wish this could be different." Tears started to form, and Jess prayed that they would go away.

"Me too, Jess. Me too."

They paused in the doorway before Jess stepped out and closed the door. She walked down and let the comforting numbness return as she waited for her Uber to arrive. Tears started to form in the car ride home as her conversation with Jack began to sink in. All these emotions were too much. Between her work stress, lack of sleep, and the emotional roller coaster of Jack, she felt herself collapsing.

She arrived at her apartment and went straight to the bedroom, not bothering to brush her teeth or wash her face. She needed her bed, right now, needed to sleep, needed to break into a million pieces. She cried as she let it all release and barely noticed when she drifted into sleep.

Chapter 30

THE NEXT FEW DAYS PASSED, AS DAYS DO. SHE AND HER TEAM HAD worked all weekend to get the project back on track, and now it was. Barring anything major happening, everything would be set for the opening that Friday. This close to the end, Jess took vague comfort in knowing that most of the tasks that could have turned south had already occurred without incident.

The time and space from Jack, coupled with the progress on Jumbl, resulted in something that felt like relief. She wasn't sure if it was pure relief—it was too emotionally complex to be that easily defined—but that pressure in her chest had lifted somewhat. By the time that Wednesday morning rolled around, she was functional enough to make coffee. It was a straightforward task, the grinding of beans and the pouring of water. It was funny, she thought, that she should be relishing in something so mundane as making coffee. But in her fragile state, having something comforting and familiar was essential. It didn't really matter what it was.

She went over to her bay window as she waited for the coffee to percolate, mentally running through her tasks for the day. She was due to be on-site in an hour, which meant no time for her to exercise. That felt fine to her. It amazingly felt fine, more than fine, to take it easy today.

Everything seemed on track with the design, and she had a glimmer of hope that things might go smoothly through the opening. She and her team would work steadily until then, but that was fine, normal for this stage of the process. There was even a part of her that was getting excited about how everything was looking. So often, artistic vision exceeded what you were able to accomplish with actual design. With this project, though, she'd come close. The campus would be peaceful and soulful while also functional. It was perfect. Donathan had seen a few of the designs but nothing close to final. She couldn't believe how sincerely he'd meant it when he said he was okay not being involved. He was set to come by Thursday, to check out the site before the opening party. She knew he'd be impressed, and the certainty of that knowledge comforted her, made her feel like herself. This work was what she was here to do. It was time to remember that.

She'd thought of Jack a few times since their breakup but hadn't reached out. True to her word, she'd had Moira deal with any last-minute logistics that needed client approval. After Friday's opening party, she and Jack would have no reason to interact. He'd be out of her life for good.

Her phone buzzed with a text from her mom. *How is the project going? You must be so excited!*

Jess replied that she was, despite the exhaustion. After she pressed send, her mom called.

"Hi Jessy, figured I'd take a chance that you were around this morning and wanted to catch you before you got busy for the day. How are you?"

"I'm fine, Mom. Tired, but fine. Starting to see the light at the end of the tunnel. How are you?"

"Good, same, boring. Catch me up? What's the latest with Jumbl, the aquarium, Jack?"

Jess felt her chest get tight at the mention of Jack. "Well, Mom, I guess, first things first, there is no more Jack. We broke up."

Diane gasped. "What happened? Are you okay? Aw, Jess."

The words of comfort from her mother brought a fresh wave of tears to Jess's eyes. "I don't know, Mom. I feel completely in over my head. I don't know what the right choice is any more."

"Aw, Jess, honey. Talk to me. I'm here for you."

Hearing those words let something inside of Jess collapse. It all came pouring out then. She told Diane what had happened, with the aquarium, with Jumbl, how she'd felt claustrophobic, like all her dreams had been crashing down around her, how she felt like she had to get back on course quickly to save them, how she'd been falling for Jack, really falling for him, and how she thought he had been, too, but how the timing wasn't right. She felt like she had this choice: either her business could thrive with her staying single, or she could let herself fall in love and watch her dreams fail.

The act of talking and crying to someone who understood and supported her pulled Jess back from her state of numbness. She was returning to herself, slowly, some warmth returning to her fingers and toes. It was an odd sensation to notice. She hadn't been aware, in her dissociation, that they were even cold.

"Jess, I'm so sorry it's been so stressful," Diane cooed. "At least it's over soon?"

"Yes, but then I start right away on the Aquarium of the Bay! If I can even go through with it. I feel like I need to redo all those designs before I proceed. I don't know, Mom." Jess let her head hang heavy. "I sometimes wonder what I was ever thinking leaving Unoa."

There it was, the grim truth. She didn't know if she could handle this. Maybe this was too much, setting out on her own. Maybe it would have been better if she had stayed put at Unoa, always playing second fiddle to Rebecca's vision but at least never having to feel like this.

"Jess, it sounds like this week has been awful, but you don't need to go down that road. You know why you left Unoa. You never were going to be what you could be if you stayed there." After a pause, Diane continued. "You know, I've been thinking about our talk since you were here a few weeks ago ... Are you afraid to be with Jack because you'll walk away from your career like I did?"

Jess began to respond but stopped. It was unusual for her mother to be so direct. She must have been thinking about this for some time. "I don't know, Mom. I think, maybe? Bridget would certainly say so. I know that you said that I have more choices and that you had other reasons for leaving medicine, but I don't know that that's true for me. It still feels like I have to choose. Even if I thought I didn't have to, this week has taught me that I do. Maybe it's easier on women now, but for me personally, I became so distracted by Jack, and I …" Jess was talking more quickly now, feeling the anxiety around the loss of Jack come up again.

"Jessy," Diane said softly, soothing some of the tension that was building within Jess, "I don't think there's anything wrong with you. The beginning of a relationship *is* distracting. And then it starts to settle, and you find your rhythm and it all works out. It sounds like Jack really understands that it's a hectic time and isn't trying to pressure you. You've always been pretty hard on yourself. Even in school, when you had all that trouble focusing, I don't think you would have had such a hard time if you'd just embraced that about yourself instead of trying to make yourself fit in. You're a special girl. Except it turns out that, like everyone else, you are capable of getting swept off your feet. You'll land soon, and you'll be happy he's by your side."

"Mom," Jess squeaked almost inaudibly, "do you think I made a mistake?"

She heard her mom inhale. "I don't know that I can answer that for you, honey. Do you think you love him?"

Jess let the words move through her tears. "I think I do. Every positive thing that has happened this week, I've wanted to tell him about. And I keep picking up my phone and wondering if he's texted, but he hasn't. But I don't text him. And I feel sad. It's like everything is now working out with Jumbl, but I have no one to share it with."

"Mm-hmm," Diane soothed. "Jess, maybe you should reach out to him. Maybe it's not too late to tell him how you feel. Everyone does things they regret sometimes. We all hurt each other in relationships, and we have to hope that the other person understands."

"Even if I did, even if we talked things through, the problem is still there. I have no idea how being with him these next few years could possibly work. No, I have to accept that Anicca has to be my life right now. It's just, for the first time in my life, I feel sad about it."

Diane was silent as she let Jess cry into the phone. After a bit, she spoke, hesitantly. "Jess, I don't know if that's for you to figure out, all alone. If Jack cares about you like you do about him, he'll want to support you in your career. And, somehow, you will both figure it out. I know you're learning from this experience, but I'm not sure you're learning the right thing. Doing everything all on your own doesn't seem to be working for you. Maybe the lesson isn't that you have to keep doing it all on your own and cutting others out. Maybe the lesson is that you like having support, and that that's okay. You *are* taking on some big projects, and hopefully more of them to come. It's okay to want support for that."

Jess looked out her window for a moment. Diane's words rang true. She *did* want support. It was so obvious once someone said it. Jess wondered why that idea had felt so much like failure before. "I have a lot to think about, I think."

"I think you do. You'll make the right choice. My sweet Jess, you always know what to do when you listen to yourself. Even when you were small, you knew who you were. I always loved that about you. It's only when you tried to change who you were for someone or something else that you had trouble."

"You're right. I just have to remember that."

"I think you will. I love you, Jess. Let me know how it goes this week, okay?"

"Okay, I love you, too, Mom. Goodbye."

Jess hung up the phone and looked out her window again. Her mom was right. Maybe the answer wasn't that she needed to dig in her heels and do everything on her own. Doing that felt terrible. She was becoming worried that Jack's words were true and that needing to prove herself in order to belong was an endless cycle that would never feel complete. Belonging didn't feel like the right goal if, in the end, she would still be alone.

The possibility of another option relieved some of the angst that Jess was feeling. Maybe she *could* get some support. Maybe that wasn't failing. Maybe that was what she needed to succeed.

Jess scanned the sky and watched as it changed color, a darker blue to the west of the city as it subtly became lighter towards the east, in the direction of the sun. She saw the sunlight reflect off the different buildings around her, highlighting the vibrant Victorians that gave the city the character she loved. The city felt alive, the dance of energy from one part to another creating this electricity that woke her up. Jess felt some clarity come to her through that vibration.

Everything seemed so simple. The sun was beautiful on its own, but the interplay of the sunlight with the trees and the clouds and the buildings made it even more interesting. It was okay that she didn't want to work alone. It was easy to admit, once she let herself. She didn't want to work alone, and the best part was, she didn't have to.

For the first time in a few weeks, Jess felt present. Her body was hers again. Her life was hers, based on her choices and her dreams.

Jess picked up her phone again. She had a couple very important phone calls to make and didn't have any time to waste.

Chapter 31

"Jessica Tyler, FaceTiming me on a Sunday morning? To what do I owe the pleasure?"

Jess shifted to make herself more comfortable. "Hi, Rebecca. Hope you're doing okay. Is now a good time to talk?"

"Sure; now works. What's up? Heard you got the aquarium project, by the way. Congratulations!"

"Thanks!" Jess exhaled as she prepared to speak. She knew she could trust Rebecca, but that didn't necessarily make what she was about to say easier. "That's actually what I'm calling about. I was wondering if you'd like to collaborate on it."

"Are you serious?" Rebecca asked. "Jess, not that I'm not honored, but what's going on?"

"Don't worry; everything is okay. It's just," Jess paused, "I miss collaborating with you. I started Anicca because I needed to go out on my own, and I'm happy I did, except now that I'm here, I realize ... it's kind of lonely." Jess took another breath before continuing. "There's so much to be done for the aquarium. I keep second-guessing my designs, and even on days that I like them, the thought of executing them feels daunting after the Jumbl project. I'd rather not do it all alone."

"Jess," Rebecca said, "I get it. Actually, of all people, I probably get it more than most. Being a creative is hard. The second-guessing, the pressure to come up with something as good as the last time, the struggling with what you want and what the client wants and what is possible—it can all be very isolating. Eventually you get to the point where, even though you know you *could* create designs all on your own, you don't want to. There's no joy in it, or at least not the type of joy that you crave … Did you know that's why I expanded Unoa?"

"What do you mean? I thought Unoa had always been your firm." Jess was surprised to hear that Rebecca once felt like she did. She always seemed so confident and independent.

"It has; it has. But it used to be smaller, just me. Believe it or not, I can be a little bullheaded."

They looked at each other seriously for a second before bursting into laughter.

"You, bullheaded?" Jess played. "No way."

"Ha ha, aren't you such a comedian this morning!" Rebecca shook her head but had a smile on her face. "*Anyway*, yes, so we both know I have that tendency to me. When I first started Unoa, I thought it would be perfect, just me, no one else, doing things my way. And then, after a few years, I looked around and no one else was there. I had everything my way, but no one to share the joy with. I wasn't doing my best work. I benefited when I had others to bounce ideas off of, to take my idea to the next level. That's why I always appreciated having you there, by the way. I always thought you were incredibly gifted at seeing what a design needed to become even better."

"Thanks, Rebecca. But then why didn't you let me have full control over some projects?"

"Hey, I said I liked to collaborate, not that I wasn't protective of my own brand. And maybe a bit controlling too. But in this industry, your reputation is all you have. You can't afford to let something slip. It's a ton of pressure."

"Yes, it really is." Jess thought before continuing. "Would that work, then, us collaborating? Wouldn't the same desire to control your brand come in? I want a real collaboration, Rebecca, different from Unoa. Equals."

"I think I'd like that, too. No, your being at a different firm now means that *your* firm's reputation is on the line, so it's different. The pressure's not all on me, so then neither is all the control. Maybe you having your own firm is what we needed to work together all along. I have to say, Jess, this is a real honor, you asking me to work with you on the aquarium. It means a lot that you would want to do this together."

"Rebecca …" A series of emotions overcame Jess, a blend of gratefulness and relief and excitement and hope. "Rebecca, I would honestly love it. It would feel amazing to work together again."

"As equals," Rebecca added.

"As equals." Jess smiled. "Okay, I'm finishing up the Jumbl project. The opening is on Friday. It's kicking my ass, by the way.

But after that, I'm turning to the aquarium. I'll figure out how to let them know about the collaboration. We'll have to work out details. I'm sure they won't want to pay more, but we can come up with something that will work."

"Sounds good to me. Good luck this week. Ugh, the last week of a major project. Not jealous."

"You know, if I were you, I wouldn't be, either." Jess laughed. "Thanks, Rebecca, for everything."

"You're welcome. And thank you too."

They hung up. For the first time since she had taken on the Jumbl project, perhaps even for the last few years since she left Unoa, she felt lighter. There had been moments where she felt less tense before, moments when she even thought she had relaxed, but now that she really did feel like she had options, she experienced a level of relaxation that she had forgotten had existed since she founded Anicca.

It was going to be okay. She was going to be okay, more than okay. Why had she thought she needed to do this all by herself, as if she had something to prove? The knowledge that she *could* do it alone, that she didn't *need* someone else to succeed, took the pressure off. She had nothing more to prove now. She *wanted* to work with Rebecca because doing so felt better. She was collaborating because she wanted to, not because she had to, and having that choice was liberating.

She decided to sneak in a run. She didn't have much time before she headed to the campus, but she hadn't gone running in a while. It felt important to be outside. Working with Rebecca had been the right call. She felt excited about the aquarium project now, whereas before she had felt mostly dread and pressure. Design was something she loved, truly loved, and for these past few months, she'd forgotten that.

She laced up and headed out the door. There was one more call she had to make when she got back home. For right now, though, what she needed was to feel free. She ran up along Steiner Street in the direction of the Marina, pausing on Fulton to catch a glimpse of City Hall, one of her favorite views of the city. It felt good to be here, like she had direction again. She continued to run, taking in the character of the Victorians, the parks, the people—all the things that she had loved when she came here as a child that she still found comfort in after all these years. She ran up to Lafayette Square and then just over the hill to catch her first glimpse of the bay and the Golden Gate Bridge. She was here. She had made it. As she looked around, for the first time in a long time, she didn't feel alone at all.

Chapter 32

That Thursday, Jess anxiously checked her watch: 1:00 p.m. Donathan would be here soon.

She had sent him a text the day before inviting him over for a late lunch, and he'd agreed. Since then, she had spent what little time she could drawing some sketches to make a last-minute amendment to the design. By no small miracle, the rest of the Jumbl project had gotten back on track and was in good shape for the opening event the next day. This change would not make too much of a difference, at least not to anybody but her. She could only hope that he would agree to it.

Jess glanced at her phone again to check the time: 1:05 p.m. He was supposed to arrive at 1:30, and every minute in between now and then seemed to drag. Her nerves were almost too much to bear. To distract herself, Jess took the takeout she had ordered and laid it out by one of the tables by the lake. Finally, Jess got a text letting her know that he was there.

"Guess you wanted me to come check out where I'm putting all my money!" Donathan gave Jess a hug as she came out to greet him. "Looks great from out here. Can't wait to see what's inside!"

"Thanks for coming to meet me!" Despite her nerves, Jess could not help but be caught up Donathan's his good mood. She was reminded of how friendly and easy he was to talk to. They were a strange pair, he and Jack, Donathan's warmth to Jack's aloofness. She wondered, if they hadn't met when they were kids, would they still have become friends?

"Of course! I know I've been hands off. Well, maybe even more than that. What can I say? I stay within my zone of genius. All this design stuff? Sure, isn't it? Besides, I know Jack would tell me if there were any problems, and he hasn't, so …"

Jess walked him over to one of the outside patios. "Well, that's actually what I wanted to talk to you about. Not the design, necessarily, but Jack."

Donathan took a seat at a table overlooking the lake. "Jack? Hey, if you wanted to let me know that you're dating, don't worry. He filled me in." He looked at the scenery. "This is awesome, by the way. I think my employees might actually forgive me for the move if it means being able to look at this all day."

Jess sat down next to him. "Thanks, I'm glad you like it. The thing is, Donathan," she paused to collect herself. Talking about this with Donathan was more difficult than she imagined it would be. "The thing is, we're not dating anymore. I broke up with him."

Donathan raised his eyebrows. "You did? You dumped Jack? That's a first. Jack doesn't usually get dumped. He more does the dumping. I mean, don't get me wrong. He's not an asshole. But he knows what he wants, and when he realizes you're not it, he lets you know. He seemed to really be into you, though, more than I've ever seen him be into someone before, actually. Why'd you break up with him?"

Jess felt a pang as she heard his words. Jack had really cared about her. She had sensed that his emotions went deep, but having it confirmed by his best friend was something else. It was becoming more and more clear to her that Jack didn't open himself up to many people, and yet he had to her, and she had hurt him. The thought of his heart in pain made her heart ache too.

"That is a very good question," she said, distributing the take-out boxes. "And it's complicated to answer. Miscommunication, thinking I wanted one thing but realizing I was wrong, taking him for granted, all the reasons why we hurt people when we don't want to."

Donathan nodded thoughtfully. "Go on."

"I thought I couldn't be in a relationship and have my career grow the way I wanted it to. I panicked, basically. I was stressed and not at my best, insecure. I'm realizing, though, that maybe the choice between relationship and career isn't the one I really needed to make. Maybe it was another choice all along. Anyway, I know that sounds cryptic, but I'm still figuring it out on my end. The important thing is that I made a mistake, and I need your help fixing it."

Donathan grabbed some chopsticks as he listened to what she was saying. "Interesting. What is this, by the way?" He gestured at the boxes.

"Shanghai Dumpling King." Jess had ordered from the famous Inner Sunset dumpling spot. "Figured I needed to bribe you with dumplings to get you on my side."

"Ha, very clever. I do love that place. You've chosen your bribe wisely." He ate a dumpling while he thought. "So, the thing is, Jess, that Jack is not the type of guy who forgets things easily. I've known him a long time, and I know him maybe better than anyone in his life. He tries to come off as all cool and friendly, and he is, but he also isn't one who forgives and forgets. I don't know what went down between you two, but I know he doesn't trust people easily."

Jess sighed. "I was worried you'd say something like that. I know I've only known him a short time, but I felt like we had a strong connection. I'm hoping that will mean that he can somehow forgive me."

Donathan placed his chopsticks down, his face pensive. "Yeah, maybe, Jess, maybe. He's an odd dude. He's got some old family drama, shit about not fitting in, always ending things because he thinks people can't understand him. I mean, I don't know how much understanding it takes to get what it's like to be a privileged white guy, but that's his whole story anyway. Feels like an outsider. You seem to have really gotten to him, though. I've never really seen him be broken up with before, so I'm not sure how he will react, but my sense is that you probably hurt him pretty badly, and … I don't know, Jess, he won't just let it slide because you had some epiphany."

Jess's face dropped. She was worried that Donathan was right. "I hear that, Donathan, but … I'd like to think of it as not just 'I had some epiphany,' but I guess that's right in some sense and almost certainly how he would see it." She put her chopsticks down, not hungry anymore. "It's really not like that, though. It's not so much I had an epiphany that, wow, made me realize something. It's more like I had a kind of breakdown, and, in a super fragile state, I made a mistake, and I wish I could take it back."

Donathan was thoughtful. "I get that. Hey, Jess, you know, I've been there, too. But I have to ask, as his friend, what makes you sure it won't happen again?"

Jess had anticipated this question. Donathan, for all his friendliness, was far from naïve. Jack was his best friend, and while she sensed that Donathan truly had some empathy for where Jess was coming from, he wasn't going to help her out unless he thought it was in Jack's best interests.

"I've thought about that and what I would say if you asked me that. Please believe me when I say that I won't. I love Jack. I didn't let myself admit that before. Now that I have, everything is different."

Donathan considered her. His warm brown eyes looked into hers. Jess sensed his strong energy, wielded with so much control and discipline. This was a man who was incredibly aware of himself, had known pain, had known what it took to overcome pain, how it never left but only changed, how you grew to relate to it differently. He looked around the lake, lost in thought, before speaking. "Okay, Jess, I'm on your team. But just so it's clear, if you ever hurt him again, I will always take his side."

"I would expect nothing less," Jess agreed.

"You gonna call him up?" Donathan opened up a new box of dumplings. "You better act fast on these dumplings, by the way, because I can't guarantee that I'll leave you any."

"Thanks for the warning." Jess chuckled as she loaded a few more onto her plate, appreciating the shift in conversation. "No, I'm not going to call. I have something better in mind. But I need your help. That's another thing. I'm kind of all about asking for help these days."

"Interesting. Alright, lay it on me."

Chapter 33

FRIDAY.

The opening event.

It was here.

Jess reflected on how much had happened since her write-up in 7×7. It felt like a lifetime ago. Jumbl. Jack, the new direction of Anicca, so much had changed. She had changed. And now here she was, her design complete. She was a mix of excited and relieved, nervous and overjoyed. More than anything, though, she was ready.

It was set to be a huge event. Jess had only invited Bridget and Rebecca, as well as, of course, Moira and Charlie. Donathan, though, had hired a publicist who had invited basically every big name in the SF/Silicon Valley tech world, and most of them had said yes. Donathan, it seemed, was well liked in the industry. That didn't surprise Jess; he was one of the most likeable people she knew. Even so, his gravitas, and the number of people who would be seeing her work, was a lot to prepare herself for.

But the swarm of people who would be there wasn't what was making Jess nervous. Her nerves were about one person in particular: Jack.

They hadn't communicated since the breakup a week ago. Out of respect for him, or maybe out of embarrassment on her part, Moira had continued to be the point of contact all week. To her credit, she had not given Jess a single "I told you so" or anything resembling that. On the contrary, both she and Charlie had been nothing but kind, which had meant more to Jess than she could say. By this point in the design, though, there were really not many decisions that needed Jack's approval. Everything had been decided; now it was simply a matter of execution.

The idea of seeing Jack tonight put Jess on edge. She spent longer than usual getting ready, which involved much less of actually "getting ready" and much more of pacing around in anticipation. After what seemed like an eternity, she heard her doorbell ring and opened the door.

"Your date is here!" Bridget exclaimed, flowers in hand. "You look fantastic, by the way. Ready to go?"

Jess took the flowers and gave Bridget a hug. "Thanks, Bridge!" She ran to get a vase for the flowers. She'd asked Bridget to come take her to the opening, and, now that Bridget was here, Jess was gratified that she had asked for the support. "These flowers are gorgeous. Thanks so much for coming. I'm so anxious!"

"How could you not be? Jack's going to be there, right?"

Jess had caught Bridget up on the Jack situation during the week and had received an unsurprising response ("Well, you sure blew that one, Jess.") Bridget's directness didn't mean that she wasn't kind or caring, though, and Bridget had listened with understanding while Jess had explained what happened. She knew the plan that Jess had in store for tonight and was on board, more than on board, actually. She was thrilled to see Jess put herself out there. In Bridget's opinion, and perhaps Jess's, now, too, it was much overdue.

"He sure is." Jess put the flowers in the vase. "Okay, shall we order an Uber?"

"No need. I put in multiple stops on mine."

"Okay." Jess gave Bridget another hug. "Thanks again, Bridget, for, well, everything. Okay, let's do this."

"You're welcome. Let's go!"

• • •

Whatever Jess thought the opening would be, she hadn't imagined this. Donathan's PR team had planned a verified gala, red carpet and everything. While Jess had been aware of what the team was planning, seeing it all actualized like this was something else entirely.

Jess and Bridget gave each other a knowing glance as they emerged from the Uber. With all the hullabaloo, Jess was even more grateful that Bridget was by her side. This moment was something she wanted to share.

Jess scanned the crowd to see if she could find Jack, only to experience a combination of disappointment and relief when she didn't spot him. Perhaps it was better this way, she reasoned, to get her bearings before seeing him again. But Jack always had a way of making Jess feel comfortable, and as nervous as Jess was to see him, she craved that comfort nonetheless.

"Jess!" She heard someone call out and turned around to see Donathan. "This place looks amazing! Nothing but rave reviews so far. You've managed to do something extraordinary. Folks at Jumbl are *excited* about the move to the new campus. I didn't even think that was possible. I've been singing your praises to anyone who will listen. Everyone wants you for their projects now, too."

"Thanks, Donathan." She gave him a hug. "It means so much that you put your trust in me. You've changed my life. I hope you know that."

"Hi!" Bridget, who had been standing quietly next to Jess during the exchange, jumped in.

"Oh, I'm so sorry." Jess introduced the two of them, "Donathan, this is Bridget, my sister. Bridget, this is Donathan, the founder and CEO of Jumbl."

"Hi, Donathan, nice to meet you." Bridget shook his hand. "You seem to be quite the visionary."

"I try. Tell me about yourself," Donathan released Bridget's hand.

As they continued, Jess caught sight of Jack talking to a woman at the other end of the main lobby. She turned to Donathan and Bridget.

"Sorry, you two, I hate to be rude, but do you mind if I leave you both for a moment?"

Bridget saw Jack and looked at Jess meaningfully. "Yes, of course. Go do what you have to do."

Donathan looked to see Jack behind him in the distance. "Sure thing, Jess. Hey, whatever happens tonight, I'm always going to remember what you did for me with this project, okay? You have a friend over here."

"Thanks again." Jess braced herself. "Okay, here I go. Wish me luck."

As she made her way over to Jack, her stomach turned. A wave of worry washed over her, concern about what would happen when she saw him. He could very well want nothing to do with her. Donathan had said he wasn't sure if Jack was the forgiving type. Still, the urge to see him compelled her more than the fear of him turning away. It was time, now or never. Hopefully he understood. Hopefully he was willing to give her a second chance. But if not … at least she would know that she had tried.

"Hi," she approached him with some hesitation. He turned to see her, and her heart melted. Seeing him there, so close, made her realize she had missed him more than she even thought.

"Hi." He looked guarded, not necessarily upset to see her but protective of himself. That block in his energy that had dissipated during their relationship was back, present more than ever before, rendering him cold and a little aloof. "Jess, this is Alice. Alice, Jess. Jess is the one who designed this masterpiece."

Jess felt momentarily foolish. This could very well be his date. Jess found it hard to believe that he would do that to her, bring a date to her big event, but the possibility that he was then or could ever be with someone else caused her to almost wince in pain.

A wave of embarrassment flashed over her, and she briefly considered turning around and reaching out to Jack another time. But Jess was not here to play it safe. She had something to say to Jack, something she might never have the chance to say again, and she needed to let him know how she felt even if there was the very real possibility that she would be hurt. "Hi, Alice," she forced herself to say. "Lovely to meet you. I hate to be inexcusably rude, but I need to steal Jack away from you. Something urgent." Jess hoped that Jack would agree to come with her. Please, she silently prayed, if he had ever really cared for her, let it all not have faded now.

Jack was taken aback. He stiffened his lip slightly but didn't protest. They said goodbye to Alice and moved to where they could talk.

"So, I take it you want to talk to me?" Jack's tone was stern but not furious. Jess could work with that. "Not furious" was a good start. As for stern, well, what could she expect, knowing that any defensiveness that he now had resulted from how she had hurt him.

"Yes, I ..." Jess had thought about what she'd say, how to convey what she was feeling while also preserving some part of herself in case he had moved on. But here now, seeing him, there was no concern about any of that. There was only one concern, that he'd never know how much she cared about him, that she'd give anything to take what had happened back.

The words came straight from her heart. "I messed up. I really messed up. I got so overwhelmed, and I made a mistake. I hurt you. I'm so, so sorry."

Jack breathed in sharply. "Jess, I ... Yeah, you did. It's ... it's been a shitty week."

Jess shook her head, looking up at him, not wanting to break the eye contact that he was somehow maintaining with her. "I'm hoping that you can give me another shot. I'm hoping that you can forgive me. If you've moved on, *un*-move on. Please. If you care about me, about us, please give me another chance."

Jack broke their gaze and turned away. "I don't know, Jess. Nothing's changed, really. Your career is still at the same place it was, even busier so after tonight, I bet. And I'm still who I am, with all the baggage that comes with. Everything you said before is still true. And," he tensed, "I don't know if I can set myself up like that again."

Jess ached then with the knowledge of how much she had hurt him. He was afraid ... of her, afraid that she'd hurt him again. The truth sat with her, uncomfortable in its heaviness.

"Is Alice your date?" she asked timidly.

"Yes." Jack's tone was sharp. Seeing the hurt in her face, though, he added, "But not like that. I had to bring a plus one, and Alice has worked with me at ShineStar a long time. It's not romantic."

Emotion washed over her. He hadn't moved on. There was still a chance. "Come on, I have something to show you." She reached for his hand, and he took it, hesitantly. She led him out of the lobby and into another room, heading down a hallway as she spoke. "It's not directly an answer to your question. I'm trying to work on things, and I can tell you how. But first, I wanted you to know something." They arrived now outside of another room. "Go inside."

Jack slowly opened the door and stepped inside. It was a room painted black but with vibrant photographs on the wall and videos set up next to headphones. In the middle of the room, elevated so that the words were visible from all around, was an art piece stating "#LoveIsPermanent."

"I pulled different pictures and stories from this hashtag off Jumbl and created this room. It was something to remind the people who work here what life is all about, easy to forget in the ephemeral world of social media." Jess brought Jack over to one of the videos. On the screen was a video of Jess, paused. She lifted the headphones and handed them to Jack. "Press play," she whispered, her voice barely audible. She was exposed now, completely, and the courage of that left her with little strength left to speak more loudly.

Jack put the headphones on and paused, his finger hovering over the play button, before pressing. Once he did, the video began, and Jess's voice came in through the headphones.

"What does #LoveIsPermanent mean to me? It's funny because my whole life it meant one thing, and, now, it means something else. I'm an interior designer, and my whole aesthetic is based on Wabisabi, this idea that nothing is permanent. And really so much of life is that way; most things change. But when it comes to love? If you would have asked me six months ago, I would have probably said that love fell in that category of impermanence too, the whole fairy tale romance that isn't real. But since that time, I met someone and, despite my resistance and belief in what I 'thought' was best for me, I ended up falling in love. And I feel forever changed by that. Now, I think I understand something I didn't before. Love is permanent. The idea that we love, that we can be loved, that it's something we have always, the best part of being human, all of that … it's the one thing that's permanent."

Jack took the headphones off and slowly turned to look at Jess.

"I love you." The words came pouring out of her mouth. "I fucked up, and I hurt you, and I don't ever want to again. But I realized that I love you, and I want to be with you, and I want to try harder. Please, please say that you're willing to try."

"Jess, I don't know. What we had before, you threw it all away so easily. How can I trust what you're saying now?"

"I know. And Jack, all I can give you is my heart. This is my best shot. So here it is. When I met you, I wasn't looking for a relationship. Actually, it was more the opposite. I was avoiding one. But then I met you, and I fell for you, and every step of the way, I've put these roadblocks up. I was completely oriented towards what would happen if I were with you, all that I could lose, what it would say about me. But then I lost you, and I saw that all my fears were about the wrong thing. I was afraid of falling in love. And now that I have, and I've lost it, I see that falling in love is not nearly as terrifying as losing the person that you love. I can't guarantee I won't hurt you. I'm sure I will, and that you'll hurt me, at times, because that's what happens when you open your heart to someone. You can't have love without vulnerability, and you can't have vulnerability without the possibility of being hurt. But what

I can promise is that I won't take you for granted again and that I will do everything I can to earn your trust back. I love you. I was so terrified to admit that to myself. I'm not anymore."

Jack hesitated. "Jess … I love you, too. You know I do. But is that enough for you?"

Jess grabbed his hand. "Come on, I have one more thing to show you."

She ran with him, through the crowded room, up the stairs, to the door opening on to the roof deck. "I wasn't sure how to let you in." She placed her hand on the handle. "Well, I'm trying not to block you out anymore." She opened the door and pulled him out onto the deck.

"Hammocks," Jack said. He laughed, despite the heightened emotions running between him and Jess. "All overlooking the lake."

Jess nodded. "Yes. It was a good idea, Jack, and I was saying no to it out of principle because I didn't like the idea of you being part of the process. Design is so personal to me, and, I don't know, I guess having you involved in it felt too much like you taking me over, if that makes any sense. But the thing is, you already have me, every part of me, and once I stopped fighting that, everything became so much easier. Please, Jack. I'm sorry I hurt you. I don't want to do that anymore."

Jack closed his eyes and shook his head. Jess saw a lifetime's worth of emotions pass through him, his energy expanding and contracting at a rapid pace. After what seemed like a never-ending amount of time, he opened his eyes and looked at her, briefly, before pulling her in close. He embraced her, urgently, as if he'd been drowning before and she was his first experience of land. "Jess, Jess." He tilted her chin up so that he was looking her in the eyes. "Please don't ever do that again. I love you too much to go through the pain of losing you."

"Never, Jack, I never want to lose you, either."

He kissed her then, passionately, her lips molding to his and her body relaxing. This was right. This was where she had to be.

"Now, I don't suppose I could talk you into a Tiki bar? Great corner for it, over there." Jack pointed to the edge of the roof closest to the lake.

Jess laughed, the thrill of being with him bursting forth through every one of her cells. This was too much happiness. She was glad she had his body next to hers to help her hold it all. "Don't push your luck, Stinson," she joked.

"Come on, now." He kissed her. "Those paper umbrellas, you open them up, you close them down, up, down, constantly changing—it's perfect."

Jess groaned as she led him over to the edge of the deck. They stood there, overlooking the lake, kissing and laughing and watching the sunset over the green-blue water.

For Jess's entire life, she'd been searching for a place she fit. Here, in his arms, looking out over the water, she felt none of that uncertainty. Here, in his arms, she had finally found what she was looking for.

Epilogue

BEEP!

Jess was startled by the sound of the alarm. She had been in a blissful sleep, having the most exquisite dream. She wondered, if she didn't fully wake up, could she somehow fall back asleep and finish the—?

Beeeeeep!

Jess groggily turned off the alarm. It was 6:00 a.m. She had long ago gotten used to starting the day this early, but it never managed to feel easier.

Jess sighed as she peeked open her eyes and looked at the sky: still dark. She stared at the sky, trying to will it to turn lighter.

"No, turn it off; it's not time yet."

Jess turned over to see Jack strategically place a pillow over his eyes. He squeezed her tightly, not letting her get away.

Jess scooted closer to him and placed her face against his chest. It was warm near him. She loved the feeling of his hands around her.

"Come on, sleepyhead. It's our only time today." She looked up as he squeezed his eyes more intensely in mock sleep. Her heart jumped as she looked at him. Even now, after all this time, seeing him made her feel alive. "Promise I'll make you weekday pancakes when we get back."

He opened his eyes then and quickly removed the sheets, the abrupt wave of cold air shocking them both awake.

"Pancakes? Alright, let's do this. I wonder if I should be harder to persuade …"

"No, never," she burrowed her head into his chest. "You can't take away my pancake superpower."

He squeezed her and kissed the top of her head. She almost fell back asleep then, despite the cold. He tilted her head up. "Jessica Tyler, now it's my turn to hold *you* to your word. Let's get this over with." He gave her another kiss before sitting up. She sat up, too, and they prepared for their morning run.

She was right, after all. It was a busy day. In the little more than a year since Jumbl, so much had changed. Jess was an established top designer with more projects than she could handle. She'd expanded her team so that there were now seven of them, and she'd finally given Moira and Charlie the promotions they had deserved a while ago. Her Aquarium of the Bay project with Unoa had been featured in MOMA, part of an SF arts and sciences collaboration. It was already being heralded as an innovation in design, and cities outside of the United States were reaching out to her. It was an interesting blend of projects, and Jess was content spending her days doing something she loved. Jess enjoyed working in partnership with Rebecca. It was easier, much more fulfilling, when she wasn't working on her own. That lesson had come forth loud and clear on the Jumbl project, and she had been infinitely happier since learning it.

Equally close to Jess's heart, though, was her collaboration with ShineStar, Jack's solar company. Jack had obtained investor buy-in for the solid-state battery manufacture that would allow the solar batteries to hold more charge, but he ran into challenges when the company tried to create the rest of the house in a way that was economical, aesthetically pleasing, and easily manufactured and transported. Jess had organically become involved with the project, collaborating with Jack's team to come up with a sustainable design for the houses. Today, after their run, they had a joint meeting at ShineStar headquarters to present the new design.

It had been one of the scariest things she had ever done, letting go of her old way of thinking and embracing the new, letting someone in so deeply, so fully, that she honestly wondered if she could ever go back to how it was before Jack. Her life was so full now. It's funny how the process of change always feels painful, even if the change turns out to be for the best. She showed Jack, through words and actions, that what she had said the day of the Jumbl opening was true. She loved him, and she wanted to put the work in. Their relationship wasn't always easy, but they made it a priority to talk about what was hard and to come back, time and time again, to each other. The work that they put in, they got back tenfold.

She and Jack made their way to the front door, avoiding her moving boxes while doing so. It had been less than a week since she had moved into his apartment, and her stuff was everywhere. Jack didn't seem to mind, though. He made her feel welcome, more than welcome. He made her feel at home.

They went over their route as they went down the elevator: up to Lafayette Park and then along Pacific until they reached the Presidio. If they had time, they'd make it all the way to Baker Beach, but it'd be tight, especially if they wanted to squeeze in pancakes.

It was a different route than she'd had from her old apartment, but she was getting used to it. It was a different life than she'd had a year ago, but she was getting used to that too. Different didn't necessarily mean worse. Sometimes it meant better.

As they started on their run, she looked up at Jack. She hadn't known she could love someone this much. He caught her looking at him and leaned down to give her a kiss. Her breath caught at the contact. Every day, she felt how much he loved her. She knew that feeling would never go away.

Yes, sometimes different meant better, much better. Jess felt herself at peace, understood, accepted, loved.

Today was going to be a pretty great day.